The Dragon Heir

The Dragon Heir

Book One

Amelia Wood

Hardback: 979-8-9853665-0-1
Paperback: 979-8-9853665-1-8
Ebook: 979-8-9853665-2-5
First edition

The Dragon Heir is a work of fiction. The names, characters, businesses, places, events, locales, and incidents are either products of my imagination or used in a fictitious manner. Any resemblance to actual persons, living or dead, or actual events are coincidental.

Editing by Judi Weiss
Cover art by Theá Magerand
Typesetting by Sarah Beaudin

To Mom and Dad.
Thank you for always believing in me and encouraging me to
pursue my craft. I will forever be grateful
for your support through this process.

Love,
Amelia

Part One

THE DAUGHTER

She was a storm in the night

Dry lightning over the sea

She was the wind in my hair

None I loved more than she

She was the sun in the sky

A bird high in a tree

A whisper in the woods

Wild, uncompromising, free

My daughter, my love

My everything

—A POEM TRANSLATED FROM THE OLD LANGUAGE.

A daughter is to be all the things her mother is—

proud of herself, respectful of those greater, and above all,

faithful in worship of the Phoenix.

—TAKEN FROM THE JOURNAL OF

A FORMER EIADEN NOBLEMAN.

Chapter

ONE

Ember Ignis sat across from a Dragon.

Not a true Dragon, of course.

It was only her mother in the carriage with her, and Ember watched as she gently moved her hair out of her face, fingers brushing through a gray streak near the front, something that would be dyed later, hiding it. Ember shared her mother's eyes, a vicious, molten gold, and had no doubt that her own dark hair would one day be just as silver. Her mother, Verity, wasn't old, necessarily, but she wasn't exactly young, either. Plus, she had been the House Draco matriarch for nearly thirty years. That took a toll on a person. Verity's hands were folded in her lap, her tattoo on full display. The House Draco crest, matching the one on Ember's shoulder. A proud sign of the power that Verity held. Power that would eventually transfer to Ember.

They were matriarch and heir of the highest house in the kingdom, second only to royalty. Verity was the king's highest—and most trusted—advisor, and Ember was waiting patiently for the day she would hold that position.

Verity tapped on the roof of the carriage, and the driver snapped the reins. They pulled out of the drive, leaving their darkened estate house behind them. Only two windows on the second floor had candles flickering in them, giving the impression of two narrowed eyes.

"Who had the baby again?" Ember asked, leaning against the window as they passed over a particularly smooth portion of the road. The smell of apple perfume filled the carriage as Verity turned her head to look out the window.

"Lord Yvlin of House Corvus."

"Another fledgling for the nest, I suppose. How many does this make?"

"Six. Each with a different woman, and none of them his wife."

"The king really will throw a ball for any occasion. Even a child out of wedlock."

"Crows typically mate for life, too. Which only makes it more despicable." Ember shrugged, reaching up to touch her hair. Unlike Verity's, it hadn't been left down. Instead, it was in a simple updo, secured with a Dragon-head knife. It would keep her hair from tumbling down while she danced, as well as giving her a bit of extra protection should she need it.

"At least he has plenty of heirs for when one of them inevitably sinks a knife in his chest." Verity gave a soft laugh.

They were close to the palace already, as the Draco Estate was always occupied by the king's most trusted advisor. He needed Verity close by, and by default, Ember.

"Looks like a full house tonight," Ember remarked, and her mother shrugged in response as their carriage came to a stop. Every candle in the castle seemed to be lit, making it a beacon against the dusk sky.

"It won't be," Verity responded. "Nobody cares that much about House Corvus. Most of them will be here for the food." The castle was, by far, the most impressive structure in Eiad, their home continent. Perhaps even in all of the three continents.

After all, who could possibly claim to have something more regal? Certainly not the far and middle continents, with their war-torn cities and plagues. No, Eiad was the most beautiful of the three, and the palace was the most beautiful structure in Eiad.

Six towers were dark shadows against the night sky, seeming to scrape the heavens themselves, as though they were desperately trying to reach the Phoenix. It was all made of a dark green stone that had long become a precious commodity, worth thousands of ovum, Eiad's currency. The towers were connected by a walled walkway, and when Ember squinted, she could make out archers perched on them, ready to shoot down anybody who dared threaten the royal family. The whole palace was centered around a ballroom large enough to hold all twelve houses. During the warmer months, the roof was removed, letting in the natural warmth of central Eiad. But now, during the winter, the roof was up, and twin fires burned on either side of the ballroom, making the entire thing far more intimate than it would've been during the summer.

"Congratulate Lord Yvlin if you end up near him. But ignore his wife. She'll be out for blood tonight, and we don't want a repeat of last time." The last two words were accompanied by a pointed look from Verity, which Ember returned with a wide smile. Lady Corvus was far too easy to provoke, especially when there was a new baby involved. The carriage doors opened, and a palace servant bowed before retreating.

"I'll see you later," Ember said, stepping out of the carriage and following a crowd of people into the ballroom. A servant took her coat as she walked in, taking stock of her surroundings. The green walls were hung with deep blue tapestries with a screeching silver Crow woven into the center, for House Corvus. At the far end of the room were the thrones, three of them intricately carved by the same stone the palace was made of. The king and queen's were empty, and Ember quickly located them near Lord Yvlin, cooing over the newborn baby wrapped in his arms. His wife was near him, arms crossed as she stared at the infant. Ember steered away from her and the hatred— almost bordering on madness—in her eyes. Ember and her mother joked, but she didn't cross people who had that extent of madness surrounding them.

The only occupied throne was the teenage prince's, and he was half asleep, the firelight rippling across his face and making his golden crown shine. A brown-and-white hound dog was sprawled at the foot of his throne, lazily watching the crowd with one eye.

The floor of the ballroom was made of the same green stone, cool underfoot, and far slicker than the marble at home. It didn't matter. Ember wouldn't fall, even though she was barefoot.

"Lady Ember Ignis," someone behind her said. Ember turned on her heel, steadying the knife in her hair and crossing her arms.

"I'm sorry, do I know you?" The boy gave her a smile, and Ember studied him for a moment. He wasn't unattractive, necessarily—those of the houses hardly ever were—but Ember had definitely seen better. And far more interesting. Fair skin, golden hair, blue eyes, and a suit that was most definitely a hand-me-down. The stitching was torn near his underarm, and Ember resisted the urge to chastise him about it. She was taller than him by at least a few inches, even barefoot. His hair was slicked back in a hideous style that hadn't been popular in several years. Even still, Ember had no doubt he'd one day make a fine husband for some rich, houseless woman who sought to elevate her position.

"We met at the Race of Heirs, Lady Ember, at the first snowfall. I'm Viper Trunca of House Serpens." Ember racked her mind but couldn't remember seeing him at the Race, a holiday that took place during early winter. She'd been too focused on making sure she came in first to pay too much attention to any of the other competitors. Even the heir who'd come in second hadn't been fast enough to grasp her attention. She squinted, and he gave her a nervous smile.

Oh, wait. She remembered that tentative smile, and she remembered him. The boy who'd attempted to break her horse's legs only minutes before the race had begun, who hadn't even been punished as the king was too drunk to do anything, much less kick a lesser, unimportant son out of the Race. That's how it always was at holidays—the royals and lords and ladies got drunk, and the heirs attempted to attack each other.

"Your parents really tried on your name, didn't they?"

"I'm the seventh child out of eleven. Compared to my little sisters' names, Viper is nothing to sneeze at. My littlest sister's name is Adder," he said with a light chuckle. His laugh was low and slightly wheezy and completely annoying. Even a houseless woman couldn't look past—or rather hear past—such an obnoxious sound.

"Can you tell how little I care?" Ember said, turning away from him and stalking toward the food tables. She nearly cringed as his footsteps continued after her. He was obnoxiously loud, heels slamming against the polished stone floors.

"Have I done something to offend you? I apologize if I did. I was only trying to make conversation at this dull party."

"You do realize that you are speaking to the future matriarch of House Draco, correct?"

"I— Yes. I know who you are. Everybody knows who you are. It's not exactly a secret, Lady Ember."

"And you, the seventh child of eleven, have the gall to talk to me? To pretend that you are on the same level as me? How dare you." Viper backed up a step as Ember took another forward. She willed him to be quiet in her mind. If he was any louder, someone was going to notice, and then things would get out of hand, and Verity would notice as well.

Ember couldn't let her mother see this—disgracing their house by fighting with someone below her station.

"I'm sorry. I was just told to approach you—"

"Tell whoever gave you that idiotic instruction to take it and shove it down their throat." Viper's eyes narrowed, and for a brief second, Ember wondered if he was armed.

"You do not want to bring the wrath of House Serpens upon you."

"Let me tell you something, Viper of House Serpens. If you ever—and I mean even in the slightest look, or the most minute gesture—dare to threaten me again, I will not hesitate to shove a knife into your throat. And nobody will miss you. In fact, I do believe they'll ship your body to one of the islands for the vultures. Do you understand? I am your superior. Have I made myself clear?"

"Crystal, Lady Ember." He gave her a short bow before retreating from her side. Ember turned back to the impressive spread of food before her, laid out on a blue silk runner. It would be stained and torn by the end of the night, but the palace had plenty more on hand. A servant in black stood behind each dish, patiently waiting for instructions.

A whole roasted goose—they would have to be careful to make sure House Olor didn't mistake it for a Swan—was stuffed with fat and glistening berries. The goose sat on a bed of fine greens and some sort of sauce that was a soft brown color. Ember's mouth watered. Being the first house of twelve meant they ate exceptionally well every night, but this sort of feast was something only the palace could produce. Various silver platters and bowls held sides that were almost too beautiful to eat. A bowl of mashed root vegetables with seasoning from the far continent, a platter of savory pastries overflowing with thick cheese and herbs that no doubt came from the islands. A bowl of red jelly, berries distended in it. Beside all of it was a tower of small blue-and-silver cookies that had been baked especially for House Corvus. Ember resisted the urge to grab one and shove it into her mouth. She picked up a blue porcelain plate from the end of the table and considered her options.

"They really have outdone themselves today, haven't they?" Ember jumped as her mother slid in beside her, tattooed hand picking up a silver plate.

"For a bastard child, yes. Is House Olor here?"

"No. I think that's why the king decided goose was allowed. They would have a tantrum if they mistook it for a Swan. You know how dramatic they get." Ember made a face as she studied the roasted goose.

"They should be here, dramatic or not." Verity dipped a small tasting spoon into the red jelly and hummed softly as she considered what Ember had said. Or perhaps she was considering the taste of the jelly—Ember wasn't privy to her mother's thoughts, no matter how hard she tried. The lords and ladies trusted nobody with every one of their secrets, not even their children. Verity certainly didn't share anything with the other lords and ladies—their position painted a target on their backs, and few of the houses would hesitate to stab them in the center.

"We're here, as are House Tigris and Pardus. The king needs nothing more than his top three advisors for something like this," Verity said, holding her plate out for a black-clad servant to fill, and pointing her tasting spoon at the jelly. "Give me half of that bowl." The servant had the audacity to gape for a minute, but then went to fill Verity's plate with the jelly. Something silver flashed around the woman's neck as she bent, an animal pendant Ember didn't recognize, but she brushed it off. She had an eye for things that glittered, but if a servant wore it, then it certainly wasn't worth her time.

"I suppose. Have you seen the baby yet?" Ember asked, holding her plate out to the servant as she finished with Verity's. She pointed at the goose, and she supposed that the way she was looking at the cookies gave her away, as the servant gave her one of each, along with several thick slabs of meat, thoroughly covered in sauce, and a spoonful of seasoned vegetables. Finally, she handed Ember a small cheese pastry, which she bit into without hesitation, sighing softly as flavor flooded her mouth, soft cheese and flaky dough melting on her tongue. Phoenix above, she was hungry.

"Yes. Hideous little thing. Looks something like a bug, but it doesn't look like any of his mistresses, which is good, because his wife already wants to strangle the miserable thing." Verity was staring across the ballroom, eyes trained on something in the far corner. Ember followed her gaze, frowning when she noticed her mother's attention was fixed on the king. Certainly she spent enough time looking at him during meetings? "Or burn it alive, perhaps." Ember snapped back to the conversation, moving her eyes off the king and allowing them to rove around the ballroom, taking in the party. Servants just like the woman who had served Verity and Ember, lined the walls, interspersed with the occasional guard, although Ember knew there were more, staying in the shadows and out of sight, but always watching.

Ember, who had grown up in the court, had gotten used to silent guards and hidden protectors, although she highly doubted any of them would stop Lady Rostro if she attempted to kill the newborn.

"No, that'd be putting it out of its misery. She'd do something much more horrible," Ember said, and Verity snickered. There was commotion by the door, the king's joyful greeting carrying over to them, and they both turned to see a family of redheads walk in.

"House Vulpus just arrived. I'm going to go greet them. Enjoy your meal." Ember took her plate back from the servant before finding a seat against the wall. This was where she usually spent parties until the dancing started, eating, observing, watching the other houses as she tapped her foot against the green floors.

Viper was on the far side of the room, arms crossed as he looked anywhere but her. He banged his head against one of the deep blue tapestries, disturbing the woven Crow and his slicked hairdo. She couldn't help the small smirk that crossed her face as she watched him, scraping her plate clean and delicately licking her fingers to remove the rest of the sugar from the cookies. Sometimes, she absolutely adored the power she held over the other houses.

There were only half of the houses present tonight—Draco, Tigris, Pardus, Serpens, Vulpus, and Corvus. Enough to fill nearly half the ballroom, since the other six houses were missing.

The band played a soft tune, not quite fit for dancing yet, rising above the low conversation centered around Lord Yvlin and his new child.

As she ate, Ember watched the crown prince on his throne, shifting this way and that as he too watched the proceedings. He let out a yawn, and Ember frowned. She would've made a far better princess than he made a prince. The man—boy, really—was constantly drunk, the stench of alcohol following him wherever he was. Eiad needed a crown prince that would actually move the country forward, not bring it to a grinding halt, or worse, erase some of the progress his parents had made. Ember knew for a fact she was stronger than him in more ways than one and sleeping during a ball only proved that point further.

And of course, had Ember been the princess, she would've become the most powerful person in Eiad rather than the second. Verity was content with being second to royalty for the most part, but Ember had higher ambitions.

The prince adjusted his crown as he laid back in his throne and closed his eyes again. The dog at his feet yawned, revealing two rows of sharp teeth, then settled back down, just as lazy as her master.

Ember looked up again, and Viper was gone from the wall. It didn't take long to find him, quickly striding toward the exit, and she watched as he walked out of the double doors, away from the ballroom and away from her.

Ember smirked as she watched him leave. Dragon beat Serpent, every time.

Chapter

Two

E MBER RUBBED HER FEET in the carriage while she and Verity headed home. She had laid back completely, absorbed by the velvet of the seat. If she sat up any longer, she was afraid of falling over onto her mother.

"You were quite the dancer tonight," Verity said, and Ember chuckled.

"I figured I might as well. The House Vulpus heir dances wonderfully, but he's usually snatched up by someone his age. It was nice to have a mature partner who was completely focused on the dance."

"As opposed to what?"

"My position," Ember said simply, tracing the wood engravings on the carriage. All Dragon carvings, of course. "Where did you disappear to all night?"

"Lord Ivin and Lady Alex and I spent the night together. Lovely to speak with them about something other than politics. I suppose we all need a break from being courtiers." Her lip twitched, and Ember furrowed her brow. Her mother's lip twitching meant one thing, and one thing only—a lie.

So who had Verity spent the night beside? Ember wanted to ask, but that would be a mistake. Verity would explode if Ember attempted to catch her in a lie, and they were having such a pleasant evening.

"The baby was annoying," Ember said, eliciting a laugh from Verity.

"Wasn't it? I nearly drowned it in my wine glass. Send it straight up to the Phoenix before it could grow up and become like its father. I probably should've, in retrospect. I would've been doing the miserable thing a favor."

"Oh, and take that privilege from Lady Rostro? She'd be out for blood." Verity laughed, tapping her lap to indicate that Ember could put her feet up. She rubbed them softly, and Ember sighed in relief, sinking further into the carriage seats.

"You're the best, Mother," Ember said, and Verity shrugged.

"I try, darling, I try." Ember studied the tattoo on the back of her mother's hand. The gold Dragon eyes staring up at her, eyes like Ember's and Verity's.

"Mother?" Verity was completely concentrated on rubbing Ember's feet and hummed in response.

"Is it easy?"

"Easy?"

"Being the lady of a house."

"No, it's not easy. There's a lot of pressure related to leading a house, especially ours. But you already knew that. So why did you ask?"

"I always need more information on running our house. I'm not going to ruin House Draco's legacy because I'm unprepared." Verity shoved Ember's feet off her lap and leaned forward, eyes burning like twin suns.

"You think I left you unprepared? You think I haven't taught you enough to keep you afloat, even if this carriage toppled over and I died this very instant?"

Ember recoiled slightly. "That's not what I meant. But I don't want to inherit the house in the same position you did."

Verity softened slightly at that.

"Your grandmother was murdered because she wasn't vigilant enough. She was far less cautious than I am now. She genuinely thought she could trust the other lords and ladies, and the men she entertained, when trusting is the last thing any of us should be doing. Plus, she had more enemies than I do. Or, at least, she had bolder enemies." Ember laughed at that. Her grandmother, Ferra, had been found with a knife in her back, a beautiful Dragon-head knife that was currently in Ember's hair.

"Plus," Ember added with a smile. "If someone dared to kill you, they'd have me on their scent until they all bled."

Verity patted Ember's knee and smiled back. "I have no doubt that you'd make them pay."

Ember let out a long breath, watching it mist in the cold night air. The house behind her was still golden and warm with flickering firelight, as Verity was still awake, but Ember could only let off energy and emotions in one productive way, and it wasn't something she could do inside the house.

She tromped through the snow toward the end of their very dead garden, two wooden targets shoved under her arms. There were servants in the house, of course, but she didn't want anybody's help for this. What was the point in trying to focus when somebody was constantly hovering over her shoulder, asking her if she needed anything? She didn't want to accidentally hurt any of them. She didn't care for them, exactly, but...

She wasn't a monster, after all.

Ember placed the targets in the snow with a soft thud, pushing them as deep into the snow and frozen dirt as she could, fingers trembling with cold, although they were fully gloved. She moved back to where she had stood initially, reaching down into the bucket at her side, pulling two of the objects out.

Twin throwing knives, gleaming softly in the candlelight streaming from the windows. Their blades were sharp enough that they would easily stick into the hardened wood of the targets, and heavy enough for the wind to make little impact on them. The handles were simple, with little decoration, carved of a deep, black wood, a sharp contrast to the silver of the blades. They were designed to be thrown but could just as easily be used to slit a throat or carve a piece of meat.

Ember flipped one blade in her hand, angling it toward the sky, the handle flat in her palm. She adjusted her stance, placing her right foot slightly in front of her left. She let out a long, slow, breath, watching it mist in front of her, before pulling her arm back.

She swung her arm forward, releasing the knife as it came down.

It flipped through the air, catching candlelight on the blade, before sinking deep into the wood.

She moved the knife in her left hand to her right and held it exactly as she had with the other, pulling her arm back to throw it. When it hit the target, it hit true, and she reached into the basket at her feet for two more.

Ember threw those too and two more when she was done with those. It was an easy way to work out the stress and tension in her body. She threw herself completely and entirely into it, practically losing herself in the easy rhythm of picking a knife, angling it, shifting her hips, and then watching the knife fly through the air, thudding into the target with a satisfying noise. She had always been like this, as long as she could remember. It hadn't always been knife throwing, but there had always been something she used to forget her daily stresses.

When she had been small, she had played with the other heirs and lesser sons and daughters when their parents were together. She hadn't been allowed to run completely wild, but Verity had still allowed her to play with the other children. At the age of ten, however, something had changed, and Ember grew up slightly. By then, Verity had started preparing her for taking over House Draco, and through that, Ember learned to ride a horse. She wasn't very good at it, and the horses made her wary, but she practiced constantly, building a tentative bond with the horses kept in House Draco's stables.

After the horses had come the dancing. Ember found dancing easier than riding horses. For one, she didn't have to be worried about being bucked off an animal five times her size. She quickly learned waltzes and quicksteps and foxtrots, allowing herself to spend hours upon hours perfecting every turn of her wrist or swing of her skirts.

Dancing was not as important as other skills Ember learned, but she enjoyed doing it, and it was something she could use to escape, to slip into a world that wasn't quite her own.

Now, it was the knives. She still danced at parties and balls, and occasionally by herself, when she wasn't in the mood for throwing knives.

The relief that came from exercising, regardless of what she was doing, was essential to Ember. She could control where the knives struck and how far they sank into the target. She could control the steps of a dance, the gentle touch necessary to guide a horse around a corner. Ember could grasp it. Keep it close to her chest and perfect it. She couldn't control what the king and queen did, couldn't control her mother. But this was something she could hold onto.

She threw her last two knives, watching them arc through the air and slam into the target before going to collect them, putting everything away before slipping inside, stamping snow off her boots as she touched the Dragon knife on her arm. She hadn't thrown that knife, and never would, not only because it was not made to be thrown, but because the knife, and all it symbolized, meant everything to Ember.

Chapter

THREE

MBER WAS GOING TO a palace meeting. She was dressed simpler than she had been a week ago for the party, opting for a soft yellow shirt that looked like flickering candlelight over a pair of tight black pants. Ember wore her hair down, pinning back the front with a ruby pin. A light brush of gold across her lips, to try and offset her pale skin, and a pair of soft black flats and her knife strapped to her forearm. Even with the weapon, she looked far less intimidating than she had at the party two days ago. Which was the goal, of course. She wasn't the House Draco matriarch yet, and it was best if she stayed in her mother's shadow until her own time came. But it was still important to present herself the way Verity presented herself, and that was constantly done up, looking her best for the court.

Ember was well aware of how highly House Draco was held in the eyes of House Phoenix, the royalty, and she'd be damned before she ruined her reputation. She hadn't missed a meeting since she was ten. Nothing could keep either her or Verity from fulfilling their duties except death itself.

Fifteen minutes later, Ember sat behind her mother as they waited for the meeting to start. All along the walls sat the children of the various lords and ladies of the court. Behind them hung tapestries depicting all twelve of the patron animals, woven in their house colors. Ember ran her hand down the House Draco tapestry, fingers brushing over the golden Dragon against the deep, black background. She relished the feeling of the soft wool, then slipped her hand underneath it to touch the cool, green stone. It was similar to the floors at the Draco Estate, but even the Dragon didn't have the luxuries the Phoenix did.

The court's meeting room was far bigger than the ballroom, with one large table in the middle that the lords and ladies sat around. At the head was another table, where the royal family would sit. Windows lined the room between the tapestries, letting in weak winter light. Because of it, lanterns had been lit around the room, bathing it all in a strange glow.

The king and queen had yet to make an appearance, but the prince sat on his green throne, a stack of papers in one hand and a glass of an amber liquid in the other. Ember studied him for a moment. He was the opposite of Viper Trunca in every physical way—dark skin, dark curly hair, dark eyes. And far more handsome, too. With a better name—Asher. Like a Phoenix out of the ashes. His hound dog was again at his feet, asleep as the tip of her tail moved slightly.

She could feel Viper's eyes on her from where he sat six houses away, in front of a bronze tapestry depicting a violet serpent poised to strike. Ember was surprised he was even there. She figured one of his older siblings would've made an appearance, since usually only the firstborns—the heirs—came to the weekly meetings. These could be dreadfully boring, if there were no international issues or internal conflict. For the most part, it was the same thing repeated, week after week.

Verity stood up in front of her, and Ember immediately rose as King Whelyn and Queen Feather—a common name among House Passer members—entered the room. A small but meaningful glance passed between Verity and Whelyn, and Ember resisted the urge to frown openly at her king.

"Thank you, Great Phoenix, for bringing your patron animals to us, loyal and proud. Please, sit," Whelyn said, finishing his short prayer, and as one, the group fell back into their seats. The queen remained standing, though, holding a roll of parchment in her hands. Roll call, in order of how powerful each house was. House Draco was the highest, wielding more power than the ones below it. House Passer, of the Sparrow, held the least power.

Ember outranked everybody in the room except for the three royals, and her own mother, and took a great deal of satisfaction from it. The other houses could do nothing when it came to what she said or did.

"House Draco, of the Dragon?"

"Present," Verity said, and Ember watched as Verity and the king shared a small smile. They were close, it seemed, but Ember had always thought Verity and the queen were friends, not Verity and the king. She'd seen them interact before, certainly, but there was something different about this. It was as though something had...shifted.

"House Tigris, of the Tiger?"

"Present." The Tigris patriarch had a scar that marred half his face, and his eldest son behind him had one to match. A rite of passage determined by the Tiger, who decreed that physical pain was the only way to prove true loyalty, and his house followed his lead. A road paved by blood and tears. Ember respected the Tigers for what they went through to prove that they were truly dedicated to their house.

"House Pardus, of the Leopard?"

"Present." House Pardus members were neither male nor female, choosing instead to pick their gender at the age of eighteen. The current leader was a male-born-female, and the heir was a born female that some people were sure would become a male. There were even bets on it.

"House Ibis, of the Owl?"

"Present." Members of House Ibis were small. Their current matriarch barely came up to Ember's breasts. The current lady of the house wore spectacles that made her eyes gigantic, as though she were a humongous insect.

"Hurry up already," Asher said from where he lounged, and his mother shot him a glare before starting the roll call again. He rolled his drink in his hand, ice clinking against the sides of the glass, but his eyes were fixed on his mother's back. He at once looked bored, terrified, and completely nonchalant.

The terror was interesting, but perhaps even the untouchable feared something.

"House Equo, of the Stallion." Ember couldn't help but agree with Asher, although she kept her mouth shut, unwilling to turn the stares of the houses upon herself. It was clear that all twelve houses were there. They always were. Nobody would dare miss a weekly meeting. And yet the king and queen insisted on taking roll every single time they gathered. An odd sort of paranoia Ember had never understood.

"Present." The Stallion's house was made up entirely of males. Females who married into it, or had the unfortunate pleasure of being born into it, weren't accepted as true members of the house.

"House Alces, of the Elk." Ember couldn't help looking in that house's direction. The daughter sitting behind her mother was the source of her attention. Amber Forrest. And next to her... her brother, Allen. They had been friends, once, before Verity had decided Ember ought to grow up. Both of them were shy and reserved, although once Amber was given something to drink... she came alive.

"House Serpens, of the Snake," Feather said, and Ember did her very best not to look at Viper and his father. She failed. She wondered if he'd told his father about their encounter last night, or if he had been too embarrassed to speak about it. Judging by the fact that his father smiled warmly at her when he caught her looking, she guessed the latter.

"House Vulpus, of the Fox." The slyest house in the court, made up entirely of redheads. Usually the king's spies if he needed them. Even in the meeting, they all wore slim throwing knives at their sides, ready to defend themselves and House Phoenix should the need arise. None of the other houses trusted House Vulpus, but they were good in a crisis.

"House Olor, of the Swan." Sharp cheekbones, shock white hair, and silver eyes...except for the heir son. He had dyed his hair a violent shade of blue, going completely against the way his family strove to present themselves. Ember hated that. There was a way things were done. If he wanted blue hair, he would leave the family. Let his little brother become heir. At least he could be trusted to present his house in an appropriate manner. She didn't even want to think of what Verity would do to her if she dyed her hair or wore obscene clothing. But, perhaps, Swans had less dignity than Dragons.

Not that it mattered. Her black hair wouldn't hold a color. "House Aranea, of the Spider." A pair of twins ruled the tenth house, sitting side by side. They didn't have a current heir, either, leading many to speculate that the twin sisters were barren. If that was true, there was fear of the Spider's house disappearing completely. That couldn't happen, of course. Only the Phoenix could disband a house entirely. A solution would be found.

"House Corvus, of the Crow." Lord Yvlin nodded at the queen in answer, clearly exhausted by his wife's response to the newest addition to the nest. His eldest son sat behind him, head resting on his hand. He looked tired, too, and Ember speculated that Lady Rostro's fits of rage had kept the entire house on their toes all night.

"And finally, House Passer, of the Sparrow." The queen gave her former house a soft smile. She was a Phoenix, now, but it was easy to see why she would keep a piece of her heart to her family's house. They were the smallest, and the most peaceful. Ember was sure it was easy to exist with people like that. People with no backbone, who would bend over backwards to ensure everybody got along.

People who were weak.

"Great, we're all here," Asher droned, and Ember held back a small snicker as the queen took her seat. Queen Feather whispered something to Asher, and to Ember's surprise, he flinched away from her words, taking a long drink from his glass.

The king sat forward and picked up the stack of papers in front of Asher. He shook his long braids out of his face before pointing at the House Equo patriarch.

"Charles, you had a request?"

Charles Palin stood, holding a paper in his hand.

"Yes, Your Highness. Thank you. Is there any chance we could have more palace soldiers for our estate perimeter? As you know, the patron circle is surrounded by small villages. During the winter months the villagers get...restless. They have a tendency to attack us—especially the higher houses—when they become hungry, ignoring the fact that it's not our fault. We don't need too many more guards—my sons do a fine job—but with my two eldest gone, we need two more soldiers to replace them." The king nodded as Charles sat back down.

"A reasonable request. Granted. One of my scribes will write up an agreement for you later. I would pray to the Phoenix too, that you may be protected until the Silent Duels." The Phoenix was the main object of worship in Eiad, and a religion the king spread to all countries that Eiad conquered. During the Silent Duels, lesser sons and daughters were conscripted into the royal guard as officers, helping to protect where they grew up. Heirs were able to prove that they were physically superior to the others.

Ember and Verity exchanged a glance. Requests like this were common during the cold months, when peasants saw that their stomachs were empty and those of the twelve houses— and the royals'—were full. The close proximity of the Draco Estate to the palace meant they frequently got some of the worst of it, no matter what the lower houses claimed. Their home had been defaced more than once by eggs, by paint, by bricks through the windows.

But the price they paid if they were caught was far higher than a loaf of bread or an apple to fill their child's belly. Those who were caught hung for their crimes. Ember herself oversaw the hangings of peasants who attacked her beautiful home.

Nobody ever touched the Phoenix Palace, though, because those who did faced a punishment far worse than death. Far worse than a hanging. There were bloodstains in the palace because of those foolish enough to attack it.

The king shuffled through his papers before coming upon one that seemed to be of some interest to him.

"The price of glass has gone up," he said, and the court muttered to themselves.

"The little glass Eiad produces or the glass from Gleoj Swesh?" Lady Victoria Soo, of House Aranea, asked. Gleoj Swesh, a desert country of the middle continent, supplied Eiad with most of their glass, as far as Ember knew. In fact, the windows in the very room they sat in were made in Gleoj Swesh. They had advantage, what with being located in a country built upon sand. All one had to do to get glass in Gleoj Swesh was light a match and drop it into the ground.

"The glass from Gleoj Swesh. It's nearly doubled in price."

"How dare they," Verity hissed. "When we sent our own young people to help liberate them from the far continent. They understand how quickly those soldiers could turn around and stab them in the throat, correct?"

"It is odd," the queen agreed, giving Verity her support. "They haven't done anything like this since they became free. There must be some reason."

"Could be that idiot they put on the throne. I'm sure he already forgot what we did for him," Lady Alex Taya, of House Pardus, said.

"We helped them put 'that idiot' on the throne," Verity spat back. "Watch your mouth when you speak about their leader. We did support him."

"Oh, please, Lady Verity. We all know we only supported him because he was the lesser of two evils and because the temple backed our decision. Honestly, I'd rather have an absolute moron on the throne than a dictator, and that's why we backed him. It's been almost a year and a half. It's up to the people now to choose who they want to lead them. There's no use in meddling anymore. They're on their own."

"I still think we should send soldiers down there," Verity suggested. "To sort things out and figure out why they doubled the price of glass. Or we could double the price of lumber, since we provide them with almost all of their lumber. They'd certainly come begging if we cut supply lines. Nobody else will support them."

"We're not going to do that," King Whelyn said, interrupting Verity. Ember watched as her mother's eyes flashed with anger and betrayal for a quick moment before schooling her emotions again. He looked up, locking eyes with Verity. Ember watched her mother's hands clench underneath the table once before relaxing. "We'll just send a delegate down there to figure things out. The Phoenix wouldn't want us to attack what we so recently defended. Lord Ivin, would your son be willing?"

"Yes, sir," the lord of House Tigris said. "He'd be happy to go." Verity and Ember exchanged a glance but said nothing as the king turned back to his papers.

The meeting wrapped up, the king led a prayer to the Great Phoenix, and Ember and her mother stood to leave. Verity excused herself for a moment, going to speak to the king, leaving Ember by herself. She rolled an uninterested eye over the court and the servants against the walls, standing out in their black clothes, separated by royal guards in red and orange.

And that's when Ember saw her. At first, she simply looked past her, to the next servant in the line, but something drew her eyes back. Standing against the wall, wearing the same black clothing as all the other servants. Brown hair pulled up in a tight bun at the nape of her neck, bright green eyes. Ordinary. Average. And yet...not. There was an odd magnetism about the girl, who looked up when she felt Ember's eyes on her. Ember suppressed a gasp as she and the girl made eye contact. Gold meeting green in a sharp, dangerous clash. The servant immediately dropped her gaze, but Ember's eyes lingered on the girl's face, trying to find anything familiar about her, or something that truly separated her from the rest of the servants on the wall, but... nothing. She was wholly and completely ordinary.

Out of the corner of her eye, Ember saw Asher watching the servant girl too, and a wave of unfamiliar emotions immediately passed over her. It wasn't jealousy—Ember knew jealousy. She'd never wanted Asher in any way other than to become queen, but she'd still always thought of him as hers, even if there was no official betrothal in place.

She didn't know who the green-eyed servant girl was, but it didn't matter. There was something about her that Ember didn't like in the slightest.

Chapter

FOUR

A SHER CINIS SAT AT his father's left hand and picked at his braised lamb. He took a long sip of his wine as Whelyn roared in laughter at something the House Vulpus lady said.

"That's an excellent joke, Scarlett. If being the matriarch of your house doesn't work out, I'll hire you as my court jester." The whole table tittered with fake laughter, all desperate to hold themselves in a high position in the king's eyes. Asher drained the rest of his glass and snapped his fingers at a servant to refill it. He dropped his other hand to the top of the dog's head at his side.

His constant companion, Hazel. A hound dog who had come into his life a few years prior, as a gift from a visiting dignitary. A hunting puppy, who had ears that were too big for her head and a long, fluffy tail that was always getting in her way. She was the only living creature in the room who didn't constantly judge Asher for who he was. And she was a good companion to have when he was physically alone or when he was in a setting like this, surrounded by people but still alone. She was allowed in the dining room only because Asher had trained her well, but even still, his mother, Feather, cast dirty looks toward her every so often.

Asher didn't even know why he was at this dinner. There were no heirs at this table, only the current lords and ladies of their houses, gathering for something other than a weekly meeting. They were all too happy to sit around the palace's green tables and eat the palace's food on the palace's golden plates.

Happy to push aside the dead and forget them, so long as it suited their needs.

Well, that wasn't exactly true. At least not for there being no heirs. Ember Ignis sat beside her mother, quietly eating her lamb, her strange eyes seeing everything, even as she said nothing to the group. Every so often she would whisper something to her mother, or the other way around, and a pang of jealousy would flit through Asher. He didn't have that sort of relationship with either of his parents. His father was too busy for him, whether with running the country into the ground by taxing the people out of everything they had, or with the other women he entertained, and his mother was distant most of the time, too lost in her own little world. Too lost in memories of her childhood in House Passer, before she became the child bride of a child king. The rest of the time, she was violent, angry, and completely bitter about her own life.

Asher flexed his shoulders, feeling the scars there stretch. A reminder. Feather wasn't always distant.

Verity and Ember sometimes seemed more like sisters than mother and daughter, and Asher dropped his gaze to his dog, shoving down the jealousy.

"This is simply divine, King Whelyn," Lord Yvlin said, shoveling lamb into his mouth as though it were his last meal.

"Slow down, Yvlin. You act like you have another baby coming tomorrow," Whelyn said, and there was another round of laughter at the table.

"I might," Lord Yvlin said, and there were a few uncertain chuckles. Nobody could really tell if he was joking. His wife's face seemed fixed in a permanent scowl, and she viciously stabbed her vegetables, as though they'd personally wronged her. Asher threw back half his glass in one go, fending off a dirty look from his mother. His head wasn't even cloudy yet, which meant he was going to need more wine.

The table fell silent as everybody ate, the only sound being the scrape of forks against plates and glasses hitting the table. There were a few murmurs as people asked servants for more peas or a new fork, but for the most part, the table was quiet.

Asher stared across the room at the servant girl that stood against the wall. He had noticed her yesterday, at the weekly meeting, when he had seen Ember looking at her. Now it was like he couldn't look away. She was beautiful in a simple, organic way. Although most peasants didn't have green eyes that seemed to bore into your very soul. Perfect figure, if a bit too thin. Probably from hunger or overworking. That was common for most palace servants, as many were recruited from small, poor villages. He'd never seen her at the palace before, but that didn't mean she hadn't existed. He probably wouldn't have noticed her at all had it not been for Ember.

Asher looked back over at the Dragon, frowning as he tried to figure out why Ember had been so interested in the servant. She had even less reason than he did to notice palace servants—she didn't live with them. She sat stoically, like a stone carved from the blackness of night and the gold of the sun. The edge of a knife, designed and raised to be the perfect heir, and eventually, the perfect lady.

She looked up, eyes meeting his, and he dropped his gaze. Ember was the type of pretty he was used to. Court pretty, where the flashy clothing and heavy makeup drew the viewer's eye. There was nothing particularly special about Ember's appearance, except for the Dragon knife strapped to her arm. He'd noticed it when her sleeve had fallen back, and she'd left it in plain view for a few moments before slowly fixing her sleeve. A clear display of power. Not that it mattered. Nobody would question a Dragon. Especially not with the woman who sat at her side, eyes darting across the table coolly, as though daring someone to make eye contact with her.

Ember was a good match. She was smart and pretty enough and came from the most powerful of the twelve houses. A perfect match on paper. There was practically a silent betrothal in place—everybody simply assumed Asher and Ember would end up married at some point, producing an heir that would combine the highest houses. But even if he didn't marry Ember, there would always be heirs and lesser daughters in the other houses. His father would probably even approve a match with someone from a lower house, so long as they provided something useful. His mother had helped House Passer become stronger, silenced the laughter that erupted whenever House Passer was mentioned. Feather had done well in that aspect, even if Whelyn quickly lost interest in her.

Three of the other houses, besides House Draco, had daughters old enough for Asher to marry. Daughters were his only choice, even if he had been interested in men—the kingdom needed at least one heir to continue the Cinis line and keep House Phoenix strong. House Alces had Amber Forrest, who generally seemed to prefer females, if Asher's assumptions were correct. House Pardus had female-born Lilith Taya, but they weren't much good to him if they chose to become male. And House Corvus had a young woman—not an heir, she was the second child— that was Asher's age. And that was it. No other house had a female heir old enough for him to marry. And none held the power Ember would one day have.

But Asher wasn't remotely interested in Ember. He'd grown up with her, both of them children at the same time. She'd been intense even then, so focused on propriety and tradition that she rarely let herself relax. Asher couldn't imagine living with someone like her for the rest of his life, being forced to bear children with her, running the country at her side. Or, rather, in her shadow—Ember would never allow Asher to stand in front of her. She would be queen, and he would be pushed aside.

Not that it would be such a bad thing, being pushed out of the light and into the shadows.

Plus, he was pretty sure Ember wasn't a dog person.

"Asher, what do you think?" Asher ripped his gaze up from his plate, looking around the table frantically. His mother had asked the question, but he had no idea what it had been about.

"I'm sorry. I'm afraid I didn't hear the question," he said, and Feather narrowed her eyes. He could read the threat in them. She'd cut off his alcohol supply if he made her look bad. His mother only made time for him when he'd displeased her, and past experiences had often left his face stinging from a blow. She put on a good show, Feather did, but there was an anger that simmered just below the surface.

So long as she didn't go after his dog, though, he could handle it. As long as she didn't strike an emotional blow, he could handle it.

So long as Feather didn't mention *him*, Asher could be okay. "We were talking about our favorite places in the far continent. Lord Forrest said he preferred the spa on the ocean, in Sal, and Lady Soo said she enjoyed the lush forests of Tali. We wanted to know what you think." Asher racked his memories from his time in the far continent, but the only thing he remembered was how exceedingly bored he was. Most of the time he was there he was working, and the time he wasn't working he was drinking.

"Honestly, I think the rum in Prajan. It was nothing like I've ever had before. Simply divine. If you get the chance, you must go." Feather hummed, satisfied with his answer, and Asher slid back in his chair, relieved. He'd passed the test. He felt a pair of eyes fixed on him, and, hoping it was the servant girl, looked up. But it was Ember, glaring at him with such intensity that he almost felt afraid. Almost.

That's when it clicked—Prajan wasn't part of the far continent. It was part of the middle continent. He had gotten it wrong. But, surely, a simple geography mistake wasn't enough to warrant that kind of anger, was it? Nobody else had seemed to care. He finished off his third glass and snapped again for it to be refilled.

Asher held her gaze for a moment longer before she dropped it back to the plate in front of her.

He shrugged it off. He had better things to worry about.

Asher sat as his desk, a bottle of whisky in one hand and a book he wasn't reading in the other, cringing as his mother's footsteps crossed outside of his bedroom, followed by those of several soldiers. He couldn't tell for certain, as the other footsteps were masking it, but he had a sinking suspicion that the captain of the guard was with her. He'd spent years memorizing the exact patterns of the way his parents walked, as well as the captain of the guard, and the servants who most often spent time near his bedroom. He could tell who was coming down the hallway without ever calling out to them.

And now his mother and the captain, General Moreci, were coming to his room for some unknown reason, and things were probably going to get ugly, very quickly. He risked a glance at Hazel, curled up in the center of his bed, sleeping soundly. Feather hadn't gone after Hazel before, but Asher wouldn't put it past her. Not when she was in a rage like this.

Feather didn't knock when she came in, but Asher hadn't expected her to. Moreci followed close at her heels, all golden skin and black hair shot through with silver, although he couldn't have been more than fifteen years older than Asher. She closed the door behind her, not saying anything for a long while. Moreci lingered by the wall, one hand resting on the hilt of his sword, and the other on a leather whip, the handle branching into multiple strips of leather.

Asher flexed his shoulders again, watching Moreci. He was watching Feather—the hunger in his eyes as he stared at the queen made Asher sick.

"Where's Father?" Asher asked, leaning back in his chair, attempting to act as though he didn't care. He was bracing himself for both verbal and physical retaliation for the stupid answer he'd given to her question at dinner, or perhaps retaliation for the question he'd just asked.

"Out with some woman," Feather muttered, coming further into the room. Her hand lashed out, striking the glass in Asher's hand. It flew across the room, shattering against the far wall and immediately staining the carpet with brown liquor. Hazel jumped at the sound, letting out a small bark.

One of the shards stuck in his hand, and it began bleeding. Asher cursed under his breath and stood, moving into the washroom that joined his bedroom. He wrapped a towel around the wound, tying a knot with his teeth before sitting back at his desk, glaring up at his mother.

Asher forced himself not to say anything, even as fury simmered in his stomach. Phoenix above. She got like this every so often, when his father was being especially unfaithful, and she wasn't able to handle that in any way other than taking it out on Asher. He was tempted to offer her a drink to help ease her anger, but that would've resulted in more violence, and he was only interested in getting her out of his room as quickly as possible, although he knew she wouldn't go easily. She'd brought Moreci for a reason, and he wasn't particularly looking forward to figuring out why.

"It's not my fault," Asher spat, reaching for another one of the glasses he kept on his desk. He watched Hazel as she turned in a circle three times before settling down once more. She was watching Feather, though, amber eyes keeping track of the queen's every move. "I didn't introduce him to whoever she is." Feather's hand came down upon his desk, but Asher barely flinched at her reaction. He'd gotten used to this over the years, and he only truly got worried when Feather came at him with her fists, or when she sent Moreci at him. But there was nothing substantial in what she was doing at the moment, and he continued pouring himself a glass, even as she began ranting. He was tempted to tune her out, but the harsh words she'd hissed to him still rang in his ears.

You useless excuse for a crown prince.

His mother knew exactly how to get to Asher, and she exploited that at every possible opportunity. There were certain lines she occasionally crossed that pushed Asher over the edge, but she mercifully hadn't done that.

Yet.

"She's part of the houses," Feather said, beginning to pace. A sharp contrast to the calm, collected woman who sat through palace meetings and dinners and holy days, who presented herself as a queen should. As a steady presence who could be trusted to lead the country, should something happen to his father.

But there was nothing steady or calm about the woman that was tugging on her hair as she stomped around his room. She muttered under her breath, stopping in front of him. He took a long sip of his drink, looking up at his mother. A single tear escaped Feather's eye, but she hastily wiped it away.

"Who is she?" Feather asked, turning to Asher with desperation in her eyes. She looked broken, and because she was so broken, she was dangerous. A person with nothing to lose would lash out however they chose. She moved toward the bed, toward Hazel, and Asher sprang into action.

"Mother," Asher said, standing and pointing at the door. "Stop. Leave." Feather rounded on him.

"I am your mother!" she screeched, and Asher flinched then, taking a step away from her. Someone was bound to hear her soon, someone who wasn't already accustomed to this side of her, and then everything would fall apart. "I am the queen!"

"I understand that," Asher said, some of the anger in his stomach spilling out. "But you're doing nothing except raging around my room and knocking drinks out of my hand. If Father is out with another woman, then it's probably because you're absolutely insufferable and nobody can stand you." Feather moved faster than Asher could react, her hand cracking across his face. The liquor already in his stomach numbed some of the pain, but it still stung, and he slammed his glass down.

"My useless son," she spat, her lip curling. "Why couldn't you have taken your cousin's place? He wouldn't have insulted me. He wouldn't have disappointed all of us the way you do." Asher held his breath, and Feather opened her mouth again, more venom flying from her mouth, alongside spit.

"I wish you had been the one who died."

All of Asher's rage boiled over at that comment. Nobody, not even his mother, was to mention his cousin to him.

"Get out!" He hadn't expected it to work, but to his surprise, Feather stormed out of the room, hissing something to Moreci, and then closing the door so violently behind her that the glasses on Asher's desk rattled from the force.

Moreci moved towards Asher, and he braced himself.

"Let me guess," Asher said. "She wants us to bond?" He forced his tone to be mocking, light-hearted. To hide the fear that curled in his stomach as he watched Captain Moreci release the whip from his belt. A slight smile played on his face.

Ah, what a good lapdog he made.

"I must ask that you remove your shirt," Moreci said, a finger running over the whip as though it were a lover. "Get on your knees, and place your hands on the bedpost."

"I'd rather not," Asher said, eyes trained on the whip. The sound of it whistling through the air haunted his nightmares. The sound of it hitting his flesh was often enough to drive him from sleep.

"Comply," Moreci said. "You outrank me, of course, but not your mother. And I have direct orders from her. Remove your shirt."

"Or what?" Asher challenged, his heart sinking when Moreci's eyes flicked toward Hazel.

"Or I take out the punishment on the dog," he said, his lips curling into a wider smile. "Your choice."

Asher didn't trust Moreci not to go after Hazel anyways, and he grabbed the dog's collar, hauling her into the washroom. He slammed the door, ignoring her cries as she tried to get back through the door. Even she knew what was coming.

He slowly unbuttoned his shirt, balling it up and throwing it on the bed. He slowly lowered himself to his knees, allowing Moreci to bind his wrists to the bedpost with a strip of fabric. Another was placed in his mouth for when he would undoubtedly scream. He always screamed, always cried out for help.

None ever came. Moreci's guards were loyal to a fault, and the rest of the floor was deserted. Any servants would be forced to keep their mouths shut. Besides, who would help him? Who would dare cross the queen?

Asher flinched as Moreci brought the whip through the air, the sound making him shiver.

He didn't have time to brace himself before the whip came down, splitting his skin.

It was as though fire had exploded over his skin, the pain unbearable and consuming. Asher bit down on the fabric, unwilling to scream just yet.

When the whip came down a second time, tears sprang to his eyes, hot and bitter. Asher didn't know how many lashes Feather had ordered—it varied. Once, she'd stood in the corner, allowing it to go on until Asher had collapsed completely.

The tears began to fall when the whip came down again.

Asher cried out the fourth time, his back sticky with blood as Moreci took his skin in slow, painful strips, cool air kissing his back between lashes.

Moreci was a master of torture, leaving just enough time between each lash that the pain truly started to set in, somehow sharp and aching all at once.

Another lash. Asher prayed to whatever gods there were, be it the Phoenix or not, to end it.

The whip came down again, a sixth time, and this time, Asher screamed into the gag, his voice hoarse and cracked.

Make it end.

Behind him, Moreci let out a cold, high laugh, and then, mercifully, Asher heard him sheath the whip.

His hands were unbound, the gag removed from his mouth, and then Moreci was gone, leaving him alone and bleeding on the carpet. Asher collapsed, his breaths coming in short, quick pants. The door opened, closed, locked, and gentle hands were upon him. Servants, sworn to silence. Servants he didn't know the names of, didn't know the faces of. The pain blurred his vision, and he couldn't help the scream that tore from his throat when those same hands guided him into a bath, cold water running over his wounds and making them burn like hellfire. Hazel pressed her nose to his hand, cool and comforting, but he couldn't bring himself to reach out to her—the pain was unbearable.

Oh, Phoenix save him.

He screamed and cried and thrashed as the servants gently washed his wounds, and then bound them, thick strips of bandage wrapping around his chest and back. They were gone, then, leaving him alone in the bathroom with his dog, who nosed him anxiously. He stayed there for a long time, forcing himself to breathe.

Asher stood, tears springing into his eyes as his back cried out in protest.

He could do this.

Slowly, steadily, Asher moved back into his bedroom. A drink. He would be okay if he got a drink.

He settled back in his chair, picking up his deserted glass, swirling the liquid. He didn't let himself think of the wounds on his back. If he didn't focus on them, he could get through this.

Asher made himself think of his parents instead—someone to blame. Moreci delighted in the torture, but he wouldn't be bold enough to go after Asher if not for Feather's approval. She was to blame.

Feather was normally distant, keeping to herself when she wasn't forced to be on display. But there were times like this, when she exploded from the weight of everything that was on her shoulders.

And that explosion almost always ended in new scars on Asher's back.

Asher could remember a time when both of his parents had been loving and doting, but that had stopped after he was around twelve. The stress of the kingdom upon the two of them—especially his father—had worn them down and turned them almost unrecognizable.

And Asher had taken the worst of their anger and fear and sadness. He tried to imagine himself as king, wearing the crown his father only pulled out for ceremonial events. A wife at his side. Would he, too, crack under the pressure? Would the strain of running an entire country eventually make him unfaithful, or would his addiction only grow deeper?

Or worse, would he become like his mother, cruel and violent to the end, with only a care for herself, and nobody else?

Nothing drew Asher toward the crown. Nothing made him wish that he would one day sit on the throne and be king. He truly wished his cousin had survived to take the throne.

Asher didn't want the throne. Not in the slightest. Not if it would turn him into his father, or his mother.

Chapter

FIVE

ASHER REACHED UNDERNEATH HIS mattress and felt around until his hand closed over a fistful of fabric. He quickly shimmied out of the clothes he had on, stuffing them into his closet. He didn't think anybody was going to come into his room while he was gone, but he still hid the clothes on instinct.

On went the clothes that had been under his bed—a servant's uniform—and he called Hazel to his side, flinching as the shirt glided over his new wounds. He slipped out of the room, keeping his head lowered as he walked down the hallway. A few small bottles of liquor clinked in his right pocket, enough for what he needed, but not so much that it would raise suspicion. In the other, he clamped his hand over a single key.

Nobody paid attention to him, except a singular guard, who pulled away from the wall and followed at a distance, but that was to be expected. Servants rarely got attention in the palace, and when they did, it usually wasn't for a desirable reason. Hazel drew some attention, but other servants, especially stable boys and hound-keepers, kept dogs at their sides, and even she was ignored by the few people they saw. The single guard behind them kept his distance, and Asher paid him no attention. He was used to always having one guard on his tail, and he fully planned on losing the man once he was on horseback.

Down the servants' stairs, Asher's back protesting with every step, he descended once more, moving toward where the servants' quarters, the kitchen, and the staircase to the prison were. Hazel's nails clacked loudly on the stairs behind him, her tail wagging excitedly as they headed to their new adventure.

This also happened to be the way to get to the stables without being noticed, and that was exactly what Asher wanted. If someone recognized him, he'd be in trouble. Most of the servants were happy to keep their mouths shut if they caught him doing something he wasn't supposed to, but there were still plenty that would go running to his father, or worse, his mother. The guard was one of the few that rotated when it came to following Asher around and ensuring his safety, and he hoped the man wouldn't say anything. When would he, after all? He was too busy following Asher.

That wasn't a conversation he wanted to have with either of his parents. It would most certainly result in some sort of physical retaliation from his mother, and his alcohol supply would be cut off. Two things he'd avoid if he could.

Nobody stopped him as he made his way down the hall-way, however, removing all possible threat of getting caught by his parents.

The stables were directly connected to the hallway by a broad door. As soon as Asher opened the door, the smell of hay and manure hit his nose. Comforting. Familiar. A dozen stalls lined the main walkway of the stables, each housing one of the palace's beautiful mares and geldings. It was heated and cooled just as well as the rest of the palace, to ensure the horses' comfort throughout the seasons.

Horses neighed softly to each other and stamped their feet as Asher made his way through the rows. The royal family each had a horse they were given at birth, or the day they married into it. They were kept at the very end, closest to the doors that led outside. Asher's horse, Siliros, had his back turned to the walkway, black tail swishing as he gobbled down whatever the stable hands were spoiling him with.

"Siliros," Asher whispered, opening the stall door. Hanging on the far wall were the horse's saddle and bridle, but Asher didn't trust his own shaky hands with all of the buckles and buttons, and knew he could ride Siliros without either.

Besides, they were unnecessary for the short ride Asher was about to take.

Asher coaxed Siliros out of the stall with a handful of oats, backing up until his back hit the doors. He swore at the pain, cursing both his mother and Moreci with words that would've curled a sailor's hair.

Hazel wove between the horse's legs, coming to stand beside Asher as he fumbled for the handle, just as Siliros stretched his neck out for the oats. The door gave way just as

Siliros's tongue lapped up the oats. He followed Asher out of the stables and into the cold embrace of Eiad's winter. The door closed softly behind them, and Asher dragged a small stool over from the side of the door, brushing snow off it and hauling himself up on Siliros's back. The guard was still in the stables, saddling up his horse. Asher took his opportunity.

"Ready?" Asher whispered, bending close to the horse's neck. He gently kicked, and Siliros trotted forward, leaving deep prints in the snow. Asher shivered, pressing himself further on the horse's back. The faster they got to their destination, the better.

Hazel kept an even pace at the horse's side, tongue lolling out of her mouth in her excitement.

He guided Siliros towards the back road, which had been mercifully cleared of snow, that led out of the palace, which was used primarily by soldiers, servants on errands, delivery carts. It wouldn't do to have those types of people going in and out of the same entrance as the royals, the houses, and visiting dignitaries. It was just one more way Asher's father kept the people at arm's length.

The back gate, unlike the front, was only guarded by a single soldier and was always left unlocked, as most deliveries came in during the earliest hours of the morning, when the world was still dark. Asher had spent hours examining the rotations of the guards, which carts came in on which days, at what time, and who drove them. Plenty of servants came and went during the night, although most weren't allowed to use a horse.

Luckily for Asher, servants were sometimes issued passes to use the horses. Not Siliros, necessarily, but one of the spares. It was so dark though, and everyone was so cold and tired, that nobody was going to do an in-depth look at which horse Asher was on.

The soldier at the gate barely looked over at him, simply holding his hand out for the pass. Asher slipped it from his pocket, handing it to the man. He gave it a quick glance before handing it back. He looked down at Hazel with an unimpressed gaze.

"Be back by sunrise," the man grunted, and then Asher was free, sitting up and spurring Siliros on. The horse responded with little urging, taking off down the road. His hooves clacked against the stone that paved the way. The way that took him from his parents, from the social pressures that came at him from every angle. Hazel took off beside them, disappearing down the road with a bark of excitement.

Nobody could tell him that he was a disgrace of a prince where he was going. Siliros wouldn't look at him with disappointment every time his glass was refilled.

He could leave his title behind, and simply be Asher.

Asher allowed himself to smile as the palace gradually disappeared behind him.

It didn't take long for Asher to find his destination, even as the small road in the woods was covered almost completely by the snow. Someone had made a half-hearted attempt to clear it, as evidenced by the rather large piles of snow on either side, but there was truly no point of clearing a small, practically unused road during Eiad's winter.

Asher guided Siliros on the smaller road, staying low on the horse's back to keep from getting hit in the head with low-hanging branches. Hazel was keeping pace with them now, panting from both exhaustion and exhilaration.

Iron gates, underneath a large archway, appeared at the end of the small road, and Asher slowed Siliros to a walk, dismounting when they reached the gates. He brushed snow off the lock, fumbling in his pocket for his key, hands trembling from drink and the cold. He should've worn gloves. He tipped his head up, reading the words inscribed in the archway.

Et non solum dormientes.

They are only sleeping.

The gates creaked open, giving just enough room for Asher and Siliros to walk through the gates. They clanged shut behind them, and Siliros spooked, trotting a few feet away as Asher took a deep breath.

The royal cemetery.

One of the few places Asher felt he could truly be himself. It was rare for the cemetery to have visitors—the last time Asher had actually seen it with anybody other than himself, Siliros, and Hazel was after a distant cousin had died and was laid to rest inside of it.

It was beautiful, in the macabre way cemeteries so often were. Especially now, during the winter, when a perfect layer of snow had fallen over all the headstones and the mausoleums. Hazel was bounding through the snow, annoying Siliros.

The cemetery was centered around a reflection pool, which was currently frozen over. The oldest graves were closest to the pool, spreading out in a circular motion from there. The mausoleums were set around the edges, built up of the great, green stone that the Phoenix Palace was made of. They were for kings and queens only, often laid to rest together. Asher moved toward the center of the cemetery immediately, to the reflection pool. During the summer months, the cemetery was alive with bugs and small creatures, slinking between the graves as they called to one another.

During the winter, however, the cemetery was quiet, and the only sound was Siliros stomping around the snow near the gate, and Hazel chasing her own tail near him.

Asher let out a long breath as he settled by the frozen edge of the reflection pool, watching his breath mist in the air. He sat there for a long moment before standing and moving away, towards a headstone that was far newer than the others. He settled on the ground, cupping his hands in his lap before knocking snow off one of the headstones, eyes dancing over the name inscribed there.

Vax Cinis.

A cousin who Asher had one day found dead by his own hand, having spiked his own drink intentionally. It had been only two days after they'd buried Asher's aunt and uncle, the former dead from a drowning accident, and the latter from heartbreak.

Asher tucked his knees up to his chest, staring at the headstone for a long moment before beginning to speak, words hanging in the still air.

"Things aren't getting better," Asher said. "Actually, I'm fairly sure they're getting worse." His words died only a few inches from his mouth, dropping into the snow.

"All of it, I mean. The alcohol. The pressure. All of it," Asher said. "I can't stay here anymore, Vax. My parents. They just... Everybody expects me to get better. And I can't get better. None of it is getting better. Everybody expects me to be you, but I can't be you. I wish you could've taken my place."

Hazel bounded over, settling comfortably in the snow beside him. Asher buried his hand in her fur, using her to ground himself.

"All I have left is the liquor, and Hazel and Siliros. That's all." Asher dropped his head to his knees, unable to stop the small sob that ripped out of his chest.

Oh, Phoenix. Asher didn't know what he was waiting for—there would obviously be no response. Not from the dead. Vax was only ashes in a golden vase at this point, cremated by the Phoenix Flame, the last bit of magic in the world. He couldn't respond.

But that didn't stop Asher from coming back to where he was laid to rest, to tell him how badly his own life was spiraling out of control. He reached in his pocket, his hand closing over one of the bottles of liquor. It had been Vax's favorite, and Asher had taken to it after Vax had died. It had been the start of his craving for alcohol, to numb the pain. To fill the hole that his cousin's death had left.

It was partially Vax's fault. Asher couldn't blame him, even if it would've been justified. He'd been furious, at first, at his cousin for abandoning him. But now...now, he could only blame himself.

"I have to get out of here, Vax. I don't know where I'm going. Not yet. But this isn't the place I'm meant to be," Asher whispered, the words coming out of his chest with great effort. He bottled everything inside of him, and even when he was only overheard by a dog and a horse, he still had difficultly speaking some of his innermost thoughts out loud.

Asher uncorked the other bottle of alcohol, knocked it against the one on Vax's grave, and drank the entire thing in one toss of his head.

Chapter

Six

"DID YOU NOTICE THAT the prince was drunk last night?" Ember asked Verity as they sat by a roaring fireplace, a knife and a whetstone in Ember's hand, and a stack of financial reports and an apple in Verity's. It was always apples with Verity—the smell of her apple-scented perfume filled the entirety of the Draco Estate.

"Yes. I didn't think anything of it." Ember looked up from her knife, hoping her mother wasn't being serious.

"You're joking. He's the prince for the Phoenix's sake. He shouldn't be getting drunk at palace dinners. He looked ignorant when his mother asked him about Prajan. It's common knowledge what countries are part of the far and mid continents, especially with the education he's no doubt received. Especially of a close ally, like Prajan or Qin. Doesn't he own a map? Honestly, Mother, I don't see why you're looking past this."

Verity glanced up from her papers, adjusting her glasses. She'd started wearing those recently, when her eyesight had started to go. And yet she only wore them when she was alone with Ember. Dragons were not supposed to show any physical weakness, and going blind was most certainly a weakness. "You're reading too much into this. He might've just been having an off day. Plenty of people drink when they have bad days."

"Princes do not have off days. Phoenixes do not have off days. If I were the princess, I would never get drunk. He's an embarrassment."

Verity slammed her apple on the table, and Ember jumped.

"You will not speak about the crown prince that way. He does outrank you. It would do you good to remember that. Especially since you're going to be the lady of House Draco one day. You have to learn how to bite your tongue, even when your royals act stupidly."

"That's hardly fair. If someone is more fit to rule the country, they should be allowed to. Half the time I think *you* want to rule. Plus, he can't meet other leaders drunk. We'd be the laughingstock of the entire world, us and our king with his nose in a bottle. He'll drink himself to death without an heir and that'll be the end of us."

"Don't speak of him like that, and don't speak of me that way. I'm not power hungry, Ember. I'm content with what I've been blessed with and what I've worked for. He could clean up, you know. He's still young, like you. His parents will rule for years to come—he has time. And I care for the king more than you'll ever understand." Ember snapped her book shut and glared at her mother. She had half a mind to chuck one of the silk pillows at Verity's head but dismissed that thought quickly. She enjoyed being alive.

What did she mean by care for the king?

There was no time to ask, however, Verity was awaiting Ember's response, looking at her with a bored expression.

"How likely do you think that is? He drinks like a fish, Mother. People like that don't 'clean up'. They end up passed out in a dirty tavern to be robbed and murdered. And you and I both know he's the only heir. What happens if he does get murdered? What happens if he doesn't clean up? Am I expected to sit idly by and watch him ruin Eiad?"

Verity sighed, rubbing the space between her eyes.

"I don't want to talk about this anymore. Go to bed, Ember."

"I'm not done talking about this. It's ridiculous that the prince continues to get drunk in front of the entire court. We deserve a prince who cares about us, who cares about our country. He has to care about something more than alcohol if he wants to lead the same way his father does. Half the country is going to flee to the mid continent if Asher takes over."

"Did I ask if you wanted to keep talking about this?"

"No. But I thought—"

"You thought wrong. Go to bed, Ember. I won't continue to be so kind if you refuse me again." Ember dipped her head at Verity in response before backing up a few steps, and then fleeing out of the room, refusing to allow Verity to see the tears in her eyes. Her mother was the only person that could provoke tears from Ember, a fatal flaw Ember was desperate to shake off. She couldn't have weaknesses, and she couldn't cry.

No Dragon would be caught dead crying.

The next morning dawned cold and dark for Asher. He wasn't even entirely sure it was morning when he woke up, as the sky was still dark and there was only one servant in his quarters, slumbering soundly in the little servant's bedroom that was off Asher's. He didn't feel like waking the man, though, and instead donned his robe and slippers before grabbing the whiskey bottle he kept on his bedside and slipping out into the hall. He left Hazel in the room, the dog still sleeping on the floor beside his bed.

The hall was fairly empty, too, and the woman standing guard outside his room offered him a small nod as he walked past her. She would follow him, Asher knew, but ignored her anyways.

He uncorked the bottle as he walked, taking a deep swig of the whiskey. It left a pleasant burn in the back of his throat, something comforting and familiar to him.

The palace wasn't quite awake at this hour, as it wasn't time to prepare breakfast yet, and the cleanup from dinner had been completed hours ago. It was quiet. Peaceful. The only sound was the soft pad of his slippers against the thick carpet and the rustle of his silk robe as he roamed the hallway. There was no screaming or crying, no anger echoing down the long halls.

Asher didn't really know where he was going. He knew he wasn't going back to the cemetery—the sun was going to be coming up too soon, and he wouldn't be able to make it back in time.

At first, he headed toward the kitchen, but then realized he had no idea how to prepare himself a snack and decided against it. His next idea was the gardens, but the frost over the windows made him quickly discard that.

He wandered through the halls as though they were foreign to him, taking a few moments to appreciate the portraits that lined most of the palace walls. Royal portraits, yes, but also those of the twelve house lords and ladies, and their predecessors, hidden down forgotten hallways. Lady Verity Ignis, a Dragon curled around her shoulders, smoke billowing from its mouth and leathery wings flared. Lord Charles Palin, sitting astride a magnificent Stallion. Lady Scarlett Evet, her face dappled by the sunlight through trees. A Fox's eyes peeking over her shoulder. Lord Yvlin Rostro, surrounded by a flurry of black feathers and beaks, coolly gazing out of the frame. All of them, beautiful and cold and violent, perfectly suited for the Phoenix Court.

In between the portraits and around the rest of the palace were stained glass windows, each made up of the patron animals' colors. Gold and black for House Draco, black and orange for House Tigris. During the day, they cast magnificent patterns over the carpets, but the moon didn't come through them, and they were simply dark and slightly glittery.

Asher came to a stop outside a heavy set of wooden doors. He hadn't meant to come here. It wasn't an easy place to be in, most of the time. But even still, he pushed the doors open and entered the temple, taking another drink from the bottle.

A massive, white stone carving of the Phoenix towered over the space, wings outspread as though it intended to protect the devout. Her mouth was open in a silent screech, eyes wide as she gazed down at the sanctuary. Her face was dappled in flickering shadows.

Underneath it burned an everlasting fire, called the Phoenix Flame, that was fed by blood. The white stone pit holding it was lined with knives, each a different length and sharpness, so the devout could offer their own blood to the Phoenix and choose how painful it would be. The fire had been brought down from the peak of Mount Saffi, where the first temple had been created. Supposedly it was the spot the Phoenix ascended from Eiad, cleansing the continent in fire and fury.

Vax had been cremated by the Phoenix Flame, but they hadn't bothered to move his body all the way up Mount Saffi. They'd just lit a torch from this Phoenix Flame and dropped it on his body.

The floor was made up of a gem mosaic, depicting the Phoenix's final ascension from Eiad into Her home in the sun. She was done in reds and oranges and yellows, the background a deep green and blue. The only black was the Phoenix's eyes, cold and unfeeling as She stared up at him from the floor. Immortalized in ruby and emerald and onyx. Priceless gems that so many shoes had stepped on.

Along the walls were statutes of the twelve patron animals in various fighting positions. A Tiger baring its teeth, a Snake coiled to strike, a Leopard ready to pounce. Ready to defend the Phoenix from all who dared attack it. Carved from solid white stone, the same that held the Phoenix Flame. He paused for a moment to look at the statue of the Dragon, wings outspread in a magnificent display of fury and power. Similar to Verity Ignis's portrait in the hallway.

The temple was easily the largest part of the palace, even larger than the conference room, since it held nearly the entire staff on holy days. His father had commissioned the entire thing almost as soon as he came into power, proving to the temple that he was committed to his faith. Rows upon rows of white stone benches bolted to the floor. There were no windows on the walls, but the entire ceiling was a giant dome of glass, arching over the temple. It let in plenty of light during the day, and apparently during the night, as Asher was able to see every detailed carving on the benches. Violent carvings, of the Phoenix cleansing the world with fire and taking Her leave. Gentle carvings, of the Dragon, curled up beside the Phoenix and sheltering Her with their wings while She wept for Her lost children. Delicate carvings, of the Fox stepping through high grass, the Sparrow perched on a high branch, singing a soft song. Dangerous carvings, of the Tiger and Leopard facing down the Bear and the Wolf.

The statue of the Phoenix seemed even more imposing during the night, where shadows from the moon and the flickering fire caused it to look less like a kind spirit and more like a vengeful deity.

Asher took a few more steps forward before noticing *her*. She clearly hadn't seen him yet, as her head was bowed as the knelt at the fire. Her mouth was moving but no sound came from it.

Asher strode forward and placed his hand on her shoulder. She jumped, nearly falling into the flames and barely catching herself at the base of the Phoenix's statue, her hand only inches from the hungry fire, which would quickly devour her, gobbling her up until she was nothing more than a rotting pair of pants and strands of bloody, brown hair. Maybe leaving her green eyes at the bottom of the flames, so everybody could remember the idiot girl who fell into the Phoenix Flame.

"Apologies. I didn't mean to scare you," Asher said, although he absolutely meant to scare her. He rarely got a rise out of people, and in a sick way, he found it fun to make servants jump. His words were a little slurred, and she looked at the bottle quickly before responding. He figured she was thinking he shouldn't be near an open flame. Not one as powerful as the Phoenix Flame, at the very least. Even from where he stood, he could feel the power of it—it was the only magic Asher could believe in. The Phoenix Flame seemed to reach toward him like a beast of flame and fury, rather than teeth and claws.

It feasted on blood nonetheless.

"It's quite alright, Your Highness."

"You're not allowed to be in here. Only the houses and the priests are allowed." That wasn't entirely true. His father left the doors of the temple unlocked at all times so anybody who needed it could use it. But the servants' quarters had a small statue of the Phoenix they were supposed to pray to. That was all that belonged to them—the patron animals were only for the houses, and by extent, this temple.

"I'm sorry. I didn't know. I just desperately needed to pray, and I couldn't remember where the smaller statue was. I misplaced my personal Phoenix charm while I was unpacking a couple days ago. I'll be sure to ask somebody tomorrow morning. Good night, Your Majesty." She moved to walk past him, but Asher held his hand out, stopping her with the bottle.

"What's your name?" Her eyes flared wide with fear. He blocked the only door, and the only thing behind her was the Phoenix Flame. Not to mention the fact that she could hang if he told anybody she had been in the temple.

But he wasn't his father. He wouldn't force this girl into bed to buy his silence. And he wasn't his mother—he wouldn't strike her. Asher refused to make her truly afraid of him. A small scare was one thing. Terrifying the poor girl was completely different.

A rabbit, caught in a trap.

"I'm just curious. I'm not going to report you." She let out a breath before responding. He'd lifted the door, and she had scampered out.

"My name is Juniper, sir. Juniper Farley." Asher watched as she turned and disappeared from the room, those strange green eyes burned into the back of his mind.

Ember woke early, determined to get rid of the sting of her mother's words before she and Verity had to speak to each other. She threw for well over two hours, moving the targets and her own position, attempting to throw with her left hand,

and even, at one point, trying to throw while she was moving, which went spectacularly wrong.

But even all of that, even the bite of the bitter cold and the feeling of knives against her palm, wasn't enough to drive what Verity had said from her mind. Ember didn't know why she had latched onto it, why she was unable to forget the cruelty behind Verity's words. Her mother had spoken to her like that before. It wasn't common, exactly, but it had happened, and Ember had been able to recover from it then.

But this time...she couldn't forget. Couldn't work off the frustration still burning in every one of her muscles.

Ember let out a frustrated sigh, gathered her knives, and began to throw again.

Chapter

SEVEN

"**P**HOENIX FLIME YTU," A priestess murmured in the old language, lighting a stick of incense as she danced around the statue of the Phoenix. "We thank You, Great Phoenix, for the blessing of Your patron animals among this place. For the Dragon, the Tiger, the Leopard, the Owl, the Stallion, the Elk, the Snake, the Fox, the Swan, the Spider, the Crow, and the Sparrow." She dumped a bowl of blood into the Phoenix Flame, probably from some poor initiate, or maybe an animal, whispering more soft words in the old tongue. The flames surged higher at her words, gorging itself on the blood. Only those of the temple knew how to speak that forgotten language, and even still, it was only the words of the temple they remembered. Nobody used it to converse anymore.

"Thank You, Great Phoenix, for protecting Eiad, Your blessed country, from the dark evils of the Eagle, the Wolf, and the Bear." Another stick of incense was lit, and Ember's eyes watered from the strong smell and the smoke it produced. The incense and the Phoenix Flame had created a thin cloud of it that was constantly aggravating Ember's nose and eyes.

"Thank You, Great Phoenix, for keeping our children safe during the Race of the Heirs, during Your blessed first snowfall. Continue to protect them and make them strong, so that they may serve You, and their patron animals, with pride and strength."

"Thank You, Great Phoenix," the temple repeated quietly, with one voice that reverberated off the stone walls and disappeared near the skylight. The priestess raised her hands, cupping the Phoenix's spirit in her upturned hands. At least, that was what Ember had been told she was doing. It looked stupid to her. Even still, she could admit that in the sunlight, she looked almost like a deity, completely awash in golden light. Ember fidgeted in her seat. This priestess was slower than the person they'd had last holy day, and her small breakfast wasn't enough anymore. She willed her stomach to be quiet as she sat in the second row.

The priestess picked up a long, serrated knife with a bone-colored handle from near the Phoenix Flame, slicing her right palm open with it. It hardly made a sound, but Ember could see her blood bubbling up from the deep wound. She squeezed her palm over the fire, and it climbed higher, devouring her blood. To the priestess's credit, Ember noticed, she hadn't cringed when the knife had dug into her skin. That said something about temple training. A few scraps of her skin fell in, and Ember swallowed down her small breakfast. She wasn't squeamish, usually, but there was something incredibly unsettling about someone cutting their hand open without so much as blinking.

The priestess wrapped her hand in a bandage she produced from the inside of her silver robe—the color of temple neutrality—and wiped the knife off, placing it back in its spot.

"Now the temple is invited to say prayers to their individual patron creatures, to ask them for blessing upon their houses. I also invite King Whelyn, Queen Feather, and Prince Asher forward, to offer their blood to the fire. After the service, any who are willing may approach the Phoenix Flame and give an offering to Her." Verity bowed her head as the silent prayers began, but Ember barely dropped hers, keeping her eyes on the row in front of her. Asher hadn't bowed his head either, nor moved to give his blood, and Ember frowned. She knew she wasn't quite the picture of a devout follower—she certainly wasn't priestess material—but she believed in both the Phoenix and the patron creatures. There was no reason they couldn't exist, and they had gotten her this far.

Asher hadn't said any of the prayers the entire time. She had noticed. He'd even had the audacity to cough when the initial stick of incense had been lit. And now that he was refusing to slit his palm for the Phoenix, she was even more upset about it. His parents could do it—why couldn't he? It didn't matter to Ember whether or not he actually believed, but it looked good for him to at least pretend that he cared. One of the best things his father had done was make the temple strong again, making them almost a built-in support system should the king need them.

Asher couldn't—no, wouldn't—destroy all of that because he couldn't fake believing in the Phoenix. Ember simply wouldn't allow it. She'd do everything in her power to ensure the temple was still slightly swayed towards the palace.

Ember had also noticed the green-eyed servant girl in the farthest row when she had come in.

She seemed to be everywhere, lurking in the back of every hallway in the palace. She unsettled Ember, making her feel unsafe in the safest place on the continent. The Phoenix Palace was quite possibly the safest spot on all three continents, and there was no reason for the girl to make her feel that way— what power did a servant, a houseless nobody, have against a Dragon? But Ember couldn't shake the feeling that there was something very off about the girl, and that in and of itself was enough to make her wary.

Ember muttered a quick prayer to the Dragon while she stared at the back of Asher's curly head.

A very pointed cough came from behind her, and Ember slowly turned her head, afraid that if she moved too quickly Verity would notice and chastise her brutally later. Nothing physical, of course, but Verity's talent lay behind her lips, and with her wicked tongue, and Ember didn't feel like being subject to harsh words again.

They hadn't quite made up from their fight yet. In fact, Verity hadn't spoken a word to Ember since the argument two days ago, making the mood of the Draco Estate sour like bad milk. Servants scurried around them with their heads down, reluctant to mention Verity to Ember, and the other way around. A thick cloud hung over the estate while Ember and her mother refused to acknowledge the other person. Dragons were remarkably good at holding grudges. However, it was rare that Ember and Verity went more than a day without speaking to each other. Certainly not two days. It simply wasn't practical to do so when they had to work in perfect harmony to keep House Draco running smoothly. It didn't feel right for there to be so much space between Ember and her mother.

Viper glared at her before giving another cough. To anybody else, it would just sound like he was having issues with the sweet smoke. But Verity was far too smart to mistake a pointed cough for an accidental one. Verity shifted a bit, and Ember quickly turned back around and dropped her chin to her chest, and pretended to pray, tracing the mosaic on the floor with her eyes. She locked eyes with the Phoenix just as the priestess broke the silence.

"Go forward, and may the Phoenix protect you," the priestess said, and the temple stood as one, chattering and laughing with each other. The royal family mingled in the crowd, the king and queen quick to say hello to the members of the houses that didn't come to the weekly meetings, like younger siblings and close cousins. Thanking the lords and ladies for keeping their smallest children quiet while the priestess spoke. Now, however, children ran between the rows of benches, shrieking with laughter and chasing each other down as they tumbled over the floor. Ember figured it was lucky for them that the mosaic was underneath a strong sheet of clear stone, or else those children would hang for defacing palace property.

Not truly, of course. The houses could be vicious when necessary, but none of them went after children.

They were many things, after all, but not demons.

Verity stood, brushing nonexistent lint off her red dress, straightening her posture. She didn't look at Ember as she spoke. "I'm going to speak to the king for a moment. Go to the carriage if you want, I'll be out in a minute. Or don't. It doesn't truly matter to me. You could walk for all I care." Ember turned away from her, walking out into the main hallway, trying her best not to stomp like a spoiled child. Her mother did know how to get on her last nerve.

Ember walked out of the temple, dodging righteous members of the houses that tried to place blessings and fire oil on her forehead. She'd received enough blessings to last her entire lifetime, and she certainly didn't need any more sticky fire oil spread on her skin. She'd just washed this morning. But that came with being House Draco's heir, when everyone who was anyone wanted to claim part of her future success, whatever it would be.

She fully intended on walking out of the palace and waiting in the carriage, but a sound from one of the side hallways caught her attention, and she ducked down it, padding noiselessly down the hallway. It took her another left turn before coming upon the source of the noise.

Ember hid behind the corner, peering into the slightly dark hallway. The stained-glass windows let in little light, and the portraits on the walls put a slight damper on it all. Former matriarchs and patriarchs, looking out of their frames with little more than entitlement in their eyes.

Asher was easily recognized, since he was facing her, leaning against the wall, and there was a strong scent of liquor floating toward her. That smell was a dead giveaway for him. The hound dog at his side was another. It took her another second to figure out who the other person was, and once she did, she had to resist the urge to interrupt their little meeting.

The green-eyed servant murmured something to Asher, and he laughed sloppily. Ember suspected he'd already had far too many drinks for this early in the morning. Especially on a holy day, when there wasn't supposed to be any drinking.

"You're funny, Juniper Farley." Asher said something else, too, but Ember had pressed herself against the wall, controlling her breathing and counting the red Phoenix crests in the wallpaper to calm herself down.

She shouldn't have been upset. It wasn't like there was a betrothal in place or anything like that. The Phoenix hadn't promised her that she would marry Asher, and neither had the king.

And yet...even his father had chosen House Passer. He hadn't dared marry somebody outside of the houses. To defy the will of the Phoenix by marrying outside of Her chosen few. They were lucky, by all accounts, and he would throw that away if he wasn't careful.

Ember was overreacting. Asher didn't belong to her, for the Phoenix's sake. He wasn't hers, and she wasn't supposed to get him until there was an official statement of betrothal. And yet, Ember so desperately needed her mother's approval that she couldn't afford to lose Asher to a houseless girl. She'd be disgraced. Mocked by the lower houses. Her mother would have to produce another heir and would cast Ember out. Or, worse, she would be given a pity wedding. Forced to marry House Tigris's heir or perhaps someone even lower.

All because a servant had decided to show up and ruin everything. Asher was Ember's way into royalty, into the position of queen. She couldn't lose that.

Something made a noise down the hallway, and Ember slipped her knife from her sleeve, peering into the darkness of the hallway behind her. She took a step forward, fully intent on cutting whoever it was.

And yet the dagger at her throat made her stop in her tracks.

Chapter

Eight

ASHER BRUSHED SOME OF his curls out of his face as he spoke to Juniper. It had been chance, actually, that he'd caught her in this back hallway, while he was trying to avoid speaking to the house leaders. Holy day conversations were completely dull. He didn't need any more fire oils anointed on his forehead, and he certainly didn't want to hear "the Phoenix protects you" one more time.

It wasn't that he didn't believe in the Phoenix. But he also knew that his success—whatever he accomplished—would be self-made.

And above all, he didn't want to see his father flirt with half the court while his mother fumed.

Juniper had been walking rather quickly, arms swinging at her sides, completely focused on wherever she was going.

He didn't have any reason to stop her. But he did anyways since Juniper was ridiculously pretty and seeing her was like a shot of the strongest whiskey. Exhilarating, almost. Breathtaking. Burning.

"How are you today, Juniper Farley?" Asher asked, stepping into her path. Hazel, who had been waiting for him outside the temple, sniffed her curiously, tail wagging with excitement. Juniper gasped, stopping to speak to him.

"I'm good, Your Highness." Asher leaned up against the wall, making sure to give her enough room to get around him if she really wanted to. Juniper's fingers were twitching, and she bent forward to run them through Hazel's fur as Asher watched.

"Where were you going in such a hurry? There's usually nothing interesting going on during holy days. Just extra prayers in the temple, if you want to give blood, and random blessings in the hallways."

"I just wanted to go out to the gardens for a moment, sire. To get a breath of fresh air. The kitchens are remarkably stuffy." Asher looked at her, a bit shocked, and quickly glanced out the nearest stained-glass window. As he suspected, mounds of snow covered the castle grounds, pushed off the main paths to provide walkways. Even still, he had no doubt her shoes would get soaked through.

"You want to go outside dressed like that? You'll freeze to death. It snowed last night, you know." Juniper was only wearing the standard palace servant uniform—a simple, long-sleeved black shirt with a matching pair of pants. The uniform Asher used to sneak out was identical; the material was thinner than paper and provided about as much warmth. During the winter months, it wasn't unheard of for some poor servant to freeze to death after being locked outside for the night.

"Ah, then at least I won't have to go back into the kitchens."

Asher chuckled. "You're funny, Juniper Farley."

"Please, sire, just Juniper. It isn't proper for a prince to know my full name."

Asher nodded. "Fine. Then just Asher. Don't worry about calling me sire or Your Highness or anything. And who cares how proper it is? It gets old after a while. Here, let me walk you outside. I can get another servant to bring me an extra coat for you. Would that be okay?"

Juniper gave him a soft smile as she answered. "Yes, please, sir. I would like that."

"So tell me again about your brothers?" Juniper laughed, fully engulfed by Asher's warmest winter coat. It had been a bit of a fight to get her to wear it, and Asher had to take a small bottle of clear liquor out of the pocket, but eventually she'd folded and allowed him to lead her around the dead gardens. Hazel ran wild in the garden, hunting some poor animal through the flowers and bushes as Asher and Juniper continued to speak.

"I have four, and I love them to death, but sometimes I wish I was an only child. Like you. Aspen, Huon, Pine, and Beech. Aspen and Huon are older than me, and Pine and Beech are younger. And, yes, I'm well aware that our parents named us all after trees. People love making that connection.

My parents are from the middle continent. They grew up in the forests, so it only makes sense, honestly." Asher didn't dwell on her comment about him being any only child. There had been a period of time when he had a cousin who was more like a brother than anything. But he didn't know Juniper enough to confide in her about something as personal as Vax.

"What do they do for a living? Your parents and brothers?" Asher asked, enthralled by Juniper's story. He rarely got a firsthand account of somebody's life outside of the houses, much less a servant's story. The welfare of the people was supposed to be his mother's domain, and in the future, his wife's.

He took a little sip from the small bottle he'd found in his coat pocket and then corked it again. He didn't want his head to be fuzzy during this conversation. But the warmth was welcome in the frost-covered gardens. He offered it to Juniper, but she shook her head and waved it away.

"Well, we have a farm, like I said before, so during the spring and summer they're all fully occupied. During the colder months, Aspen works two jobs to support his family—he's married and has a daughter—and my other brothers and I work odd jobs around town. Just doing what we can. Huon is studying to become part of the temple, but that's not a job that makes anything. They feed him, though, and give him a place to sleep, so at least it's six mouths instead of seven. Dad chops lumber during the winter. Mom used to help, but once she had Beech, she couldn't lift the axe anymore. It nearly killed her, not being able to help. This palace job is the steadiest work we've ever had. It definitely helps with the monthly taxes."

Asher shoved his hands deeper in his pockets. He was beginning to lose feeling in them, as with his toes, but there was something fascinating about the girl that walked beside him, feet delicately stepping through the light snow, moving as quietly as a rabbit. By comparison, he was obnoxiously loud. *Crunch, crunch.* She didn't even seem to be bothered by the cold, even though it was seeping through Asher's bones, even with the weak warmth from the noon sun. Winter in Eiad was unforgiving. Religious zealots claimed it was the Phoenix's grieving time. Asher just thought it was brutal. Constant snow and ice for nearly four months. He couldn't imagine living through it outside of the warm palace.

"How much of your paycheck do you send home to them?" Juniper hesitated, as though she wasn't sure how to respond.

Crunch, crunch. "All of it. I get fed here, have a place to sleep, just like Huon. I don't even have to buy my own clothing. So all of it goes to them. It helps them a lot. Usually we have to go into debt to pay for the taxes, but with this extra money it helps. Keeping us out of debt means keeping us alive, honestly. Tax collectors in the smaller towns are terrible, and loan men are worse."

Asher rolled that information over in his mind, considering. His father had begun taxing the people heavily when he'd first come into power, pouring the money into the palace's temple as well as the battle still raging in the far north. Asher knew they were high but...so high that they were unlivable? That couldn't be.

"Are they hungry still? Even with your paycheck, and their work?"

"Yes. We'll always be hungry. There's no getting around that fact. Most people are hungry once you leave the patron circle. Sure, there's an outlier here or there, a rich widow or what have you. There are people who make a fortune from running pleasure houses and taverns or capitalizing on a particular trade, but that's the exception. But my family will always want for more. Almost everybody I know will want for more."

"But you own a farm."

"A small farm. Most of what we grow has to be sold for other necessities—clothing, soap, candles, payments on the house, since we took a loan to purchase it. Which is ridiculous, honestly, since there are only three rooms. I shared a room with Beech until I moved here. And besides, the farm doesn't make anything during the winter. All our crops are gone by the Race of Heirs. And honestly, sire, nobody wants to eat the same thing day after day. You grow weary of it."

Crunch, crunch. They had made a full circle around the garden and now stood in front of the doors leading back inside. Asher fiddled with the bottle in his pocket, knowing that their walk was over but unwilling to accept it. He really didn't want to go back inside, to a palace that was swarmed with the devout. The devout who would feed him to the Phoenix Flame if they saw he had been fraternizing outside of the houses. Flirting outside of the houses. Flirting with a girl who was as dazzling as winter sun on snow.

"I need to go back to the kitchens," Juniper said, shrugging off Asher's coat and handing it to him, shivering a bit as the cold air embraced her. "I do appreciate the walk, Prince Asher. It was good to talk. I haven't made too many friends here yet.

Perhaps I'll see you around. Have a nice day, sire." She turned away, but Asher grabbed her arm. Juniper's eyes flared as she looked at his hand around her arm, and he immediately dropped it. When he saw the red mark on her skin, he pulled away a bit before taking her hand gently in his.

"I'm sorry if I hurt you, but I enjoyed this talk. Thank you for sharing your story with me." Without thinking of how he came across, he brought her hand to his mouth, pressing a soft kiss against the back of her hand. Juniper gasped quietly, drawing her hand away and tucking it into her pocket, and gaping at him a bit.

"Have a wonderful day, Juniper Farley." Asher turned away from her and headed into the palace, Juniper still gaping at him.

NINE

EMBER IMMEDIATELY GRABBED THE wrist holding the knife, twisting it as far as she could before thrusting the person away from her. She sent up a quick thanks to the Phoenix for how lucky it was that the halls were carpeted.

"Yes, please, I would like that," came floating down the hallway, and then the sound of Asher and the girl—whose name was apparently Juniper Farley—retreating down the hall.

Ember turned to face her attacker, nearly clawing his throat open when she recognized Viper.

"I'm going to kill you," Ember hissed, striding toward him with her knife out. "You're such an idiot!"

Viper sheathed the knife up his sleeve, and Ember got a glimpse of the handle in the shape of a serpent in a figure eight. "I warned you about not bringing the might of House Serpens upon you. You didn't heed the warning."

Ember rolled her eyes, resisting the urge to put her knife through his stomach. "I didn't 'heed the warning' because it was absolutely ridiculous. What are you doing here?"

"I was at the service. It is 'strongly suggested' viewing, you know." Viper crossed his arms and smirked at her. Ember kept her knife out, making Viper keep his distance a few feet away from her. "I followed you over here because you were sneaking. Sneaking is a sin, you know."

"It is not. And I was not sneaking. I was simply... listening."

"Listening to who?"

"None of your business. Go slither into a hole and die." Ember went to walk past him, but Viper unsheathed the knife again. Ember's knife clanged into his, and they stood there for a moment until Viper pushed her back. Ember was severely lacking muscle in her arms, and she ground her teeth in frustration. She'd have to do something about that later.

"Tell me who you were listening to," he said, backing her up against the wall. Her free hand hit the wallpaper and the Phoenix crest that popped out from it. She traced it with one finger.

"Why do you want to know so badly? It's House Draco business. Not House Serpens business." With that statement she remembered Verity, how she would have already left, stranding her at the palace. Ember muttered a curse under her breath.

"Tell me," Viper demanded, pressing the flat edge of the knife against her throat. Ember pushed it away, allowing herself room to breathe. She considered for a moment as she looked at Viper.

"If I tell you, will you give me a ride home? My mother left without me."

Viper nodded. "Sure."

Ember groaned in frustration, slamming her head against the wall. She could lie, she supposed, but that would only come back to bite her in the rear later. Plus, it wasn't like he had anybody to tell. Nobody would take his word over hers.

"Prince Asher. That's who. Are you happy? Put the knife away, Viper." He did as she asked, but his frown never wavered.

"Prince Asher and who?" Ember was already walking toward the exit and didn't bother to turn around. She didn't owe him any more of an answer than the one she'd already given him.

"Prince Asher and a servant. It was of no importance, and none of your concern. Come on, I need to get home."

Verity was nowhere to be found when Ember arrived home. In fact, the family carriage wasn't even in the drive when Ember and Viper pulled up. Viper had somehow managed to secure the entire carriage for just the two of them, but Ember spent the entire short ride home staring out the slightly dirty window, replaying the bits of conversation she'd overheard over and over again. She didn't feel the need to speak to Viper, even if he was doing her a favor. Ember secretly hoped he thought she was simply praying. It was a holy day, after all.

Just because she didn't want Asher didn't mean she wanted to lose him to a servant. If she was going to lose him, it was going to be someone from one of the houses. At least then, the loss would be dignified.

Juniper. As if that wasn't the stupidest name she'd ever heard. Who named their child after a tree?

When the carriage pulled up outside her house, she opened the door distractedly, barely noticing Viper attempting to open it for her. His footsteps followed as she walked up to the house, and when she reached the black front door, she spun around, frustrated beyond belief.

"I told you what you wanted to know. Now go away. We're even. Goodbye," Ember said, fishing in her pockets for her key.

"You kept muttering the entire ride. Kept saying Juniper, I think? Maybe jumper? If you need someone to get you information, maybe someone from House Vulpus. They *are* spies, you know—"

"Leave me alone, Viper! Unless you have something productive to add to my situation, shut up!"

Viper took a step back. "I'm sorry. About annoying you, and about what happened at the Race. You have to understand, Lady Ember, I just wanted to win for my House."

Ember gaped at him for a moment. "First you say please, and then you apologize? Phoenix above, did you hit your head? Did the priestess really speak to you today? I'm surprised you didn't offer your blood as a sacrifice to the Phoenix Flame."

"Fine. Have it your way. See if I give a damn. Goodbye, Lady Ember." Viper turned and strode back to the carriage, slamming the door behind him.

Ember breathed a sigh of relief as she located the key in her pocket and fit it into the lock. The butler standing by the door jumped, surprised by her arrival through the front door, rather than the family door in the back. She shrugged her coat off and accepted his offer of a cup of tea.

"And, Roland," she said, as the butler started walking away, "for the love of the Phoenix and Her chosen twelve, spike that tea." The butler gave her a knowing smile, and Ember slumped against the door, careful not to slide all the way to the floor, like a child who hadn't been invited to a birthday party.

She needed her position secured. And she sure as hell wasn't going to lose it to somebody that wasn't even part of the houses. Viper had suggested House Vulpus, of the Fox. The king's spies. Sly and dangerous with their belts full of throwing knives and eyes full of secrets. Going straight to Lady Scarlett wasn't possible. There would be too many questions asked. And her eldest son was so close to taking over the house that he was out too. But he had twin little brothers, maybe thirteen years old. They would work. Enough threats of the Phoenix's wrath could scare any child into complying. So could enough money. She didn't want to take Viper's suggestion, but even she could admit that it was a good one.

Roland came into the sitting room with a golden tray with a matching teapot and teacup, and a shady silver flask that undoubtedly held something rather strong.

"Thank you, Roland. Is there any chance that, if I needed to write a letter to one of the other houses, you could deliver it for me? Would that be possible? I'd do it myself, but my duties here are far too pressing to deliver a letter on my own."

Roland nodded. "Yes, Lady Ember. I could deliver your letter. What house did you have in mind?"

"It's a letter for the young twins of House Vulpus. I have need of their...services."

Ember let out a long breath, concentrating hard on the target that had been set up at the end of the garden. After sending the letter to the twins of House Vulpus, Ember had dragged the target and her knives out, spending a few minutes stretching before she had begun to throw, each knife hitting the target harder than the last. Each was thrown with practiced control, something she hadn't had during her argument with Verity.

While her head was usually rather clear when she was throwing knives, thoughts were crowding the edges of her mind, seeking a way in.

"Enough," Ember hissed, throwing another knife and watching as it sank into the target, almost to the hilt. She wiped sweat from her brow, swung her braid over her shoulder, where it hit her back with a heavy thump, and picked another knife from the basket at her side.

This one went wide.

Ember groaned in frustration, quickly grabbing for another knife. Verity still wasn't home, and a small part of Ember wanted to have a conversation with her, to attempt to fix the rift that had been drawn between them. But the other part of her knew that if they re-entered that conversation, it could get heated again, and this time, Ember had been allowed to prepare her own arguments. Verity wasn't going to get the best of her. Not again.

She threw another knife, watching as it sank into the bullseye of the second target.

Ember would be ready to open that conversation with Verity when she got home, and she'd show Verity that she could be just as vicious as her.

There was no doubt about that.

Chapter

TEN

A YOUNG WOMAN WAS hiding in the garden. It was far past servants' curfew. She was supposed to be sound asleep, resting for the next day. In all honesty, she was tired. But she needed to be out here.

She shivered under her thin coat, rolling the small Phoenix charm in her pocket between her frozen fingers. She desperately missed the fireplaces that warmed the servants' quarters. Right now, she was as far from warm as it could get. She was pressed against the hard-packed dirt, trying to keep as much of herself out of the snow as possible. Her feet were resting in it, and she could no longer feel them.

Farther in the garden, behind a bush of dead flowers, something moved, and the woman shifted her position. Finally. Her fingers shook in her pockets from the cold, and she dropped the charm, bringing her fingers up to her face to blow warm breath on them.

The shadow moved closer, until another girl knelt in front of her. A scar crossed the left side of her face, extending from her ear to her jawline. When she smiled, the scar stretched grotesquely. Even still, they embraced in a quick hug.

"How's it going?" the girl with the scar asked, holding the first girl's hands in hers to help warm them.

"Could be worse. I've found out some very...interesting information. I think it's time we changed my mission." "To what?"

"To seduce and kill the crown prince."

At the same time, Asher Cinis let out a long breath, sprawled in the late-winter snow beside a headstone. He rolled a small bottle of liquor between his fingers, having already put one down for Vax. The last few he had left still remained, although several had frozen and then shattered from the cold.

"I don't know, Vax," Asher said. He hadn't come to speak to his cousin since Juniper came into his life, and part of him felt irrationally guilty about it. He turned his head to watch Siliros scuff the ground with his hooves as he tried to find a snack.

Everything seemed upside-down right now, in Asher's opinion. This strange servant girl, who was uncharacteristically compassionate and yet bold at the same time. Who complained about the country and the way it was run, right to the crown prince's face? Asher admired that in her, but it confused him nonetheless.

"I don't know how much trust to give her. My parents, especially my mother, are paranoid. Afraid of stepping outside of the patron circle, or even the palace. Not my father—you know how he is with women—but he doesn't confide in them. Not to my knowledge, at least. I'm fairly sure he gives them a pretty decent amount of money before and after, just to keep their mouths shut, and to keep them from killing him. This is all speculation, you know? It's just things I've picked up over the years. It's not hard to figure these things out. But my mother...she wasn't as bad before everything happened with you and your parents. But now she's so cautious. Keeps to herself, and I'm fairly sure I'm one of the only people she ever speaks to anymore, even if she's just shouting."

Asher fell silent, bathing in the silence of the cemetery. The only sound was Siliros, still disturbing the snow in search of food, and Hazel, who was rolling around in it and generally being a nuisance. He didn't know how he felt about Juniper yet; she was beautiful, that was sure, but Asher didn't feel anything toward her other than a growing friendship.

Maybe the liquor was messing with his head. He corked the bottle, setting it beside the others.

"How can I trust her? I know nothing about her. It's no secret that there are people who want me dead. In other countries, yes, but even in Eiad, there are plenty who would see my family and the houses crumble. They would murder me as a political move. She could be an assassin, sent to put a knife in my throat or poison in my glass. I just... I want to trust her. I don't want to be like my parents. And honestly, I don't think she's any sort of threat. She seems…real. I don't know how else to describe it, honestly. Maybe that's a stupid reason to trust somebody, but it's just how she is.

"I haven't had a friend in years, Vax. I desperately need one. I just don't feel *anything* about the people in the houses. Ember is one of the only heirs my age, and my parents wouldn't approve of me speaking to anybody who isn't an heir. There's Amber Forrest, I suppose, or Blue Corvu, but neither one of them seem like the type of people I'd want to be with. Maybe I'm being rude. Maybe I should give each of them a try, but I genuinely don't want to. I can't deal with the pressure. It's just a lot. You know all of these things."

Asher squeezed his eyes shut, then opened them again. He turned to look at the headstone, at the name inscribed there.

"I just need a friend," Asher admitted softly. "A living friend." With that, he drained the rest of his bottle and crushed it underfoot, calling Hazel to his side as he guided Siliros out of the gate. Only a quick ride down the road, and then the Phoenix Palace rose into view once more—all green and glittering and claustrophobic. The guard at the gate looked up, surprise registering on his face when he recognized Asher, who dismounted.

"Prince Asher!" He dipped into a low bow as Asher squirmed uncomfortably. The guard was young, probably Asher's age, or perhaps a year younger. Something dropped from the boy's pocket, and he scrambled to pick it up, even as Asher bent to pick it up, something silver flashing in the moonlight that the guard snatched from underneath Asher's gaze. He slipped it back in his pocket as he straightened up. "I'm so sorry, sir. I didn't recognize you at first. Welcome back to the palace."

Chapter

ELEVEN

"HAVE WE RESOLVED THE Gleoj Swesh issue?" Lady Nocte Specula, of House Ibis, posed the question, and it hung in the air until Asher's father spoke up.

"Lord Ivin's son has been sending us correspondence as often as possible, but unfortunately his meeting with the new king was delayed. The people are still in turmoil, and it's been difficult for anybody to see the new king. But we are desperately trying to get him in as soon as possible, because these prices are truly ridiculous."

Asher dropped his hand to Hazel's head, rubbing one of her ears between his fingers. His mother glanced at him with a look that, to anybody watching, would merely be a mother checking on her son. But Asher read between the lines when it came to Feather and knew she was disapproving of him bringing Hazel into the meeting room. Hopefully that wasn't enough to warrant a Moreci meeting. He was trying to avoid both his mother and the captain of the guard as often as possible, especially because he wanted to shield Juniper from them. If they figured out he was friends with her... No, that wasn't an option. He couldn't consider that.

"Has anybody heard from Verity Ignis?" Whelyn asked, looking around the room. Asher shook his head as his father's gaze passed over him. He hadn't seen the elder Dragon since the temple meeting the day before.

"It's unusual for her not to be here, but I highly doubt anything is wrong," Victoria Soo said, giving Whelyn a reassuring nod. "Perhaps she's gone to take a vacation, or she's fallen ill. No doubt we'll receive word from her sometime today." Whelyn nodded, although Asher couldn't help but notice his father looked strangely upset about Verity's missing presence.

"Hopefully we will," he said. "Now. Domestic issues first." Asher perked up, looking at his father as he continued speaking. "I've decided it's time to raise the taxes again." Asher immediately opened his mouth, ready to defend the people like Juniper and her family, who were unable to defend themselves against the taxes. He didn't stop to think about what he was doing—that wasn't important.

"No." The word jumped from Asher's mouth, and the rest of the table looked up at him. Beside him, Feather slowly turned her head toward him, and Whelyn shifted his eyes to him. Neither one of them said anything for a long minute, simply staring at him. The court had seemed to hold its breath while they waited, and then Whelyn spoke up, breaking the deafening silence.

"What do you mean by 'no'?" Asher swallowed, already regretting his choices.

"I've been speaking to people who aren't part of the houses," he said, not willing to name anybody in particular. It wouldn't be fair to call Juniper out, and he desperately didn't want her to get in trouble. "And they've told me that the taxes are absurd. Unlivable in places. The tax collectors, who we employ, who we pay, are insufferable. They're vicious. People can barely support themselves. They're starving. If anything, we should be lowering taxes to help the people." He stopped talking, worrying the fur on Hazel's head as he waited for a response.

Finally, Feather spoke.

"And how, pray tell, do you expect this country to continue running without the money we take in? Everything would shift and collapse. A country cannot run if the government doesn't take money from the people. Not to mention the fact that your lifestyle would change dramatically. All of ours would. These things cannot possibly happen."

"I'd be willing to give up some of my things to help. I'm not that selfish," Asher said. He tried to channel Juniper's calm demeanor, Vax's compassion, but it was difficult when his parents got like this. The scars on his back seemed to tingle as he stared at his mother.

"Prince Asher," someone said, and Asher turned to find his uncle, the one from his House Passer side, looking at him. He wasn't close to the House Passer side of his family—his mother became House Phoenix as soon as his parents' wedding ended, and technically, the only extended family Asher had had died.

"You have a gentle heart," Lord Lark Canticum said. "But even I can admit that it would be an absolute disaster to attempt to lower, or even eradicate the taxes. They hold this economy up. I'm sure you know all of this already, but it's important to consider. Yes, being kind and compassionate is important. Of course it is. But when you take the throne, the entire country will collapse if you attempt to implement something like that." Lark settled back in his seat as Feather nodded at her brother.

"He's right. Whelyn, what do you have planned for raising the taxes this time?"

Asher sat in the library, Hazel at his side and a drink in his hand. It was fine whiskey, imported from the mid continent, and sweetened with berries and honey, but it left a bad taste in the back of his mouth. He set it down, letting out a long sigh. Asher wanted to go to the cemetery, to talk to Vax about the meeting and everything he had tried to do, but his mother had not-so-discreetly assigned several soldiers, on top of the one who always followed him, to ensure he didn't do anything stupid in his rage.

He stood, pacing toward the shelves of books. They were mostly historical books and atlases for this library, contained in a single space. The oldest books were kept in a separate vault, with multiple keys, spread out across the palace, to protect it. But there were certainly books with value in this library.

Asher moved toward those books, running his hand over the spines. He'd never been much of a reader, but libraries were still a comfort, with the smell of old books and the silence.

His fingers met something smooth that most certainly wasn't a book, and Asher looked down at the shelf. There was a distinct space between two books, holding the halves of the shelf away from each other.

In between them was a knife.

Asher reached for it, pulling the blade out of the wood. The handle fit comfortably in his palm, and he ran his hand over the carvings. It looked as though it was made of something akin to bone, and at the top of the knife, an animal's head was carved. He squinted at it, trying to decipher what it was. He ran the pad of his thumb along the blade, pulling away when it nicked him.

He put his hurt thumb in his mouth, keeping blood from dripping on the books, before he flipped the knife over, still unable to figure out what animal it was. It wasn't the fault of whomever had carved it—the lines were small and exquisite, clearly made with a delicate hand. Rather, it was the fact that there were hundreds of the lines and indents, and Asher was fairly sure that some of the lines made up words in the old language. Whatever the creature was, it didn't seem as though it was one of the patron creatures, much less the Phoenix.

He took the knife from the library, running his thumb over the handle as he jogged down a flight of stairs, Hazel keeping pace with him. He certainly wasn't going to leave the knife in the library. It was high quality, and he had no doubt he could find a sheath to fit it in the training room.

Asher didn't often spend time in the training room. It was primarily used by high-ranking soldiers who served in the palace, but it was technically always open to the houses, although it was mainly used during the weeks leading up to the Silent Duels. Now, however, the room was cold and empty when Asher eased the door open, closing it before Hazel could slip in, the room lit by the windows that hugged the very top of the wall, ensuring that the majority of the walls were left open for other things.

Such as racks upon racks of weapons, glittering in the sunlight. Asher's eyes instinctively went toward the crossbows hung, one beside the other. They were gorgeous, carved of wood or forged of metal. All from the finest craftsmen in Eiad. The bolts, in their leather quivers, were no less beautiful. Asher had never been one for knives or swords; he found crossbows and even regular bows were simpler to use, and he preferred the distance they allowed him to have from whatever adversary he was facing. He didn't have to stare someone in the face moments before sinking a knife in their chest. The throwing knives, too, were an issue; he could never figure out how to aim them so that they stuck in the center of the target. He'd seen House Vulpus throw before, during the Duels, and although there was something darkly beautiful about the knives streaking through the air, like gems suspended by an invisible hand, they'd never called to Asher.

His hands itched for one of the crossbows, but he turned his attention on the knives instead. Each knife was hung in front of its sheath, but there were a few spare sheaths, kept in a small basket on the floor. He dumped the basket out, immediately discarding the ones he knew would be far too long or too short. There were some that were too wide or too narrow, and although the pile thinned drastically, he still ended up with a good six options.

They were all made of leather, although each were dyed a different color. One was a deep blue, like the color of the sea that Asher had often seen from the deck of a royal ship, although he oftentimes spent most of the time below deck— he couldn't stand the way the ocean moved. There were two that were green, although not the same green— one was of the lush jungles of the far continent, and the other was of the grass that grew in Eiad itself, which carpeted the rolling fields of the west. And still, that was not the end of the colors. Another was the red of blood dropping into the Phoenix Flame, and the last two were both shades of browns, the lighter one reminding Asher of the brown of Hazel's fur.

He chose that one, if only because of her. The knife fit almost perfectly, the top only slightly too small. It left just a bit of the blade exposed, but not too much that it would pose any serious issue toward him.

The sheath itself was designed to be strapped to his arm or leg, but it was easy to string it through his belt, where it hung comfortably against his thigh.

He ran his fingers over the handle, digging them into the deep grooves of the animal's head.

If only he could figure out what it actually was.

Chapter

TWELVE

*LICK. **CLICK. CLICK.***

Click. Click. Click.

Ember's shoes tapped against the polished wood floors of the Vulpus Estate. Verity still wasn't home, but Ember figured that her mother would've insisted on shoes, simply as a formality, and wore them anyways.

It had been one full day since Ember had missed the carriage after church. Three days since their fight about Asher.

She wasn't worried. Her mother was more than capable of taking care of herself. Plus, she was waiting for the twins to appear.

She had been sitting in the remarkably well-kept formal room of the Vulpus Estate for nearly half an hour now. A maid had told her the twins would be down in a moment. Apparently, Foxes didn't know how to keep time.

The Vulpus Estate was nice, by all accounts. But that was all it was. Nice. There was nothing particularly glamorous about it. Nothing special. She'd been in houseless estates that were better, belonging to merchants and high-ranked artisans.

Plus, while everything seemed as though it was perfect, when Ember looked closer, there were signs of the Vulpus Estate being slightly worn down, as though nobody had bothered to fix the place up. The wooden floors had obviously been cleaned recently, but there were still scuffs near the walls, there was a bit of dust on the mantle, and the chair she was sitting on made a horrible screeching sound every time she shifted her weight. It made sense for one of the lower houses to have a home that looked like this, she supposed, but it was still far below what Ember had expected from a house estate.

Ember couldn't help but feel slightly disappointed in the Fox's house. The houses were expected to keep themselves and their property up to the standards of the Phoenix Palace, and the Vulpus Estate seemed to be lacking.

She tapped her foot on the floor once more before rising from her chair. She had places to be. Things to do. With Verity gone, she'd be expected to pick up the slack on her mother's main responsibilities until she came home, and Ember didn't have all day to wait around for some children to decide she was worth their time. She'd waited plenty time for them to arrive.

Ember's hand was on the doorknob when the stairs behind her creaked. She froze, one hand clutching the knob and the other itching for the knife sheathed up her sleeve.

"Lady Ember Ignis?" A soft voice, like the pad of a cat's feet over velvet. Or perhaps a Fox's paws over grass. Ember turned. On the stairs were two redhead boys, gazing at her with such intensity that she almost felt like she should leave anyways.

"You must be the twins, right?" One of the boys nodded, and they descended the stairs, holding each other's hands. Every other step creaked, and it seemed an age before they hit the last step.

When they got to the bottom and went to shake Ember's hand, she pulled back with slight shock. One of the twin's eyes were murky blue, and he gazed around the room with eyes that clearly could not see.

"You just figured it out, didn't you?" he asked, reaching for her hand. She placed it in his grasp, and he shook it. His brother then took it and nodded at her.

"You're blind, right?" Ember asked, and the boy blinked, as though confirming her statement.

"Yes, I'm blind. And my brother is deaf. I'm his ears. And he's my eyes. Our mother says that we're Phoenix-blessed to have each other."

"A very fitting system. And she's right about being Phoenix-blessed. But, if you don't mind me asking, however do the two of you get information?" The blind boy shrugged. Ember was completely baffled as to how a blind boy and a deaf boy could possibly be part of the house of spies. Even as she looked, she could see a pair of throwing knives on the deaf one's waist, which meant that even he was as dangerous as his mother and older brother. If he could find his target, that was.

"Together, of course. My name is Bat. Well, that's not really my name. It's just a nickname. Because I can't see, but I can hear. Get it? My brother's name is Hawk. It's another nickname, 'cause his eyes are so good. Get it, Lady Ember?" Ember smiled at them.

"I do get it. Do you boys know why I contacted you?" Ember watched as Bat traced the back of his brother's hand with his finger, and Ember squinted at them.

"What are you doing?"

Bat, not even looking up, said,

"I'm translating. This is the way we talk. And, yes, we do know why you contacted us. You want us to spy, right?"

"Yes. Can we sit?"

"Sure, Lady Ember." Bat tugged on his brother's hand, and then the two of them led the way into the sitting room, taking a seat beside each other on the couch. Ember sat across from them in the squeaky chair.

"Who do you want us to spy on?" Bat asked, finger moving a mile a minute as he wrote the question out for his brother. Hawk responded just as quickly, and Bat giggled a little bit. Ember cocked an eyebrow but didn't say anything.

"A palace servant. Is that possible?" There was a moment of silence as the boys spoke to each other, and eventually Bat turned to her.

"We can do that. How much are you going to pay us?"

"I can give you fifty ovum a day, and an extra twenty for any night you spend there. Is that enough?" The boys went back to their silent conversation.

"Seventy-five a day, and thirty at night, and then we'll have a deal." Ember sighed. That was far more than she had expected to pay for their services, but if they could help her figure out who Juniper Farley really was... Worth it. Besides, it wasn't like she didn't have the money.

"Deal."

Bat nodded. "Hawk wants to know what she looks like," he said, and as he translated Hawk nodded at her.

"She has brown hair, and it's usually pulled up in a bun. Green eyes. I've only ever seen her in the typical servants' uniform. She sometimes spends time with the prince, so you'll have to be careful about that. Is that enough information, or should I keep going?"

"If you have anything else, you need to tell us before we go in, you know? We only have three days before our mother and brother get back from Sal, and we absolutely have to be done by then."

"I don't have anything else, really. And that's fine. Just get me whatever information you find." She held her hand out, and inwardly celebrated her victory as the boys took her hand as one.

Now all she had to do was wait.

Asher threw a stick for Hazel for the fifth time, watching his dog kick up huge mounds of snow through chasing it, before checking his watch. Juniper was supposed to have met him nearly twenty minutes ago, and he was quickly running out of the break time he had between meetings.

It was incredibly stupid of him to try and meet her in the middle of the day, when they were both supposed to be working. If his mother got word of it, he was going to be in a lot of trouble. Trouble that would result in bandaging his back. But he really needed to see her, and it was all because of the envelope in his coat pocket, stamped with the gold seal of House Phoenix. He hadn't even had a drink today. He wanted his head to be completely clear for this meeting. He'd have one after this, to satisfy the itch that was slowly building up in the back of his throat.

"Prince Asher? You wanted to see me?" Asher jumped, turning to see Juniper behind him. She still didn't have a good coat, and he immediately shrugged his off and offered it to her.

"Just take it. You'll freeze to death out here." Juniper opened her mouth, as though to protest, but Asher was already helping her into it, and she quickly snuggled down into the fur lining, warming up. Asher resisted a shiver as he began to get cold again. He didn't want her to try and give it back.

"Check the pockets," Asher said, and Juniper gave him a confused smile as she dug her hands into the pockets, pulling out the bulging envelope.

"What is it?" she asked quietly, and Asher knew that she knew.

"To buy yourself a coat and gloves, and a new Phoenix charm, if you still haven't found yours. And to send home to your family. To help with the taxes. I figure since I can't change the taxes, not yet, I can at least help with them. It hurt to hear your story yesterday. How much we're failing our poorest citizens."

Juniper turned the envelope over in her hands, mouth gaping. The coins clinked in the envelope as she ran her fingers over it. "Your Majesty, this is very generous, but I can't accept this." She held it out to him, fingers shaking from the cold. She definitely needed gloves.

"Take it. Please. I would be embarrassed if you didn't."

Juniper pulled the envelope back towards her. "How much is it?"

"Don't worry about that, Juniper Farley. I just wanted to give it to you, to help out. Especially since it's winter. I'm serious about buying a coat and gloves, because if you don't, I'm just going to buy one for you, and you might not like it. So please, just take the money."

Juniper slid the envelope into her back pocket. She still looked confused, but exceedingly grateful. Asher was glad she was taking it. Hopefully she'd use some of it for herself.

"Thank you, Prince Asher," she whispered, and Asher realized it was the first time she'd ever said his name like that, as though it was the name of a friend and not of a stranger. He offered her his arm as he began to lead her around the garden. She looped hers into his, warm and steady at his side.

"Of course. You deserve it," he said. They walked for a while, arms linked as they softly spoke to each other.

"Are you used to them?" Juniper asked, nodding to the guard who followed them at a distance.

"Of course," Asher said. "They've been following me around for years now. I sort of forget they're there most of the time, to be completely honest with you."

"I don't like them," Juniper confessed. "I feel like I'm constantly being watched. Like I'll never be completely alone in this palace."

Asher laughed softly. "Oh, it's always like that. If it isn't the guards, it's the other servants, or the houses. The palace is constantly full. You get used to it, after a while. Besides, it's not like they ever speak to me. They're just there to ensure nobody attempts to kill me."

Juniper nodded.

"That makes sense," she said. "The country would certainly hurt if you were murdered." For a long moment, they walked in silence, and then Juniper began to explain—with an almost comical amount of excitement, to the point where Asher was reminded of Hazel when she found something to chase—the places she hoped to see one day.

"Sal is probably one of the places I'm most interested in," she confessed. "I've never seen the ocean, and part of it is an island. It just sounds...beautiful. Oh, and the animals they have! Strange birds who look more like jewels than actual birds. Monkeys. I've only seen a monkey once, when a man from Sal brought one and charged people to pet it. We didn't have the money, so I didn't get to. But it was cute, anyways." They rounded a corner arm in arm, and Juniper stopped dead in her tracks. Asher, who had been too busy noticing the small wisps of hair that had escaped from her bun, looked up sharply as Juniper shielded her face from the scene.

"You father," she whispered, turning completely around. Asher gaped in shock at what he was seeing. His father, locked in a passionate embrace with a woman who was most certainly not his mother. To Asher's eternal relief, the two of them were still fully clothed, but it took him clearing his throat for his father to look up and lock eyes with him.

The woman turned her head slightly, her hood shifting to reveal thick, black hair, streaked slightly with gray. Asher's father immediately turned her back around, keeping her face hidden from him.

There was only one person in the courts who had hair like that. Asher immediately felt sick, backing up a step. His father stood, making his way towards him, hands outstretched as though to placate Asher.

"Asher," he called, but Asher was already grabbing Juniper's hand, pulling her through the gardens and away from the king who preached faithfulness in all he did, but was incapable of keeping his hands to himself.

Chapter

Thirteen

"YOU WANT TO HAVE dinner with me?" Juniper asked, wiping her hands on her black apron as she moved around Asher to pull a pot of boiling water off the fire.

"Yes. Tonight. Please. I'd really like to. But don't feel like you have to. I mean, if you don't, that's fine too. Like, it's not a royal command or anything." Asher was shouting to be heard over the noise of the kitchen, and it wasn't just the multiple fires burning that were making his face heat up. Phoenix, she was so hard to talk to. Juniper gently pushed him away from the fire and into the wall, keeping him out of her way as she continued to work. He swirled his wine glass as he tried to keep her undivided attention, which was difficult in the constant movement of the palace kitchen.

"I have work, sir. Plus, this is a very inappropriate place to be having this conversation." She nodded pointedly to the other servants who were watching them from the corner of their eyes. Especially a pair of redheads that were vaguely familiar to Asher, who had their eyes firmly fixed on Juniper. He pulled his collar away from his neck, dying in the heat of the kitchen. He wasn't used to being down here, and he had gotten a lot of strange looks when he'd descended to the basement level. But even still, it was better than being upstairs, where nobody was real.

He still hadn't quite forgiven his father for what he'd seen in the garden, and he didn't know if he could, or even would. Whatever he felt about his mother, he didn't condone his father being with women other than her.

There was noise all around him in this kitchen, cooks and maids yelling at each other to be heard above everybody else. Multiple pots boiled over the massive cooking fireplace, bubbling and screeching as the air was released. There were smaller fireplaces all around him, heating up teapots and boiling vegetables. Large stone countertops ringed the entire room, with a large table in the middle. People were crowded around them, chopping meat and vegetables, and washing dishes in the large sink in the very back. The servants were all black blurs around him, moving so quickly around the kitchen that it almost made him sick. If he had tried to do what they were doing, he would've ended up with flour dumped down his shirt and a steak knife in the back of his hand. All in all, complete organized chaos, and he certainly wasn't helping by standing in the middle.

"I understand. I can write you a note if you would prefer? Or not?"

Juniper nodded, guiding Asher to the door. Several of the chefs seemed relieved by that, and Asher took that as his cue to leave. They wouldn't say anything, but he knew he was in the way, taking up valuable space. Juniper stopped at the door with him.

"That would be better, thank you," she said, pushing Asher out. He ducked his head and walked out of the kitchen, grateful for the blast of cool air that greeted him.

He walked back toward his room, mulling over what he would put in his letter to Juniper. It didn't have to be formal, he supposed. It was simply a dinner between friends, nothing more and, hopefully, nothing less.

"Prince Asher! Please, wait up!" Asher turned, hoping to find Juniper, but instead it was one of the servants that handled mail, identified by the silver envelope sewed into her shirt.

"I have a letter for you, Your Majesty. It's from House Draco." Asher took the delicate letter from her, turning it over in his hands.

"House Draco? Thank you for delivering this to me." The woman nodded before rushing off again, no doubt to find a far more important letter addressed to his father or mother.

Asher ripped open the envelope, pulling out the thick, cream-colored inside. It gave off a strong scent of apples, as though the paper itself had been submerged in apple juice before being sent. The paper was thick quality, and there was the slightest smudge in the corner of the letter, where it seemed Ember had tested her ink. Gold words seemed to almost leap from the page in Ember's elegant, swirly hand.

Prince Asher,

I would be honored if you would join me for dinner at my home tonight. I apologize for the short notice. Please do not feel pressure to join me if you have a prior engagement. I just ask that you send a note to my home if you decline the invitation.

Please arrive at around seven, if you decide to come. It will be seven courses of the finest food House Draco can offer. Thank you for considering my offer.

Your Humble Servant,
Lady Ember Ignis

The letter was stamped with the House Draco crest, a scaly, gold Dragon staring up at him.

Asher turned it over, hoping for something else, but there was nothing. It simply was what it looked like—an invitation to dinner. No trick, no gimmick. Just dinner between two people that were very nearly at the same level. Not that he expected Ember to try and trick him. But it would've been better. He hadn't even accepted and was dreading it. Ember was so intense and rigid, always keeping close to rules and expectations. If she could loosen up a bit once in a while, Asher would've found spending time with her much more pleasant.

And of course, it was an invitation for tonight. When he had already asked Juniper to dinner.

He could refuse, he supposed, but if his parents got word of it, they'd be livid. Plus, it would reflect badly on him. Phoenixes and Dragons were supposed to have dinner together, to spend time together. The Dragon was the Phoenix's greatest defender, and Ember and her knife would be his last line of defense if he were ever attacked.

Asher turned the letter over again and again as he stood in the hallway, considering the merits of going to dinner with Ember rather than Juniper. He'd undoubtedly have more fun with Juniper, but dining with Ember would look good for the both of them.

And he could always reschedule with Juniper.

Asher knocked on the door of the Draco Estate, a bouquet of expensive flowers in his other hand. When he had told his mother about the dinner, she had insisted he bring a gift for Ember.

She'd settled on a dozen snapdragons from the islands, chuckling at her own joke. And, to make matters worse, she had insisted that Asher dress appropriately, in House Draco colors. Red shirt and black pants, complete with gold stitching. But he couldn't deny her that. Not when the guilt in his stomach was constantly rolling whenever he was around her. He hadn't told Feather what his father had done, and he grappled with whether or not he should. Now, standing outside of the Draco Estate, he couldn't help but feel worse. Was Ember aware of what her mother had done, or was she just as oblivious as everybody else? Asher felt, too, as though he didn't owe Feather anything, due to the way she continued to treat him, but...she was still his mother.

It was complicated, he supposed, although he figured he should've made his mind up before walking into the Draco Estate.

He knocked once more, and this time it swung open, and a butler dressed in bright red welcomed him in. Asher noticed the House Draco crest on his lapel, pinned there in shining gold.

"Welcome to the Draco Estate," the servant said, "Your Majesty."

"Thank you. I brought these flowers for Lady Ember. Could you put them in water for me?" The butler nodded and took the flowers from Asher, disappearing down some side hallway.

Asher stood awkwardly in the foyer, taking in his surroundings. He'd never been in any of the twelve estates before, as he had no reason to. The houses came to the palace to see him, not the other way around. The Draco Estate was far finer than he had expected, and far colder. He figured a Dragon's lair would've had some heat, but the entire home was barely warmer than the outside. He figured that had something to do with the marble floors retaining no heat, or maybe the fact that the fireplace he could see was unlit. The wallpaper was a cold black with golden Dragons, a hundred thousand eyes staring out from the wall at him.

"Prince Asher?" Asher looked up toward the staircase, and for a moment he forgot about Juniper, about the dinner he was forced to cancel. Because Ember was a beam of light straight from the sun, and even the crown prince couldn't ignore a girl made of gold.

She was in a pure golden dress that cinched at her waist and fanned out after that, ending just above her feet. Her hair was pulled up to reveal more of her neck and collarbones and secured with what appeared to be her Dragon's-head knife. She was barefoot, as always, and as she walked down the stairs toward him, she jingled from the many bangles around her wrists. She was resplendent but terrifying in the low candlelight, and it was easy to see why so many in the Phoenix Court admired and feared her.

And then Asher's hand fell on the letter Ember had written him, tucked in his pocket, and he immediately snapped out of it. The longer he looked at her, the more he thought of Verity Ignis. They looked similar, and he couldn't seem to get the memory of black-and-gray hair out of his mind.

He was only there because Ember was House Draco and Juniper was houseless. Ember descended the rest of the stairs.

"Hello, Lady Ember. You look lovely." Ember smiled and dipped down in a small curtsy.

"Thank you for joining me tonight. Please, come into the dining room. It's far warmer in there." She stepped in front of him, leading the way, and that was when he noticed the way her dress dipped in the back, highlighting her hips. Asher kept his eyes fixed on the back of her head instead.

This was *Ember*, for Phoenix's sake. Ember, the girl he'd spent weekly meetings with, debating the merits of raising the price of lumber. Who spoke about the far and mid continents but never about her personal life. Ember was an advisor, not a friend.

She was beautiful. But she was no Juniper, just as the Draco Estate was lovely, but it was no Phoenix Palace.

He knew that all Ember wanted from him was the position of queen, and all he wanted from her was an advisor he could trust. He didn't want to be anything more than friends, and even that was a stretch.

Asher and Ember spent the first two courses in stiff silence, broken only by servants filling up their glasses and taking their plates. The butler in red watched the whole affair with a frown. Asher speculated that he, as well as the rest of the servants, were fond of Ember and didn't want to see her embarrassed. When they had disappeared to get the third course, Ember cleared her throat.

"I'm sorry this is all very...awkward. Forced." She took a sip of her wine as though contemplating her next words. "I just thought it would be nice to talk. It was my mother's idea for me to make a friend. Or at least, regain a friend. I suppose going to you first was perhaps inappropriate, but I didn't know who else to pick. I don't really know any of the other heirs, or their siblings. And besides, most of them are afraid of me."

"Where is Lady Verity tonight? I expected her to be here, even if she didn't sit at dinner with us." Ember's face flashed with an emotion Asher didn't understand before she responded. Fear, perhaps? No, he knew fear. This was something else, something foreign to him. But as quickly as it had appeared it disappeared, Ember schooling her expression back into a neutral look. She was nothing if not a master of hiding emotions, Asher realized. Was Verity at the palace, in his father's bed? He couldn't help but wonder again if Ember knew what Asher assumed had transpired between their parents.

"She's out of town. She's visiting a temple in the east. She'll be back before the palace meeting in two days, I'm sure." She was lying. Asher didn't know how he knew that for a fact, but maybe it was the way her fingers suddenly started playing over her fork, which was Dragon shaped, or the way she couldn't quite look him in the eyes. And the fact that he was almost entirely sure that Verity had been the woman in the garden.

"I see. So. Friends. I don't have many, either. I suppose that's something we have in common. We're both of high houses. And we're both rich." The third course came out, each of them getting an entire filleted fish, in a thick, golden-brown sauce, complete with candied lemons beside it, and Asher chuckled.

"I suppose this meal proves that fact. Most families don't use golden plates, I believe."

Ember giggled, a sharp, harsh sound that Asher suspected was mostly forced. He wasn't exactly known for his biting wit. He sighed quietly and stared into the dead eyes of the fish the servant had placed in front of him. At this point in the meal, he'd trade spots with that fish in a heartbeat.

They both picked up their forks as one, cutting into their fish. Asher raised his hand, and the butler hurried over to refill his glass. It was only the third course, and he was on his fifth full glass. He was way beyond his usual amount by this part of the meal, but Phoenix above, this was excruciating. He needed his head to be foggy if he was going to finish this meal. And besides, the wine was fairly good. He wasn't going to let it go to waste.

"I do appreciate you coming," Ember said, after chewing a piece of her lemon fish. "It's nice to have company. Hardly anybody wants to come into our house. As if it's possessed or something."

"I'm sure the Dragon's Estate is an intimidating place to be. Historically speaking, people don't fare well when they face the Dragon. Especially not during the winter."

Ember shrugged, a rather out of place gesture for a girl who had been sitting like a stone nearly the entire time. "The estate is only intimidating if you know the story. How many men have been banished in this house. How many have been killed."

"What do you mean?"

"You never once wondered about my father?"

"It never crossed my mind," Asher admitted. Each house had its own way of producing heirs, but there was something odd about House Draco's. How there was only ever a mother and daughter. No father, no brother, no uncles. Even House Equo, of all males, still had females that married into it, or were born into it. They weren't officially part of the house, but they still existed.

"My mother banished him. Just as her mother banished her husband, and so on and so forth. Sons go with their fathers, to whatever hole they crawled out of. Daughters are raised by their mothers, obviously. Twins are split up, unless they're both male. A male and a female is easier. But if there are two females, the mother picks which one she wants. The father takes the other. I could have a dozen half-siblings and never meet them. I could have a twin, for Phoenix's sake, but I'd never know. My mother has a brother she's never spoken to, since he was born first. When my grandmother had my mother, my grandfather took my uncle and went back to where he grew up. We never hear from them. The men used to get murdered, until my grandmother realized my uncle would need a father. So she banished my grandfather instead of murdering him. Although we're pretty sure he's the one who stuck a knife in her back, so maybe we should pick that tradition back up."

"So when you marry, you'll pick a random man and he'll leave once you have a daughter? Or you'll kill him?"

Ember shifted in her seat.

"I don't plan on continuing the tradition." She flushed and looked up at Asher with an intense gaze. Asher suddenly understood the true reason for this dinner. It certainly was not just an innocent dinner between friends. Of course Ember had a motive. She was a Dragon. He doubted she did anything for no reason. But at the same time, he hadn't expected it from Ember, who was intense, yes, but had always seemed less so than her mother.

But apparently neither of the Dragons could be trusted.

"I should go," he said, standing and summoning the butler to bring him his coat. "I had a lovely time, but I really should be leaving now. I need to...pray. At the Phoenix Flame. Thank you for the dinner, Lady Ember. I'll see you tomorrow for the palace meeting. Please don't forget. Goodnight." Asher threw his coat on, completely embarrassed that he had even gone to this house. That he had chosen Ember over Juniper. What a mistake.

Asher threw open the door, striding out into the winter air. He heard Ember behind him, hurrying to catch him, but he kept his eyes forward as he got into the royal carriage. When he looked out the window, he could see Ember standing in the doorway, looking like a broken doll in her golden dress.

Or, perhaps, a conquered Dragon.

Chapter

FOURTEEN

ASHER LOOKED OVER AT the servant who was sleeping off his room, desperate not to wake the man as he pulled on one of the servant's uniforms he kept under his mattress. He was going out again, but tonight would be different.

Because tonight, it wasn't just going to be Asher and the animals. Tonight, Juniper was coming too.

Or, at least, Asher hoped she would want to go with him. There was an awful lot of unknowns going on with his plan tonight. He didn't know where Juniper's room was, for one. He planned on asking anybody he could about where she spent the nights and prayed that she wouldn't be too freaked out about him finding her room. And he hoped she would actually want to go with him, to spend a little more of that forbidden time with him.

They weren't even going to the cemetery. Asher just wanted to spend some time with her, to get out of the palace and get some fresh air.

Down the stairs, and back to the servants' quarters, where an open door cast yellow, flickering candlelight into the hallway. Asher poked his head in, eyes adjusting to the light. Two young servants looked up at him, a boy and a girl who were in the middle of folding an obscene amount of linens. A table was between them, a dozen candles lighting up the space.

"Hello," Asher said. They exchanged a glance, before the girl spoke up.

"Are you Prince Asher?" she asked. "I'm sorry. You look an awful lot like him." Asher nodded but didn't answer the question directly.

"Do you happen to know someone named Juniper Farley?" he asked. "She's new around here, I'm pretty sure. Green eyes, brown hair?" Again, the two looked at each other as Asher watched. They couldn't be older than twelve or thirteen, he realized. So young to be doing so much work. Were they children of servants, or had they come here by choice?

Or, worse, had they been taken?

Asher was fairly sure that all of the servants who worked in the palace were there of free will—it paid well, and, as Juniper had said, it provided clothing, food, and a dry, warm place to sleep. But even still...

They were so young. So small.

"I can take you to her room," the girl offered, handing her half-folded towel to the boy, who began folding it without even looking at it.

Phoenix above. Asher wouldn't be able to use another towel without thinking of these poor children, working so late into the night.

The girl grabbed a candle and pushed past Asher, leading him further down the hallway. Most of the doors were closed, with no light coming out of the bottom, but that wasn't the case for the room the girl stopped in front of. The door was closed, but light poured from the bottom, and Asher could hear people speaking inside. The girl opened the door and immediately, the room fell silent as Asher stepped in behind her.

"Juniper?" Asher asked, his eyes immediately finding her. It wasn't a big room by any stretch of the word—six beds, three on Asher's left, and three on his right, took up most of the space. Small pieces of wooden furniture on the ends of the beds took up nearly the remainder of the space. Juniper was on the bed furthest from him, sitting in a nightgown, legs crossed underneath her. She looked exhausted, bags under her eyes, and her hair, which had been left down, was limp and unbrushed.

It didn't make her any less beautiful, and, besides, that wasn't what Asher truly cared about. Unconsciously, his mind wandered toward her heart.

That was what made her beautiful.

"Yes?" Juniper asked, wrinkling her brow and squinting at him. It was fairly obvious she couldn't really see him. "Have I done something wrong?" Asher scrambled for words as the other five women in the room stared at him.

"Who is that?" one of the women whispered to another, and then the girl at Asher's side spoke up, voice tinged with childish pride.

"He's Prince Asher." Immediately, the women scrambled to their feet, dipping into low curtsies. Asher waved his hand, squirming uncomfortably. He despised when people did that. Why did a single word before his name make such a big difference to everybody?

"Juniper, could I speak to you in the hall?" Asher asked, trying to convey his discomfort to her. Juniper nodded, breaking her curtsy to come stand beside him. The young girl stood between them, and Juniper bent, whispering something to her. The girl's face broke into a smile, and she turned, disappearing back the way she and Asher had come.

"Is everything okay?" Juniper asked, closing the door softly behind her. "How was dinner?"

"Dinner was... It was fine. It was Ember. But I would've rather spent the time with you, so that's why I'm here right now. I wanted to see if maybe you'd want to get out of here for a little bit? Just go to the garden or something. It's beautiful out there at night, but freezing. I guess you wouldn't have gotten time to buy a coat. That's what we should do. Buy you a coat." Asher stared down at his feet, feeling his face flush as he continued to ramble on. "You're really intimidating, you know?"

Juniper chuckled, shaking her head as she looked up at him. "I'm nothing more than a servant. You're a prince. I'm pretty sure I'm not the intimidating one here."

Asher leaned against the wall, desperate to clear the fog in his head from the wine he'd had only a few hours prior.

"Would you like to go somewhere?" Asher asked. "You can say no, just like earlier today. I promise I'm not trying to command you or make you feel uncomfortable. That isn't my intention in the slightest. Sometimes people feel as though they can't say no to me, and that's not the case. It's just…an invitation. Between friends."

Juniper glanced at the door, where whispers drifted through the bottom, and then back at him.

"I'd love to go somewhere," Juniper said, leaning into him.

"So where are we going?"

Asher grinned, holding his hand out to her. Juniper hesitated for only a moment before slipping her hand into his, their fingers lacing together.

"Right this way," Asher said and pulled her away from the door.

Asher knew that there would be no way for the two of them to get Juniper a coat before the sun rose, and instead lent her one of his once more.

He pulled Juniper through the halls, the two of them sprinting past lush portraits and immaculate furniture, even as they were quite the opposite—bound up in heavy coats, hair loose, unable to stop the laughter that tore from their throats, echoing up and down the silent halls. All sense of propriety was lost as they raced each other to the door of the garden. A servant and a prince, running through a palace together. They reached the garden, where the two soldiers on either side were attempting to pretend like they weren't looking at them and failing completely.

Asher ignored them, instead turning to look at Juniper. She was grinning at him, flushed with excitement, and then pulled her hand from Asher's, pushing the door open. One of the soldiers held it open and then followed the two of them out, standing and watching from the door as Asher led Juniper further into the garden, through the snow and dead plants.

Asher stooped down, balling some of the fresh snow into his hand as Juniper watched. She frowned at the packed snow, and her eyes widened when Asher pulled his arm back and threw it at her.

The snow hit her square in the shoulder, powder dusting it. Her mouth dropped open as she looked at him, and Asher grinned, bending to gather another handful of snow.

"I'm so sorry, Prince Asher. Forgive me of my crimes, Your Majesty," Juniper said, and Asher looked up, afraid that she was going to go back inside due to him throwing snow at her, but she was shaping her own snowball, and, before Asher could react, she chucked it at his head.

"Hey!" Asher said, shaking snow from his curls as Juniper danced away from him, dipping down behind a bush. Asher scooped another ball, waiting until she popped back up. The ball hit her square in the shoulder again, and Juniper squealed, throwing snow at his head once more. It went over his shoulder, and Asher moved toward her, picking snow up as he went. He could see her between the branches of the bush, watching him approach. Before he could throw the snowball, however, Juniper burst from her hiding spot, darting away from him. She slid behind a rather large pile of snow, where Asher could hear her giggling.

"It's not fair that you're faster than me!" Asher said, throwing the snowball at the pile.

"It's not fair that you have a better arm, Prince Asher!" Juniper called back. Asher dipped, reaching for more snow, when some exploded across his back, sliding down his coat and shirt. Asher shivered, looking up to find Juniper watching him, eyes sparkling.

Phoenix above, she was beautiful. Not just physically, either, Asher realized. Her laugh, echoing across the garden, was beautiful. The way she was grinning at him, practically asking him to throw the snowball.

So he did.

And it hit her square in the face.

Immediately, Juniper's smile dropped, and panic blossomed in Asher's chest, just as quickly as a red spot began to appear on Juniper's cheek.

Oh no.

No no no.

Asher rushed to her as quickly as he could without slipping on the snow and ice, finding himself behind the pile of snow with her. Juniper's hand was covering her face, but mercifully, there were no tears in her eyes, and she didn't look too hurt.

"Juniper?" Asher asked, trying to give her space while also attempting to ensure she was okay. It wasn't an easy balance to find, and he found himself hovering awkwardly at her side.

"I'm okay, sir," Juniper said, standing and brushing snow off her coat. She unbuttoned it, handing it over to him. The air was thick with silence, and Asher cringed again when he saw the mark, violent and red, still spreading across her face.

"I'm so sorry," Asher said, stopping himself from reaching forward and touching her. She wouldn't want to be touched by him, he assumed, and kept his distance.

"It's okay. Really," Juniper said, moving past him and toward the door. Asher followed her, ducking his head when the guard at the door gave him a pitiful look.

Juniper and Asher lingered in the hallway for a moment before Asher spoke up.

"Well. Thank you for going out there with me. Are you sure you're okay?"

Juniper nodded, looking embarrassed.

"I'm sorry it didn't end as well as it started. I had fun, anyways. Thank you for inviting me." And then she was turning, walking away from him. Asher felt himself reach out, but then pulled his hand back.

What a disaster.

He turned on his heel, moving back toward his bedroom. He climbed the stairs slowly, sliding a hand up the banister. His mind wouldn't stop replaying the exact moment when the snow made contact with Juniper's face, and he cringed again as he started up the next set of stairs.

"You moron," Asher hissed to himself, turning down a side hallway. It wasn't the exact path to his room, but he didn't want to lie awake for hours and replay the memory. He would walk around for a little while and calm down, and then he could go to bed. Hopefully that would be enough.

Asher dragged his hand over the fine wallpaper as he moved down the hallway, every so often feeling the cool glass of a window underneath his fingers. He closed his eyes, attempting to blink away the memory, when his fingers met open air, and his boots crunched something into the carpet.

Asher's eyes flew open, and he looked down to find glittering shards of glass, mixed in with a small pile of snow, beneath his feet, shining innocently in the moonlight.

The window had been shattered.

Asher glanced outside, his hair whipped by winter wind as he looked down, but there was nobody there. He hadn't expected there to be—he hadn't heard the window break, and the snow was a clear indication that it had been broken for quite some time.

"Guards!" Asher called, pulling his head back into the hallway. "Guards!" He could hear them rushing toward him, the sound of his voice instantly calling assistance to his side. They rounded the corner, running toward him at full force. He put his hands out to stop them from disturbing the pile of snow and glass and nodded at one of them. He cringed slightly, hating the words that slipped out, but knowing they were necessary.

"Go wake my father and mother. They need to see this."

"Stupid, stupid, stupid," Ember hissed to herself, spinning in a circle and throwing a knife. It went wide, and she groaned in frustration. She was perfect when she stood still, when she had time to aim, but she struggled with throwing the knives while in motion. It was something she needed to practice, and to practice, she needed to clear her head.

Ember was fairly sure she wasn't going to be able to do that tonight.

She'd changed out of her golden dress as soon as Asher's carriage had disappeared from sight, pulling her hair into a plait and slipping into pants and a warm sweater, although she truly didn't mind the bite of the wind and snow. She could blame the tears in her eyes on them, rather than the knot of emotions that was twisting and untwisting in the pit of her stomach.

Ember dropped, rolled, and threw a knife, watching it sink into the outer edge of the target. At least she'd hit it that time.

She shook a clump of snow from her hair, shivering as it began to melt on her shoulders.

Ember threw another knife, thinking of Asher's face, his expression, when she'd made her intentions clear. Like he despised her. Like he was...

Disgusted by her.

With a grunt, she threw two knives at once, watching them sink into the center of the target.

She let out a long breath, striding up to the target to haul the knives out. She'd only managed to sink four of the twelve she'd thrown, and she dropped into the snow to gather the rest of them, the wind whipping her plait over her shoulder.

"Why did you do that?" Ember whispered to herself. "Why did you think that was a good idea?"

She'd done it, in all honesty, in an attempt to secure Asher's hand. If Verity didn't come back... Ember would be in charge. House Draco needed an heir, and to have one with Asher would further cement her position in the hierarchy. But she hadn't done it out of lust. She'd certainly not done it out of love. And truly, she hadn't expected a positive reaction. She hadn't expected Asher to leap from his seat and propose to her on the spot.

But she hadn't expected the repulsion in his eyes, either. Ember sheathed her knives, wiping tears from her eyes. There was no time for crying. There was a palace meeting tomorrow, and Ember was going to have to represent her house. She had work to do.

Chapter

FIFTEEN

Ember was wearing her mother's sweater, embroidered with the House Draco crest. She'd asked Roland to find it for her, hoping that wearing something of her mother's would help her through the palace meeting.

It had been over half a week since Verity had disappeared. Sure, she had gone off for a couple of days after a particularly bad fight, or maybe just because she could, but this was completely out of the ordinary. She would always give Ember a couple of days to prepare. To get ready. She certainly didn't just disappear into thin air without so much as a note.

Ember had interrogated every single servant that lived with them, and nobody knew anything, except that Lady Verity—and the family carriage—had never arrived home after the holy day ceremony.

As she warmed her gloved hands with her breath in the spare carriage, Ember turned over what her mother had done every meeting. She'd say present, to announce House Draco's participation in the meeting, and if anything was directed at House Draco, she'd respond appropriately. Ember had been observing Verity since she was ten. She had seven years of experience under her belt.

So why was she absolutely petrified by the idea of stepping into her mother's shoes?

Sitting in the empty meeting room, staring across the table at the House Passer's brown-and-green tapestry, made it real. The fact that she was no longer sitting against the wall, in her mother's shadow.

Ember sent up a quick prayer to the Dragon for guidance, deciding to go straight to her patron animal, since they were more inclined to pay attention to her. The Phoenix had given her the Dragon for a reason; she was going to use that to her advantage.

She scanned the servants lined around the room, looking for Juniper, but to her relief, the strange girl was nowhere to be found. That, at least, was something she could be glad about.

The next two houses to join her were Houses Tigris and Pardus, and they all gave her strange looks as they came in. Lilith Taya of House Pardus even leaned down beside her.

"Where's Lady Verity?" Lilith asked.

"She isn't feeling well, because of the incense they burned at the holy day ceremony. She sent me instead. She thought it would be good practice for me." The lie slipped out of Ember's mouth with ease. Thankfully, Lilith backed away with a knowing nod. Maybe if that were spread around, everybody would leave her alone about it.

She kept her head down, but it didn't seem to matter, since the blue-haired heir of House Olor tapped her on the shoulder. "Yes?" Ember said, snapping her head up to look at him. He backed up a step, as though surprised by her reaction. He was wearing the ugliest orange suit she'd ever seen, seemingly intent on ruining his family's image. Ember almost sank her knife into his stomach simply because of how hideous it was. Had it been either of his parents, she may have been slightly more inclined to be polite, but as it was, she far outranked him, and could thus speak to him however she chose.

"My mother wants to know where your mother is."

"I don't even know what your first name is, and you're bothering me for something that is, quite frankly, none of your business."

The boy nodded. "Fair enough. I'm Blue Corvu. And you're Lady Ember Ignis. I figure you already knew that, though."

"Very funny. Did you choose the hair off your name, or your name based off the hair?"

"Okay, that's seriously my name. Who crapped in your tea this morning?"

Ember's mouth dropped open. "How dare you."

Blue shrugged. "I'm not wrong. And although I'm enjoying this conversation—far more than you could ever understand—I'm frankly over it. So just tell me where your mother is and I'll go away, which is something we'll both enjoy."

"She's sick," Ember said. "And that's all you need to know. Now go away before I run you through with my letter opener. You should start praying now that I make it a quick death."

He shrugged and blew his bangs out of his face.

"Oh, and one more thing, Blue. Your hair is atrocious." He stalked away from her and back to his side of the table. Several other houses had witnessed their conversation, and Ember could feel their eyes on her as she dipped her head once more, staring at her hands in her lap. She was ridiculously relieved when Bat and Hawk walked in, passed her, and dropped a note in her lap. She unfolded it, desperate for information.

Something small and metal fell out of it, but she ignored it for now, eyes quickly jumping over the words scrawled in a child's handwriting.

> *Sorry, Lady Ember. We couldn't find anything except this. And we could only do two days since Mom came home early. There were a couple places we weren't allowed to be, so something might've happened there. But Bat didn't hear anything, and I didn't see anything.*
>
> *Sorry,*
> *Bat and Hawk*

She crumpled up the note in her lap and shoved it into her sweater pocket, picking up the metal object that had landed there. It was a silver pin in the shape of an animal. But it was what *type* of animal that was the problem. It looked similar to the Tiger, the Leopard, and the Fox, but only slightly. It didn't seem as though it was any one of the patron animals. A dog, perhaps? But who would wear a pin in the shape of the dog's head, and a slightly deformed one at that? It didn't seem as though this new clue was much of a clue at all. Rather, it seemed as though the twins had simply stumbled upon something that Juniper kept for whatever reason. A trinket.

She looked at the twins, gave them a nod to show she understood, and then worked on not yelling profanities as the king and queen walked in with Asher in tow.

Ember had entered the meeting hoping her day could not possibly get any worse.

Apparently, the Phoenix wasn't done with her yet. She was just getting started with Ember.

Juniper was in Asher's shadow, holding a tea tray. Ember resisted the urge to slam her head into the wooden table. Of course she was here. She was everywhere, wasn't she?

I'm on display, she thought to herself. *I am representing my house. I will not disgrace the noble name of House Draco.*

"House Draco, of the Dragon?"

"Present," Ember said, and the queen looked at her, visibly surprised.

"Where is Lady Verity?"

"She's come down with a terrible sickness, from the holy day incense. It's quite the event at the Draco Estate. She sent me instead. She thought it would be good practice for whenever I become the House Draco matriarch."

"Understood," Feather said and continued roll call, but when Ember looked up at the royals' thrones, Asher was looking at her. Ember began to grind her teeth as she read the expression.

It wasn't love or desire or anything she wanted him to look at her with. But with plain confusion. She had lied to him yesterday and again lied to the entire court. And the lies weren't the same. Ember knew that she was going to need to be more careful about hiding Verity's disappearance. She watched as Juniper prepared his tea, pouring it from a porcelain teapot and then stirring in three cubes of sugar.

Juniper shook her sleeve back, and Ember squinted at something she had strapped there. The light was reflecting off it, blinding her slightly, and it took Ember a moment to realize what it was. A vial of poison, and as she watched, Juniper stealthily uncorked it and began dipping it toward Asher's cup of tea.

Instead of screaming at her, which was her initial thought, Ember instead snapped her fingers, as though remembering something. It was a quieter way to hopefully get rid of the problem without drawing more unwanted attention to herself. Juniper fumbled and the vial's contents spilled over the table, but mercifully not into the cup of tea. If that had happened, Ember would've probably made a scene by leaping across the table and dashing it against the floor.

Luckily for Ember, the queen's roll call was loud enough to cover the sound of her snapping. She didn't need anymore questions today. Ember repressed a small smile as Juniper scrambled to wipe up the liquid with her sleeves. She produced the cork from her pocket and corked the vial, pulling her sleeve back down to hide it. She continued to stir Asher's tea for a moment before setting it in front of him.

Ember knew she had to tell Asher. But after last night, she wasn't entirely sure she could face him again.

Somebody had just tried to poison her crown prince, though. She had an obligation to report that. It was one of her only jobs—defend the Phoenixes.

The rest of the meeting passed excruciatingly slowly as Ember waited for it to end. She rolled the silver dog pin between her fingers several times, continuing to look up at the servant who it had been stolen from. She and Juniper made eye contact several times, but every time it was the servant who dropped it first.

When the queen dismissed everybody, Ember stood and quickly made her way to Asher.

"Prince Asher?" she asked, and he looked up, surprised.

"Lady Ember?" Ember curled her hands at her sides, steeling herself. The silver pin stabbed into her palms, helping to ground her as well.

"I know that dinner last night was...odd, to say the least. But I have an obligation to protect House Phoenix. It's the job of the Dragon to protect the Phoenix. I just watched a servant girl attempt to poison your drink. She has green eyes and brown hair."

Asher stood abruptly, shoving his chair back behind him. He leaned forward, eyes darting from her to Juniper, who stood nearby. "Do you have any proof?"

Ember's mouth dropped open. She had expected it to feel awkward to speak to him, but she hadn't expected him to not believe her at all.

"Ask her to shake her sleeves back. It was strapped on the inside of her left arm. If you look, you'll find it there. And she mopped up the spilled poison with her sleeves, so they'll still be wet."

"Juniper," Asher called, and she immediately appeared at his side. "Can you empty your pockets, please? And please pull your sleeves back." Juniper did as he asked, laying out a few personal items—a worn ring, a lock of hair in a small jar, a folded letter. She tossed her sleeves back, revealing her pale forearms, completely bare of a vial of poison. Her sleeves were dry, too. Ember gaped.

"Empty the pocket on the inside of your shirt," Ember said, praying to the Dragon that it was there, and Juniper did as she asked, laying out a dry handkerchief on the table.

Again, no vial. Not even the cork, or a drop of the poison on her arm. Ember's teeth began to grind harder against each other.

"Lady Ember, I appreciate your concern, but I'm sure with your mother missing you must be very paranoid and—"

"My mother is not missing. She is resting at home, recovering from the illness she contracted during her pilgrimage." Asher gave her an incredulous look.

"Okay, Lady Ember. Whatever you say." He turned and strode away, Juniper a pace behind him.

Ember stared after them, mouth still open as she looked between their retreating backs.

She wasn't wrong about Juniper. She knew she wasn't. Ember saw the vial, watched the girl wipe it up with her ridiculous sleeves.

So why did she feel crazy?

Chapter

SIXTEEN

"THREE HUNDRED. THREE HUNDRED and ten. Three hundred and fifteen," Ember muttered to herself, counting coins. She'd already counted them three times, but she needed a distraction as the carriage took her to the Vulpus Estate.

She was paying the twins today and considering asking them to look into her mother's disappearance. Perhaps they could find something on Verity, even if they couldn't on Juniper.

The carriage pulled up outside the estate, and Ember stepped out, immediately slipping on the ice and landing on her rear. She cried out in shock, rubbing her backside as the coachman rushed around to help her up, walking her to the front door, where she stood solidly on the stone steps, face burning.

How absolutely humiliating.

Ember knocked on the door, which to her surprise, swung open on the second knock. She expected the same servant as last time, maybe even the twins, but instead she was greeted by a very angry Scarlett Evet. The Lady of House Vulpus stared her down, nostrils flaring. Her face was nearly the same color as her hair, green eyes sharp against the red backdrop. Ember was taken aback by the fury in her eyes.

"Go away," she said and attempted to close the door, but Ember stuck her shoe in the crack and forced her way in.

"I need to speak to the twins." The woman backed away from her, and it was only then that Ember realized she was holding a small, wooden charm of the Phoenix, clutching it with slick palms. The sort of thing priests would use to cast a dark creature out of a person or a home.

"Stop pointing that thing at me," Ember said, batting her hand away. "I'm not possessed, for the love of the Phoenix. I'm a Dragon, not a Bear. Your boys did me a favor, and I intend to pay them."

"We don't want anything to do with your filthy house," Scarlett hissed, and Ember stood up a little straighter. Her eyebrows narrowed as she and Scarlett stared at each other, two proud women who were refusing to budge.

But only one of them outranked the other, and it certainly wasn't Scarlett.

"You would dare to call House Draco filthy when you live in a home that is falling apart? Everything here is covered in dust. And you dare to say those words to my face, when you know my mother has the king's favor? And that one day, I'll have the king's favor?"

Scarlett smiled, an odd, unnatural look on the face that had only been scowling up until now. "That's exactly the problem. Where *is* your mother, anyways? She hasn't been around in several days. Missing the weekly meeting was certainly odd for Lady Verity. If she misses the holy day, there'll certainly be questions. Questions I don't think you can answer, my dear. Can you?"

"I won't allow you to speak down to me when I hold twice the power you ever will. Lest you forget that House Draco is the most favored of all houses, that the Dragon is the Phoenix's most favored guard. There's a reason the Dragon owns the first house, and the Fox owns the ninth. If you have something to say, you will say it, so I can leave your house sooner."

"You will not speak to me this way in my own house," Scarlett said. "You will be welcome in this home once we get some answers about where your mother is. Until then, stay far away from my house. And my sons." Ember let out a frustrated sigh.

"Just give the twins this money, okay? If you promise that you'll give it to them, I'll leave."

Scarlett shook her head. "No. I won't allow them to touch anything that *your* hands have been on, bitch."

Maybe it was the way she said *your*, or that Scarlett had the nerve to call her a bitch, but Ember froze, a deadly calm settling over her, and then she snapped.

She had Scarlett pinned against the wall before the older woman could even cry out and forced the envelope in her hand. Ember pressed her arm into the woman's neck, cutting off her breathing. Scarlett wheezed and clawed at her arm, but Ember wasn't done. She unsheathed the knife from her sleeve, switching arms so the flat end of the knife was against Scarlett's throat, like Viper had done to her. It was a good move, she had to admit.

"You will pay the twins. Do you understand that? I don't give a damn what you think or say about my house, since you are insignificant, but a Dragon is always good on their word, and you will pay them. You might not have honor, but I do. We had a deal. They held up their end, and I will hold up mine. Is that understood?" The woman nodded, her clawing becoming more frantic. Ember stepped away, allowing her to fall to the floor, desperately trying to catch her breath. She sheathed the knife as she looked at Scarlett with disgust.

"Good. I'm glad we both understand." There was a slight noise on the stairs, and Ember looked up. The twins were staring at her, horrified. Bat's mouth was gaping open, and Hawk had covered his eyes. All of a sudden, Hawk let out a violent scream, from a voice that had clearly not been used in some time. Bat clutched his brother closer as they watched her. The hair on Ember's arms stood as she paced closer to the stairs.

"Boys. I have your money," Ember said, but they were already scrambling back up the stairs, getting as far away from her as possible.

Ember couldn't help but agree with their logic and turned to leave.

"You know," Scarlett wheezed, slowly rising from the floor, "the rest of the houses believe House Draco is cursed. You better find us some answers before we turn against you, Lady Ignis."

Ember didn't dignify her with a response.

Someone was knocking on the door of Ember's house, and she beat Roland to opening it.

She wasn't really in the mood for visitors. Asher himself could've been standing on her doorstep and she still would've closed it. At best, it would be her mother, coming home with an explanation. At worst, it would be Juniper Farley.

It was neither of them, and certainly not somebody she was expecting.

Lilith Taya stood outside the door, clearly frantic.

"Thank the Phoenix you're here," Lilith said. "Can I come in? Please?"

"If you must," Ember said, opening the door a little wider and allowing Lilith in. She and Lilith had never been friends, exactly, but there was a mutual respect there. They were both heirs to powerful houses.

Lilith was twice her size in muscle, but they were shorter than Ember, only coming up to about her shoulder. Their blonde hair was cropped to their shoulders, and they wore a simple green shirt with black pants. Leopard colors.

"Come into the main room. I'll have Roland light us a fire." Ember called for the butler, and as he did as she asked, Ember and Lilith sat across from each other, Ember in her mother's chair and Lilith in the one Ember usually used.

"Your mother isn't sick, is she?" Lilith asked, and Ember opened her mouth to dismiss them from her house, but Lilith wasn't done. Their leg was shaking quickly, rattling the chair as they leaned forward. For a moment, Ember was afraid they would actually fall out of it.

"My mother has gone missing too. And my stepmother won't do anything about it. I think she likes being the lady of the house. I don't know who else to go to. I already offered blood to the Phoenix Flame, and it didn't work, but I figured you might be able to help me."

Ember scoffed, and immediately regretted it when Lilith's face fell. That had been mean. Lilith clearly needed someone's help, but Ember was not the right person for that task.

"Lilith, you act like I'm some sort of miracle worker. Trust me, if I knew where my mother was, I'd be sure to help you. But I'm only one person. And I honestly have no idea where she is. I'm not trying to hold out on you. I'm just as lost."

"I have the same problem."

"No, you don't. You have two little siblings and a stepmother. I'm the only family my mother has. Nobody else loves her the way I do."

"I already told you my stepmother was useless. And, honestly, what do you expect a ten-year-old and a six-year-old to accomplish? Nothing, that's what. Please. I don't know who else to go to."

Ember considered their statement for a minute. "You could get somebody from House Vulpus to help you, but it's best if you don't mention my name while you're over there. Or, I suppose, Viper of House Serpens. Do you know him?"

"By name and face, but I've never spoken to him."

"He's quite the busybody. I'm sure he could weasel his way into some information for you."

Lilith shook their head. "I don't want anybody else to know about this. At least not until I get some answers. Please, Ember."

"Lady Ember. I do outrank you."

"Lady Ember. Please help me."

Ember sighed. "I can't, Lilith. I'm truly sorry. But I have to find my mother first. She's the only family I have. Now please, go. Consider my suggestions."

Lilith stood, fists clenched. For a moment Ember wondered if they were going to try and hit her, and her fingers strayed to her knife, but instead Lilith backed off, stepping a few feet away from her.

"You're making a mistake, Lady Ember," they said and spat a little on the word lady.

"Thank you for the threat. Now please, remove yourself from my home before I do it for you." That was enough for Lilith to stomp their way to the door, much to Ember's relief.

When the door closed, and she heard the carriage pull away, Ember put her head in her hands and let out a single, choked sob.

SEVENTEEN

EMBER SAT IN FRONT of her vanity as her maid brushed her hair. Her hands moved over the Dragon knife she clutched in her lap. They were shaking, even though a fire roared in the fireplace beside her. Her hands had only shaken from the cold before, and even then, she tried to keep them still.

They certainly hadn't shaken because of fear. Anxiety.

He mother had been gone for seven days, and it was becoming more and more apparent that she wasn't coming home anytime soon.

She had taken to spending more and more time alone in her room, unable to cope with the prospect of her mother being...

No. She refused to go down that road. If she did, she would lose what was left of her sanity. Ember had already gone over her options a dozen times.

To alert the king and queen of her problem, but that would expose her as a liar, so that was out.

Go to the twins, to beg them to help her find her mother. She'd almost killed their mother, though, so that was also out.

Slit her palm at the Phoenix Flame and pray for hours until she received some answers from either the Phoenix or the Dragon. She didn't like banking on the fact that they would pay attention to her, and she wasn't going to waste her blood for no reason.

Ask Lilith for help since she was missing a parent too. But after the way Ember had dismissed her? No.

She could search for Verity, herself, she supposed, but House Draco needed a matriarch. She wouldn't be able to leave without being asked questions she didn't have answers to.

She was completely alone in her little world. She dismissed the maid from her room, locking the door when she had left.

Ember threw the knife as hard as she could, satisfied when it thunked against the marble floor.

"Where are you?" she whispered. "Where'd you go?"

Of course, there was no answer. Ember collapsed on her bed, fully clothed in one of her old dresses, but unable to stand any longer. She felt as though she was going crazy.

First her mother vanished. Then Asher walked out during the middle of dinner. Juniper with a vial of a mystery liquid that was intended for the prince's tea. Lilith's desperate pleas that replayed over and over in her head.

Plus, she had barely been sleeping, and eating even less. Servants—especially Roland, who was fiercely loyal to her mother—kindly tried to feed her, but she would only eat a few bites before throwing the rest out.

At times like this, most people would go to the Phoenix and—

Crap. It was a holy day, and she was at home, curled up on her bed, as though she wasn't representing House Draco.

Ember jumped up, scrambling for a pair of shoes. She was sure that red with a black dress was a bold choice, but at this point she didn't care. No hairdo, no makeup. She didn't even grab a coat, although it was freezing outside. Servants moved to help her, but she brushed them off, instructing Roland to please lock the door behind her. Barefoot, in a thin black dress, rushing out the door and shouting at the coachman to start the carriage. When he hesitated, she screamed louder, threatening firing him, and he immediately took off.

Ember jumped into the carriage, shoes in hand, pulling them on after closing the door. She breathed a sigh as she strapped herself into the shoes. She was going to be late, but maybe she could sneak in the back. She started praying as soon as the shoes were on. They pulled up outside the palace, and Ember flew out of the carriage, completely frantic.

Ember reached for the door, but it was too late. The doors flew open as soon as she entered the palace, and everybody flooded out. The servants barely bothered to look her way, scurrying off to wherever they spent most of their time, but the houses certainly looked at her as though she was a madwoman.

Perhaps she was. She felt like one, at least. Tears began to fall from her eyes and her nose began to get stuffy, and she sniffled pathetically as she waited for the temple to clear. Maybe she would go in and cut her palm, just as an apology for missing the holy day.

Amber Forrest gave her a small, reassuring smile, tapping the Elk necklace around her neck. Showing her that House Alces stood with Ember. Or, at least, Amber did.

Nobody said anything, though, until the king and queen stepped out of the temple. They stood beside each other, not touching but still in solidarity. The king broke away from the queen's side, moving over to where some of the other members of the court stood. After a moment, Asher crossed to his mother, whispering something in her ear. The queen looked up sharply, eyes locking on Ember.

"Lady Ember," Queen Feather said. "Walk with me for a moment, my dear." Ember cast her eyes to the ground, causing more tears to flow freely. She couldn't exactly refuse. When she looked up again, she could see Asher watching her from over his mother's shoulder, a bandage wrapped around his right hand. So he had given blood.

Strange.

"Yes, Your Highness. I'd be happy to." As Ember and the queen stepped away, Ember could feel Asher's eyes on her back.

Ember Ignis was unraveling. Asher knew that much. He'd seen it, at the meeting where she told everybody her mother was sick, when only the night before she'd said Verity was out of town. And then, today, when she'd arrived late to the service. Completely out of place for her, for House Draco.

And maybe this would damn him, but Asher wasn't worried about her. She might've been the future lady of House Draco, but if anything, this proved Ember wasn't nearly stable enough to lead an entire house on her own. He flexed his cut palm, watching blood soak the bandages.

He knew Ember had been wrong about Juniper trying to poison him. Regardless of the awkwardness of the last time Asher had been with Juniper, he didn't see her as somebody who would attempt to end his life. In fact, he was hoping they'd make it up today, as he'd written a note asking Juniper to meet him in the garden after the service.

Ember's behavior today was enough evidence that she wasn't quite right anymore.

Yet there were things happening that he couldn't quite understand. He'd noticed books from the library missing. History books, mostly, which was no loss for him, but a deep wound for his parents, who used the advice of leaders from ages past to make tough decisions. He'd found more knives stuck in tables, although they weren't like the one Asher had found, and there still hadn't been a true answer for the shattered window in the hallway. Nobody could give him or his parents any answers, so the investigations were discontinued until another incident happened. So far, since the questionings, there hadn't been any more incidents. It gave Asher an odd feeling when he thought about it, as though he knew what was happening but couldn't explain it.

His mother had taken Ember aside only seconds after Asher had whispered who he'd seen his father with. His mother hadn't reacted visibly. But that didn't mean she wasn't furious or hurt inside.

He had chosen to tell her then, simply because of Ember's similarity to her mother. It had slipped his mind for the last few days, and the sight of Ember had brought it roaring back to the front of his thoughts. He had a feeling that Ember was going to ask his mother for something that dealt with Verity, and his mother, as much as he had complicated feelings toward her, deserved to know. She deserved to know about what he had seen, although he'd been sure to make it clear that he only thought it had been Verity. He didn't want to deal in absolutes.

But he had a date with Juniper in fifteen minutes, and he wasn't going to be late for that. He owed her, after all, after blowing her off for Ember a few nights ago. Plus, it would be good to see her, a little burst of happiness in a rather dull day.

Asher allowed himself a small smile as he went to meet Juniper.

Hopefully, this would fix everything.

Chapter

EIGHTEEN

QUEEN FEATHER LED EMBER down a side hallway, away from the post-service crowd, and settled on a small wooden bench, tapping the space next to her.

Ember sat, folding her hands in her lap as she waited for the queen to speak. They were still shaking, and she desperately tried to bury them in the folds of her dress, but the queen had already noticed, looking at them with a sad smile. There was something else in her eyes, too, but Ember couldn't make it out.

"You didn't come to the temple today," Feather began. "Why is that?"

"I lost track of time," Ember said, not knowing how much information to give her. She didn't really know who to trust. "I've had...a rough few days."

"Tell me about them," Feather invited.

"I—Are you sure? I don't want to burden you."

"My dear, you will never be a burden on this kingdom." Ember considered that for a moment but realized that if anybody could help her, it would be the queen. And she had no doubt the queen was able to keep as many secrets as she chose.

Her tone sounded sincere, at least, even if she was a bit distant. Perhaps that came with the position— holding everybody at arm's length.

"My mother is missing. I don't know where she is or why she left. It's been a week, and I haven't heard anything. Not even a letter. I'm really worried about her. She's never done this to me before. It's why she's been absent physically, and why I've been absent emotionally. I guess I was absent physically today, too."

"Whelyn and I suspected something was going on. It isn't like Lady Verity to disappear like this, especially with no warning, and without you. I know how close you two are."

Ember nodded as the queen lapsed into silence. She looked conflicted, but Ember tried her best not to stare as she considered what to say next.

"She's been gone seven days. Any evidence will be gone. But perhaps you can do something else for me. Lilith Taya's mother—Lady Alex Taya—is missing too. She's been gone less time. Please find her."

"We can try our best," Feather said. "But you cannot miss any more holy days or palace meetings. Nobody must know that your mother is missing. The last thing we need right now are whispers that a house lady is missing. That will rile the people into rebellion against your house, if they think they can get away with it."

"Rumors are already swirling, Your Majesty. House Vulpus is shunning me, and as far as I know, the other lower houses are too. I don't know if it's gotten out of the houses yet."

"If the people don't know, then it's okay. The lower houses will forever be jealous of the upper houses. Trust me," Feather said with a wink. She rose, and Ember rose with her, dipping into a low curtsy.

"Is that all, Lady Ember?" she asked. "Please, don't hesitate to ask."

"One more thing, Queen Feather. There's a servant girl. Juniper Farley. I don't trust her. Is there any way you could investigate her?"

The queen frowned and shook her head, her crown moving slightly with the motion. "I'm afraid not. I need a reason to pursue her. I'm sorry, Lady Ember, but that won't be possible."

Ember nodded. At least she'd won a victory for Lilith. It was frustrating, though, and she couldn't help the next words that sprang from her lips.

"I believe that she attempted to poison Prince Asher," Ember said, and the queen's eyes flashed, although Ember wasn't sure why. It hadn't been fear or surprise in her eyes, but, rather, hatred. But toward who, Ember didn't know.

"Perhaps a search can be done. I'll discuss it with my husband." Ember nodded, dipping her head to the queen respectfully.

"I appreciate all you've offered to do. I'll see you in a few days at the next palace meeting, Your Majesty." Ember turned and walked away from the queen, fingers shaking still, but not as violently.

She hesitated outside the door to the temple before pushing her way in. The priest at the front, tending to the Phoenix Flame, looked up, surprised.

"I want to give blood," Ember said, extending her quivering palm. The man smiled.

"The Phoenix smiles upon you, young Dragon," he responded, gesturing at the knives. "Choose."

Ember stooped and picked up a short blade knife with a smooth edge. She sliced it across her palm, forcing herself not to wince at the sharp stab of pain. She placed her hand over the Phoenix Flame and squeezed. The blood dripped from her in a fast torrent, and the flames climbed higher, gorging itself on her blood. The priest helped her wrap her hand with a bandage.

"May I ask why?" the priest asked, tying a knot on the bandage. "Why today?" Ember stared at the bandage, at the blood already soaking through.

"My mother," Ember said, but left it at that as the man stepped away from her.

Ember stumbled her way back to the courtyard and to the carriage, ignoring the odd looks the other house members were giving her and her bloody hand. She didn't have to explain anything to them.

She was a Dragon.

Ember boarded the carriage, looking out the window and meeting Lilith's eyes. She hoped that maybe Lilith would find out what she had done for them. That she had been able to convince the queen to send out a search party for Alex Taya. She couldn't tell Lilith herself—not after she'd dismissed them from her home as though they were nothing. She couldn't help but cling to the last shreds of her pride.

Ember turned from the window, hoping her offering of blood would convince the Phoenix to bring her mother home.

Asher jogged his leg, looking around the second-floor library as he waited for Juniper. It was the smallest of the four libraries that the palace boasted, and thus the most intimate. There were several maps spread on the table, and he hoped he could show them to her, to show her all the places she wanted to go. He really did want to fix things with the two of them. He had two glasses of wine as well but refused to keep the bottle on the table. He could have one drink, he reasoned, but no more than that.

The door opened, and Asher looked up, unable to help himself from smiling as he recognized Juniper. They made eye contact as she looked at him over one of the shorter shelves.

"Hello, Prince Asher," Juniper said, dipping into a small curtsy. She came over to him, standing awkwardly beside the table. "Can I sit here?"

Asher nodded, watching as she slowly sat.

"Is... We're still friends, right?" Asher asked.

Juniper smiled, ducking her head before looking back up at him. "Of course," she said. "It was just an accident. I hope it was, at least."

Asher nodded quickly, grateful that she didn't seem to hold anything against him. "It was. I'm so sorry I hurt you,"

Asher said. "I truly didn't mean to. I've got something to make it up to you, if you're interested."

Juniper looked down, at the maps spread on the table. "I'd love to know what you have in mind," Juniper said, already bending to trace her finger over one of the maps of the far continent.

"These are some of the palace's finest maps," Asher explained. "Of Eiad, and the far and mid continents. I have more specific ones of certain countries, as well, if you're interested. You can look at whichever ones you want. I have permission, and I can extend that to you." Asher wasn't even entirely sure that Juniper had heard him; she was smiling to herself as she moved some of the maps around.

"I don't even know where to start," she admitted. "I've never really been out of my hometown before I moved here, honestly. There's still so much of Eiad I haven't seen yet. I'd love to see Mount Saffi, to spend some time in the temple up there. I've heard that it's beautiful." Asher, who had been up to Mount Saffi so many times that he was bored of it, kept his mouth shut as Juniper pulled one of the maps out, eyes dancing over the colors that had been used on it. It certainly wasn't from Eiad, where the maps were made with black lines and dull colors. If Asher was correct, that particular map had come from the islands, colored with vibrant blues and greens and golds.

"What is this place?" Juniper asked, finger tracing the ancient language that spelled out the country's name. Asher squinted at it, trying to work his useless mind into translating it. Eventually, he shrugged, looking up to find Juniper watching him. She quickly looked away, a small blush spreading over her face. Asher's face heated, and he cursed himself for getting that flustered.

The shape of the country looked vaguely familiar, and Asher found the map of the mid continent, trying to match the shapes. Juniper, sensing his intentions, found the map of the far continent, and scoured it just as intently.

There was something about sitting with her in the quiet of the library, the only sound the rustle of the maps, that made Asher's heart beat erratically in his chest. They weren't speaking, much less looking at each other or touching, but it was rather soothing. A balm to his soul.

Vax would've liked her. The thought came, wild and unbidden, to the front of Asher's mind. He hadn't wanted to think about Vax, not in moments like this, when he was happy and content. But the thought rang true regardless. Juniper was adventurous and compassionate, and Vax had been similar.

Asher realized, as he sat there with her, that for the first time since Vax had died, he had a true friend.

Part Two

THE MOTHER

—A POEM FOUND IN AN ABANDONED TEMPLE

Chapter

Nineteen

Ember was sitting in the garden, a target stuffed full of knives across from her, when the knock came. It had finally gotten warmer outside, and since the temple service was over, she had been enjoying the change of temperature when her butler, Roland, came outside to inform her of a visitor sitting in their living room, and she forced herself to stand and go inside to greet them. Her palm stung. She'd offered even more blood today, becoming slightly frantic.

It had been two weeks since Verity had disappeared. Seven days since Queen Feather had promised to try and find Lady Alex.

Ember had been waiting for information, desperately grabbing onto every scrap of mail that came through the mail slot.

She'd taken up doing her mother's work, too, the financial reports and such, making sure all the help was paid and they had enough food and wine. She wrote letters on her mother's behalf, arranged meetings with old, rich, houseless men, convincing them that House Draco was still mighty and that if House Draco fell, so did they. Ember had managed to even order a birthday gift for Allen Forrest, sending the beautiful Elk earring to his house. It was exhausting, especially when Ember allowed herself a moment to think about all of it.

She had hoped that maybe the queen herself had come down to give her news, or perhaps a royal messenger. Even, maybe, Lilith, if they had figured out what Ember had tried to do for them. She knew wishing for the queen was a stretch, but she seriously needed some good luck.

Instead, it was Blue Corvu, wearing that horrible orange suit and poking around her sitting room. He pulled one of her mother's leather-bound books off the shelf, and Ember's fingers twitched with anxiety. Even she wasn't allowed to touch those. Verity didn't even let the servants dust those books. She did it herself. And Verity wasn't exactly one who did physical work.

Ember cleared her throat as she came in, and Blue dropped the book he was holding. He picked it up and placed it back on the shelf, putting it on top of the other books. Ember let out a frustrated sigh. She was going to have to fix it later.

"Hello," he said.

"Hello," Ember responded, then crossed her arms. "What do you want?"

Blue looked up at her, a stung expression on his face.

Ember felt a stab of remorse. She was being shorter than usual now, due to the stress, but she was using it as a shield more than anything. A way to deflect the attention. If she was unpleasant, then people wouldn't crowd her with questions about her mother.

Questions she still didn't have the answers to.

"Sheesh. I've been here ten seconds. Give me a minute."

"No," Ember said. "I don't think I will. Besides, aren't you supposed to be shunning me right now? Isn't that the new thing for the lower houses to do?"

Blue wrinkled his nose. "I'm sorry, what? Who's shunning you?"

"House Vulpus and the rest of the lower houses, I'm pretty sure."

"Crazy Foxes. Scarlett is going to run them into the ground. No, I'm not shunning you. And as far as I know, none of the other houses are either."

"Odd. But you didn't answer my question. What do you want?"

Blue sat on the couch, seeming to consider his statement before talking.

"I know your mother is missing, don't deny it. Everybody knows it. I just wanted to let you know that my father went out for a drink last night in a...seedy part of the next town over, and he didn't come home the next morning. My younger brother found his severed finger, with his house ring still on it. Pretty gruesome. But no sign of my father."

Ember sat across from him, suddenly enthralled. She certainly hadn't expected to get this type of news.

"Do you know where he went?"

"No idea. He goes out once in a while, but he always comes home the next morning. As far as I know, he's never done something like this. It's concerning, to say the least."

"Yeah, no kidding," Ember said.

"Look, all I'm saying is, there's something going on that neither you, nor I, know about. First with your mother disappearing, and then my father? Doesn't seem like a coincidence to me."

"That's not all," Ember said but didn't say anything else. She was hesitant to trust him, this odd boy with the ocean in his hair.

Blue nodded. "Alex Taya is missing too. Lilith was a wreck a few days ago. And their mother is really the only person they care about."

"Right. Lilith came by a few days ago to ask for help."

"It's definitely not a coincidence then. Maybe we should do something."

"I already asked the queen to search for Lilith's mother. Hopefully she's in the same place as mine. Your father could be there too. Does your father have any enemies you know about?"

"I don't know. Probably. He's a house lord, after all. I think a lot of people would like to see us hurt, and honestly, he was probably an easy target," Blue said. "I just thought you'd like to know that information. I'll go now. I can tell you have a lot on your mind."

Ember nodded distractedly and called the butler to see him out. She flexed her bandaged palm, sending up a quick thanks to the Phoenix for bringing Blue to her.

Verity could very well be safe somewhere, vacationing in Tali. Ember certainly couldn't fault her for that. They both deserved a break. It was odd, though, for Verity to go somewhere Ember couldn't follow to, leaving her no information and by default, no peace of mind. Ember's hands began moving of their own accord as she thought about her other options.

She could see the appeal to mercenaries to take her mother, and Lilith's. They were from the three highest houses, after all. It just could've been that Blue's father was an easy target, as he had said, what with him being drunk and out of his own territory.

Or, Ember's least favorite option, was that Verity had been attacked and died. Gone, leaving Ember without the chance to say goodbye. But that still didn't explain Alex Taya and Blue's father.

Ember supposed that maybe she should inform the queen, but rumors were quick to spread through the houses, and it wasn't her responsibility to keep up with all the going-ons anyways.

Instead, she began drafting a letter to Viper. She wasn't going to allow herself to unravel without apologizing first. He'd tried to help her before, and she was praying he would be willing to at least listen to her now.

Asher sat on a garden bench next to Juniper, their hands dangerously close to touching.

"I enjoy these talks," Juniper said, huddled in her new coat. Asher had been glad to see it when he'd met her in the garden, kissing her gloved hand before leading her to a bench in the back of the garden. When spring fully came, he planned on buying her new dresses and light coats that would fend off the chill without smothering her. Already, she had unzipped her coat, as the sun beat down upon them. They were sheltered only by the shadow of the castle, which was rapidly slipping away.

"Me too," Asher said, stretching his fingers out a bit and then pulling them back in. He wasn't quite sure if she would be okay with him holding her hand. He didn't even know what he wanted with Juniper. As the prince, he knew he could have her for one night and then discard her, but he genuinely enjoyed speaking to her, and didn't want to discard whatever this was.

This was so strange for him, so new. Vax and the other heirs had been his friends, but he'd never had to search for them—they'd been built in, in a sense, with Vax being family, and the others being equally entrenched in court life. Juniper was something different entirely, and he was curious to see where their relationship would go. He would be fine if they remained as just friends, but he genuinely hoped he wasn't the only one who thought that there might be something more between the two of them.

"Are you okay?" Juniper asked suddenly, shifting her body so her hand was completely out of reach. He cursed himself silently, adjusting his weight so it wasn't all on his scarred hand. Giving blood last week had been stupid, but it seemed to have pleased his parents, getting them off his back.

"Yes, I'm fine," Asher said, trying to figure out what he had done wrong. He began to itch for a drink but forced himself to concentrate. He was trying to stay sober, but it wasn't easy. The cravings hit especially hard at night, when he couldn't distract himself with work or taking care of Hazel and Siliros, or spending time with Juniper.

"You seem distracted. Did something happen?"

Asher looked around to make sure nobody was in earshot. There were guards, of course, but they stood by the doors, and if Asher didn't shout, he was fairly sure they wouldn't be able to hear him. Juniper looked around with him, raising her eyebrows in confusion.

"Can you keep a secret?" he asked, and Juniper nodded earnestly, leaning in closer. Asher, caught completely unaware by the motion, by the way the smell of her soap wafted over to him, didn't even hear what Juniper said to him.

"What?"

Juniper giggled. "I said, 'what's going on?'"

"Three of the house leaders—House Draco, Pardus and Olor—are missing. They found the lord of House Olor's finger, with his house ring still on it."

Juniper's mouth flew open. "You're kidding."

"Nope. Everybody in the houses is in turmoil."

"I probably would be too. It seems like the houses are... untouchable, in a way," Juniper said. "How are you taking it?"

Asher shrugged. "I'm alright. I'm not exactly close to any of them, unlike my mother. Relationships with the houses and the royals are usually professional, unless the heir of House Phoenix is looking for a partner, or maybe a friend. It's all very odd, isn't it?"

"It really is odd. I've never heard of anything like that before.

That's never happened recently, has it?"

"Not to my knowledge," Asher said. "Maybe a while back, when the houses were first established, but certainly not currently. After all, we are very powerful. I'm sure that maybe one or two lords or ladies have gone missing more recently, but not a group of them at once. Any stirring of a rebellion—which is my theory on it, at least—would be squashed. It's hard to imagine anybody would question the Phoenix's might." As he said it, he didn't really know if he spoke of the true Phoenix or of himself and his parents.

His theory about the rebellion was one he had been thinking of as soon as he'd heard the news about the House Olor lord. It was one of the only things that made sense, in Asher's opinion. The three leaders hadn't just decided to take off at the same time, and the House Olor lord had lost a finger. He'd been attacked, even if Verity Ignis and Alex Taya hadn't. There could be mercenaries, he supposed, perhaps even from other countries, but then why leave the finger?

Asher knew that his theory wasn't solid, but he was willing to stick with it until more information came to light.

"Well, I'm glad you're taking it well," Juniper said and scooted closer to Asher on the bench. She bit her lip, and Asher's breath sped up slightly. Her eyes were on his mouth, and he was oddly conscious of the way he licked his own lips and moved closer to her.

"Yeah. I'm glad you're not too distressed either," he murmured. His eyes darted back to their hands on the bench, and gently placed his injured hand over hers.

The small motion seemed to jar something in Juniper, and she immediately pulled back, letting cool air flow in between the two of them, and Asher flinched.

"I need to get back to work," Juniper said, jumping up and rushing away.

Asher sat on the bench in the same position, completely dumbfounded. His mouth had dropped open as he watched her retreat. Had he done something wrong? Maybe he shouldn't have tried to hold her hand. Asher had expected a lot of things of this meeting, but he hadn't expected Juniper to reject him completely, leaving him cold and alone. He certainly didn't think she owed him anything, but surely he hadn't imagined the feeling that flowed between the two of them only moments before?

Regardless, he curled his fist into his side and made his way into the palace, searching for a strong drink.

Chapter

TWENTY

VIPER HAD AGREED TO meet with Ember. She hadn't expected him to, but maybe he could read the desperation in her letter.

Ember waited for him as she thought of her mother, her anxiety causing her to jump when the knock came. He was ushered in, and for a moment they simply stared at each other.

"You asked to see me," he said, standing stiffly in the doorway. "Yes," Ember said. "Please, sit down."

Viper did, sitting across from her on a chair. He looked uncomfortable. Ember wasn't surprised. Even the prince himself had felt odd in the Draco Estate. Sometimes even *she* felt unwelcome, as though the Dragon wanted her out.

"Just tell me why I'm here," Viper said. "I'm not interested in your pleasantries. You want something, and I want to know what."

"You're right. I do want something. I want to apologize."

"Apology not accepted. What else?"

"Phoenix above, Viper. Get over yourself. My mother has been missing for over two weeks. I have better things to worry about than you throwing yourself a pity party. I'm asking you to accept the apology and then help me. You'll be rewarded handsomely, of course, if you agree."

"Go on," Viper said, and Ember was glad he was at least listening. She figured it would be easiest to get to him if she mentioned money. The lower houses could never resist money.

"It was your idea to talk to members of House Vulpus. And that was a great idea. I did go to them."

"Really?" Viper said, sitting forward a bit. Ember suppressed a smirk. This was too easy.

"Yes. The twins, Bat and Hawk. They weren't as helpful as I'd hoped, but it was a good idea. I still paid them. Right after I tried to kill their mother." Viper choked on a laugh, and Ember was glad she was getting to him.

"You did not."

Ember smiled, a cold, calculated gesture designed to draw him in and make him let his guard down. "Well, maybe I didn't try to kill her. But I lost it, I guess. She's okay, now."

Viper nodded. "So. Why am I here, other than to bear the brunt of your awful apologies?" Ember gave him a dirty look before changing her posture. She had relaxed too much, even for pretending.

Was she pretending?

Ember shook her head to clear the thought from her mind—of course she was pretending—and opened her mouth to say something else, but was interrupted by Roland rushing into the room, holding a letter. Even from where she sat, Ember could see the black envelope and the gold Phoenix crest stamped on the front.

Only the Phoenixes used black paper, and she knew who it was from before Roland even said anything.

"I'm sorry to interrupt, but this is from the palace, Lady Ember. The messenger said it was urgent."

Ember snatched the letter from his hand. "Thank you, Roland. I'll call you if I need to send a response back. Viper, you don't have to stay. I can't force you to do anything."

Ember tore into the letter, desperate for information, completely ignoring the fact that Viper hadn't moved. The queen's handwriting was familiar from years of reading over her mother's shoulder, all straight lines and sharp flourishes.

Lady Ember,

I have found a lead on Lady Alex Taya, in a village about ten miles from the palace. It's called Vyx. You may have heard of it during your studies. Perhaps you've been there before.

May the Phoenix be with you,
Queen Feather

"I need to go," Ember said, shoving the letter into her pants pocket.

"Go where?" Viper asked, but he stood too, chasing after her as she ran around the house, searching for her coat.

"Damn it," Ember said as she found her coat. She couldn't very well wear a lynx-fur coat to a poor village. She didn't have much experience with those in Eiad who lived in poverty, but she doubted she'd be inconspicuous flaunting her wealth in everybody's faces.

"What was in that letter?" Viper asked, following her up the stairs as she rushed to her room.

"A location," Ember said. "I have to find something to wear!"

She threw open her closet, digging through the finery to find the old dress she'd been wearing when she'd spoken to the queen.

"Looks like you have plenty to wear," Viper said, coming up behind her and eyeing the dress.

"Get out of my room," Ember said, shoving him out and slamming the door in his face. She slipped out of the gold dress she'd been wearing and put the black one on. She had to admit, it was far more comfortable, even with it being simple cotton. She rang the bell for her maid and waited patiently, turning the queen's letter over in her lap. Her hands were shaking more violently than they ever had before. This was it. If Alex Taya wasn't in Vyx, if her mother wasn't in Vyx , Ember had reached a dead end.

Ember couldn't let that happen. She was going to find something in Vyx , even if it killed her.

Ten minutes later, Ember was allowing Henrietta to pull her hair up into a simple bun as she ran the edge of her cotton dress through her fingertips.

"I really appreciate this," Ember said, tipping her head this way and that to examine her appearance. She didn't have any makeup on, nor jewelry. This was a look she wore only when she would be alone in the house all day. Which, as of late, was a look she wore quite often.

"Ready?" Ember turned to see Viper standing in the doorway. He had come in clothes that could pass for merchant clothes, so he lingered there, looking at Ember and waiting for her nod of approval. His hair had been ruffled out of its usual slick-back, and it didn't look horrible, for once.

Ember cursed under her breath. She didn't have time to waste thinking about Viper's hair.

"We'll discuss the plan in the carriage," Ember said. "We can take it most of the way and then walk into town. That'll be far less noticeable." She turned to the butler who had followed Viper into the room.

"Roland, can you—" She didn't even get to finish her sentence before Roland was out of the door, rushing to tell the driver to prepare the carriage for them.

"Henrietta, we'll be back later. Lock up after us. I have a key. Don't wait up, either."

Henrietta nodded. "Yes, ma'am."

Ember and Viper hurried through the halls and out into the cool night air. Ember shivered a bit, as they waited for the carriage to come around.

"Why are you coming?" Ember asked, perking up at the sound of horse hooves and carriage wheels.

"I have nothing better to do," Viper said, opening the door for her and closing it behind them.

"Bad answer. At least pretend to be chivalrous."

Viper made a face. "I'd never pretend to be chivalrous for you," he said.

"Go figure," Ember said, fiddling with the letter in her lap. She tapped on the roof of the carriage to signal that they were ready to go. They took off, and Ember stared out the window, watching the brightly lit estate disappear behind them.

She was nervous. Her hands itched for the knife sheathed on her thigh, but she resisted the urge to grab it. Ember didn't have any reason to get it out. Yet.

"Where are we going?" Viper asked.

"I am going to the town of Vyx. You can do whatever you want."

"I'm trying to help."

"No, you're trying to find a cure for your boredom. When we get to the town, you're welcome to do whatever you want."

"I'll stay with you."

"Pest. I hope the Bear gets you."

When the faded sign welcoming them to Vyx came into view, Ember realized she felt lighter than she had in the last fifteen days.

They stepped out of the carriage, walking past the sign and down the road, waiting for the town to come into view. When it did, Ember's eyes flew open. It'd been years since she'd left the patron circle, the section of the kingdom where the house estates were located. She'd never had any reason to leave. Even when she and Verity vacationed, they never rode through this town. They simply made their way to the coast and then out onto the sea. She'd seen more of the middle continent than she had of Eiad.

The entire town was completely foreign to Ember. Her neck began to hurt by how often she was turning it. Everything seemed a bit run-down. Broken-in windows, barefoot children rushing past them, even at this hour. Stray dogs chasing after them, barking with excitement and frothing at the mouth. A child tripped and fell, hitting his side hard. When he stood up, Ember noticed that she could count his ribs, even from several feet away. Starving horses, more bone than anything, were dozing in a stable, most of them as thin as the little boy. Several beggars slept in a nest of filthy blankets.

As she watched, a woman swept the front porch of what Ember assumed was a store. There were no lights on in the store, except for a small candle in the window, and Ember suspected it was closed. Even still, she had an odd urge to go in, to buy something from the sweeping woman. From where she stood, Ember could see the effects of hunger on her, sunken cheeks and a waist that was far too small to be considered fashionable. Everything smelled slightly of old snow and musk, along with the all-too powerful scents of human and animal excrement.

They kept walking, kicking up dust under their feet, until Ember heard something. A shout. She and Viper quickened their pace, rushing toward the sounds of a fight. A brawl had spilled out of what looked like a tavern, two women and a man, swinging at each other with bottles and fists, screaming profanities and slurs in Qinnish. For a moment they blocked the door, the two women coming at the man from either side, their bottles flashing violently through the air. He rolled away from them, narrowly missing a bottle to the head and opening up the entrance.

Ember and Viper skirted around them, ducking into the tavern.

Ember stood for a moment in the doorway, dumbfounded. The entire tavern smelled of piss and vomit, two scents that hardly went well together. Everywhere she looked, there was something new to see—an intense game of dice, two men locked in an passionate embrace, women dancing on every other table, hoisting their short skirts up, much to the delight of the men who sat below them, who cheered and hooted at them, tossing coins on the table. Their dresses were cut in a style that had been popular a few years back: slits up to their thighs and a bodice that exposed far more than Ember wanted to see. Everything was loud. From her right came a cry of success, and she looked over to see a young woman turning over a shot glass, beating the burly man who sat across from her. Ovum was passed around, moving stealthily from one hand to another.

Gambling was illegal in Eiad, but Ember kept her mouth shut. She wasn't Lady Ember Ignis here. She was not the law in this strange place. Calling the soldiers down on this tavern would guarantee that no one would help her.

A man bumped into them from behind, and Viper caught Ember's arm, spinning her into his chest. Ember sucked in a breath, wiggling away from him, but he held fast until the man had passed. His heart was thundering in his chest.

"We need to sit," he said as Ember pried herself away from him.

"Fine. Let's sit," Ember said, following him through the tavern.

Someone grabbed Ember's dress, and she whipped around, slamming her fist into the man's hand, and unsheathing her knife, holding it out in front of her. The man released her, taking a step away from the knife and eyeing it warily.

"Damn, somebody's having a rough day," he said, looking over her shoulder and seeing Viper. "Maybe you should ask your husband to work that tension out of you." He winked, as though they were in on a big joke. Ember flushed angrily.

"Mind your own business," Ember said and leaned forward a bit, dropping her voice to a hiss. "And if you ever touch me again, I will personally ensure that you swing for what I'm sure are *many* crimes." The man gulped as he took in the meaning of her statement. Even if they didn't know who she was, Ember cut an imposing figure. She turned around to find Viper staring at her.

"Come on," Viper said, this time taking her hand. Ember immediately pulled it back.

"Just give me your hand," Viper said. "It'll keep them from touching you." Ember reluctantly gave it to him, but gave him only her fingertips, brushing hers against his. His hand was sweaty, too, which certainly didn't make her want to hold it.

He pulled her though the tables, looking left and right as she stepped over puddles of mysterious liquid that gave off foul scents. There was even a load of rat droppings she had to jump over, but the rest of the tavern seemed to move around it easily enough. Maybe it had always been there. Maybe the rats always found a way back.

They found a seat tucked in a back corner, mercifully free of a dancer on the table and secluded enough that they wouldn't be overheard, so long as they didn't shout. Ember sheathed the knife up her leg, hiding it from view once again. If anybody saw the Dragon, they might realize who she was. Which was the exact thing she was trying to avoid. She didn't want to know what these people would do to a member of the houses if they caught one, but if Blue's father was any indication, it wouldn't be pleasant.

"What are we looking for?" Viper whispered, leaning close to her.

"Back up," Ember said, pushing him away.

Viper rolled his eyes. "I backed up. Now tell me what we're looking for."

"I don't know," Ember said.

Viper's mouth dropped open. "You don't know what we're looking for? Then why are we here?"

Ember sighed. "I'm here because the queen sent me a letter. You're here because you're a parasite."

"So that's what your letter was about."

"Mmhm. She said somebody in this town could have information on Lilith Taya's mother." Viper nodded, looking around.

"Who should we ask?"

"We can't exactly ask people if they've seen the leader of a house. That would cause a riot, and possibly stir them into action against House Pardus. That was the queen's main concern. Plus, if anybody does know where she is, it's not like they'd tell us. We're new. They won't trust us. Maybe we should've poked around for a temple first. They might've trusted us more than these people will."

"Fair," Viper said, flagging down a passing waitress to acquire them some drinks. "But it's not like she'll be out in the open. People don't usually show off those that they've kidnapped. So we probably will need to ask someone. And there isn't even a temple here. Most people worship in their homes, if they worship at all."

"I don't know who to trust," Ember said. "I've never been somewhere like this before."

"Generally, stay away from the men unless you know them. Especially in what you're wearing."

"Don't make comments about my outfit," Ember said. "It's not that revealing."

"It shows off your shoulder tattoo, so I'd say it's pretty revealing. That Dragon is a dead giveaway for you—who else would want one of the patron animals on their shoulder? Like I said, avoid the men. Don't talk to the waitresses and—"

"Speak of the Bear and it will appear," Ember said as their waitress came back with their drinks. She took a sip of the amber-colored mystery liquid and immediately gagged on it. It tasted a bit like watery alcohol and a bit like piss. It wasn't a great combination, but it was cold.

"That's disgusting," she said, and Viper took a swig before continuing. Ember pushed her glass away.

"No waitresses, since they go to every table. Your secrets could be around this place before you were even aware of it."

"Okay. Who else is even here?"

"The dancers," Viper said.

"The prostitutes, you mean."

"Call them whatever you want. They get around. For the right price, I'm sure one of them would talk."

"But isn't that your problem with the waitresses? That they get around?"

"It's different. Bedside secrets are different than table-side secrets." Ember braced herself as she took another sip of her ale. It really was disgusting, but in a weird way. She couldn't stop drinking it.

"How do you know so much about places like this?" she asked, and Viper shrugged.

"I get around, you know? My parents don't pay a lot of attention to me, so it's pretty easy to slip away to a place like this for a couple of nights. I've stayed in the inn above this tavern a couple times, actually. Usually just keep my head down and my hood over my eyes so nobody recognizes how nice my clothing is. It was smart of you to change before we came here. They would've jumped you in ten seconds if you had been wearing your other clothes. They might still if they recognize your eyes or your tattoo."

"I'm not as much of an idiot as I seem," Ember said. "Plus, there was nothing I could do about my eyes. And I won't cover up my tattoo. I'm proud of it."

"Nobody called you an idiot."

"It was implied."

"It was not."

"I'm not arguing with you like we're children or something. Let's just get one of those girls to help us, and then we can leave."

"Let me do that," Viper said. "They'll get suspicious if you go over there."

"I highly doubt it, but okay. Just be quick." Viper nodded and slid out of the booth. Almost as soon as he had gone, someone sat next to Ember, and she tensed. She expected another large, bearded man, but instead it was one of the dancers, a girl far smaller than Ember. Smooth dark skin, twin braids, and brown eyes that searched the room as she spoke. Her waist was cinched underneath a corset, and her skirts were so short that they rested halfway up her thighs when she sat.

When her eyes landed on Ember, she bit back her questions. There was a wildness in the girl's eyes, the likes of which she'd never seen. It was like looking into the eyes of a wild animal—uncaged and uncompromising. A storm, about to break.

Against her better judgment, Ember liked her immediately.

"Thank the Phoenix he left," the girl said, and her voice had the hardness of the desert in it, coarse sand and a rough people. "I thought he'd never go." She picked up Viper's mug and took a long drink from it, staring down into the glass with a disgusted look on her face, but she still picked it up again as Ember stared at her.

"I'm sorry," Ember said. "Do I know you?" The girl smiled, and there was more of that desert wildness in her smile. Ember tried to place the accent, the hardness of her syllables. It was most definitely not Eiaden. Perhaps from Gleoj Swesh?

"You don't need to know me. I know who you are, and I know what you want."

"You have no idea who I am," Ember said. "My name is Ferra." She used her middle name—what were the chances this girl would recognize the name of the Dragon from two generations ago?

"No, your name is Lady Ember Ignis, and the boy you came with is Lord Viper Trunca. The two of you stick out like a sore thumb in a place like this. Even that dress—it's a great dress, by the way—can't hide your eyes. Gold eyes aren't exactly common around these parts. And tattoos like the one you have, and your friend? Definitely not Vyx quality. They're far too clean, and yours has a bit of gold in it. Our tattoos are only black." She pointed at her wrist, where a daisy had been tattooed in dark ink. The girl had nearly drained Viper's glass at this point, and Ember was about ten seconds from smashing it against her head.

"Keep your voice down. If you couldn't tell, I'm not exactly fond of drawing attention to myself. Besides, you said you could help me. So help me, and I'll reward you for it. Um...what's your name, again?"

"My name is Lucasta. Lucasta Tersus. And, yes, I have the information you so desperately want. Who is it that you're trying to find? Your mother?"

"How do you know about my mother?" Ember said, but then caught herself before she told her any more information.

"Your friend is embarrassing himself," Lucasta said, and Ember looked up at Viper. She was absolutely right.

Viper had approached another table, trying to speak to the dancer on top of it, a redhead beauty with freckles scattered across her skin. She was having none of it, attempting to bring him onto the table to dance with her, pulling on his shirt and his hands. The men at the table were clapping their hands and pushing him up on the table, keeping him there when he attempted to get down again. Viper was speaking calmly to her, but she ignored him, pressing her supple body into his.

Something slithered through Ember's stomach, oily and dark, as she stared at that dancer.

"I'll get him," Lucasta offered, snapping Ember out of it. Lucasta stood and went over to Viper, who had allowed himself to be pulled onto the table. The girl was trying to place his hands on her waist, but Viper was still attempting to reject it, keeping his hands firmly behind his back.

Ember studied Lucasta. Her braids hung to her waist, and her feet were bare. Ember squinted—how were her feet not filthy? Viper nearly toppled off the table when Lucasta pulled on his arm, spinning around to face her. The other men hooted. How often was it that someone caught the attention of two dancers? The first girl was pouting, but one of the other men placed a handful of ovum on the table, and that encouraged her to hike her skirts up and continue to dance for him.

As Ember watched, Lucasta whispered something to Viper, who then looked at Ember, locking eyes with her. Ember gave him a small nod, and he slid off the table and walked back to her.

"Are you sure about her?" Viper whispered, his mouth nearly against Ember's ear. She moved away before responding, but the hair on the back of her neck stood up, much to her dismay.

"We don't have a choice," she murmured back, and Viper helped her away from the table.

"Then we trust her," Viper said. "But what does she want out of it?"

"I don't know. She didn't say anything," Ember answered.

"Lucasta?" The girl turned toward her, hands firmly placed on her hips. Ember stifled a laugh. Lucasta was a good foot shorter than her, but it already seemed as though she was twice as fierce.

"Yes, darling?"

"What is it that you want out of this?"

Lucasta smiled. "You get me out of Vyx , and I'll tell you whatever you want. That's all I need. To get out of here. Please. I'll tell you anything, about anybody."

Lucasta stuck her hand out, looking at Ember expectantly. She stared at the daisy on Lucasta's arm and let out a long breath.

It wasn't what Verity would do. She wouldn't simply trust a girl that she knew nothing about, wouldn't bring her into her home.

But Verity wasn't there, and Ember was desperate.

Viper and Ember exchanged a glance, before Ember placed her hand in Lucasta's, shaking it twice before Viper led them out of the tavern.

Chapter

TWENTY-ONE

MBER WAS HALF ASLEEP across from Viper in Verity's chair when Lucasta descended the stairs. They had decided to bring her to the Draco Estate with them, allowing her time to take a bath and change into something less...provocative. Ember didn't know how comfortable Lucasta would've been having the conversation in Vyx, where anybody could overhear their conversation and stick a knife in her chest. Besides, she was exhausted and didn't particularly relish the idea of spending the night in some disgusting inn.

Ember had changed, too, into one of her red nightgowns, but Viper had stayed in the clothes he was wearing, saying he wouldn't be caught dead in a girl's nightgown.

Ember glanced at Viper, sitting across from her. She'd moved her chair close enough that if she wanted to, she could reach out and touch him. All she wanted was to be held, and even being held by Viper seemed better than sitting in her chair alone. Verity had never been overly affectionate, but when she could tell her daughter was drained, she would allow Ember to crawl into her lap for a little while. Ember didn't move, though, unwilling to show him that weakness.

She was going to get her answers soon, and then she wouldn't have to worry about being weak.

"She's taking forever," Viper murmured, clearly just as exhausted as Ember was. His head slumped onto the back of the couch, baring his neck. Ember could see where his pulse beat, and she dropped her gaze.

She needed to concentrate.

"Who cares," Ember responded, yawning. "Thank you for coming with me tonight."

Viper shrugged. "Sure. It was fun to get out of the house. And I'm glad we found someone who can help you."

"Help us."

"What?"

"Us. You're in this too now. That's what you get for inviting yourself today."

"Okay. I'm sorry that guy grabbed you today. He shouldn't have done that."

Ember snapped out of her sleepy state. "You noticed?"

"Yeah. I was going to jump in, but you very clearly had it under control, what with that knife and all, so I just let you do what you needed to do. It was no big deal, really. Can you imagine what would've happened to me if I'd let the heir of House Draco get kidnapped? They would send the dogs after my scent."

Ember chuckled. "Ah, always the self-preservationist," she said, and Viper looked as though he wanted to say something else, but there was a slight creak on the stairs, and they both turned to Lucasta. She was in one of Ember's gold nightgowns, which looked radiant against her dark skin. Her hair was unbound, and it was only then that Ember realized there were streaks of white in it. She was strange and exhilarating all at once, and completely foreign to Ember.

Lucasta grinned at them both before rushing down the last few steps.

"This nightgown is amazing," she said, plopping into the chair across from Ember.

"I'm glad you like it," Ember said, sitting up straight and slapping Viper's arm to make him do the same. "But, Lucasta, we really need information. You said you could help me. If you were lying, you'll wish you were back dancing on tables in Vyx. You can trust me on that."

Lucasta nodded, her face becoming completely serious. Leashing the wildness.

"Where is my mother?" Ember asked. Her heart was racing. Maybe, just maybe, she was going to be able to get her mother back. To restore balance to her world, which had been so out of the ordinary lately. Her hands had been moving quickly ever since they'd gotten in the carriage and hadn't stopped since.

"She was taken by a rebel group that I'm fairly sure is operating out of the south."

Ember struggled for words at what Lucasta had just revealed to them. Viper's mouth dropped open.

"A rebel group?" Ember and Viper exchanged a glance. Rebel groups were rare in Eiad, especially after the king had finally conquered the far north and brought the entire continent under the rule of the houses.

"Yeah. I've, erm, worked for some of them, whenever they pass through Vyx. Enough alcohol and desire will make even the strongest man spill his secrets. Especially since he doesn't think I'll do anything with them. What could a prostitute do with a rebel's secrets?"

"Clever," Viper admitted, and Ember leaned forward.

"Do you know the town they're from, or anything like that? The name they operate under, perhaps?" Lucasta shook her head.

"Nobody could ever give me a real answer. They were always different every time. When somebody did, and I checked it out on a map, it doesn't exist. I have a feeling that information is... not common knowledge. Or, maybe, there are multiple camps and they're only allowed to know one of them. I'm sure they'd pay a hefty price if they told anybody that information."

"That's all you know?"

"You already made it pretty clear that if I lied to you, I would regret it. I'm not lying."

"That can't be it," Ember said, standing and pacing. Her fingers twitched.

"That's all I know," Lucasta insisted. Ember stared into the flames, eyes going out of focus as she tried to grapple with the fact that her mother could be anywhere in Eiad at this point. Viper jumped in, much to Ember's relief.

"Thanks, Lucasta," he said. "Ember, don't you think she could try and remember overnight?"

"I suppose," Ember murmured, staring into the fireplace. "Roland?"

"Yes?" The butler had appeared as though out of shadows and stood a few paces behind Ember.

"Please show this young woman to one of the guest rooms. Perhaps the black room?"

Roland nodded understandingly. "Of course, Lady Ember. Right this way, miss."

When they had disappeared from view, Viper stood beside Ember, gently guiding her back to her seat. Her mind was whirling as he spoke to her.

"What's the black room?"

"The only room that locks from the outside. I don't completely trust her."

"She gave you information on your mother. She didn't have to do that."

"Actually, she did. Had she not, I would've made sure she hung for it. Actually, no. There are worse things than death, and whoever lies to me about my mother would suffer for it."

"You're sick, Ember. She helped you, and you're locking her in. It's just gross."

"Aren't we all a bit sick? It's in our nature. The Phoenix made us a cold people. Her patron animals were never sent here to be kind. They were sent here to take the world back, through whatever means necessary. I'm just following the Dragon's example." Ember broke off and shook her head. "Here, let's get a map and see if we can figure out where we want to send spies to. I'll have Roland unlock her early tomorrow morning, before she even realizes that she's been locked in."

Viper got off the couch to help Ember get a map of their country off the wall. They spread it out on the small coffee table in the center of the room, holding the corners down with various things they found around the room. Viper's finger traced a path starting at Mount Saffi, down the main road, which was used by anyone from the royal family to merchants to bandits and smugglers. Yet it was still the safest way to travel, as there were no trees to hide thieves, and it was wide enough for several carriages to ride alongside each other, either going the same way or opposite. That was the way Ember travelled when she and Verity left the county, for business and for vacation.

"I have a feeling they wouldn't have used the main road," Viper said, his finger roaming through the patron circle, and Ember hummed in agreement.

"If they had been stopped by a Phoenix patrol, they would've been caught."

"But the Phoenix patrol controls all known roads in Eiad. So they must've taken a backroad, something that isn't on most maps. They probably have a special map memorized or something."

"Then we're out of luck," Viper said, sitting back on the couch. "We don't have a special map. Maybe we can convince someone to take the main road to the south and— What? Why are you smiling at me like that? Why are you smiling at me at all?"

"I appreciate all your help, Viper, but you don't have to come with me if you don't want to. I was just kidding with you earlier. In fact, I insist that you don't help me."

"I'm already in this deep," Viper said, shrugging. "I might as well make sure you don't get yourself killed down south. If I know anything about you—which I don't know much—it's that you're ridiculously hotheaded and are bound to get yourself in some type of predicament." Ember's smile grew wider.

"It'll be nice to have someone to help me. But it's late tonight. You can stay here, if you'd like. Or I can get the carriage to bring you home. Your choice."

"I'll just stay here, if you promise you won't lock me in."

"Promise."

"Goodnight, Ember."

"Goodnight, Viper. Pick any room you'd like. Except mine, of course. Or my mother's." She folded up the map and left it on the table before following him up the stairs, stumbling a bit with exhaustion. She had no energy to do anything except collapse in her bed, much less throw her knives just to attempt to get a semblance of control. Their little trip had completely drained her.

But it would all be worth it if she could bring Verity home.

Chapter

TWENTY-TWO

WHEN EMBER AWOKE THE next day, Viper was already gone, and the spare carriage was pulling into the drive after its use. She ran the details of the night over in her mind again, and immediately jumped up, rushing to unlock the black room. The door was already wide open, though, and she could see Lucasta inside, humming as she combed her hair. She was still in the silk nightgown, but she had washed away her heavy makeup and was barefoot. Ember stepped into the room, looking around to find that Lucasta had somehow bribed one of the servants to bring her a bottle of perfume and a small book. The Book of the Phoenix, by the look of it. Lucasta's nightgown was a stark contrast to the walls, which were deep black, broken up by an even darker black flower that repeated over and over on the walls. Even the furniture was black in this room, painted in a style that made the armoires and vanity blend into the wallpaper.

"Good morning," Ember said, standing awkwardly in her nightgown. Lucasta looked up and smiled.

"Good morning. When's breakfast? I'm absolutely starving, and I have a feeling you eat pretty well here." Ember's mouth dropped at her openness. Did she have no fear?

Ember's initial intuition about Lucasta—that she would like her—only deepened. Fearlessness was something she admired, so long as it didn't lapse into stupidity.

"Um, soon, I suppose. You can eat whenever. If you want to wait for me, I can be ready in ten minutes."

"Do you have any more clothes I can borrow?" Lucasta asked, gesturing down at herself. "One of your servants took my dress to wash, and the armoire is empty."

"Sure," Ember said, still completely baffled by Lucasta in general. This girl was a complete opposite of Ember in nearly every way. Lucasta followed Ember back to her room, whistling through her teeth.

"I thought your guest room was nice," Lucasta said, stepping farther into the room and running her hands over Ember's furniture. "I can't believe people can even live like this."

"What do you mean?" Ember asked, opening her armoire and riffling through her simple dresses.

"That you can just have all of this luxury and not share it."

"I'm confused," Ember said, turning around and looking at Lucasta. "You think we don't share this?"

"Your guest room was a little dusty. It doesn't seem like you host company all that often. Especially not company like me. Poor people."

"We have no reason to host poor people like you. I'm not saying that to be rude, it's just...that's how it is. We hardly have any reason to host anybody."

Lucasta, who had now taken it upon herself to try out Ember's bed, frowned. "You don't have family come visit?"

"Don't have any to speak of," Ember said, picking out a dress and holding it up before deciding it wouldn't look good on Lucasta.

"Damn," Lucasta said. "I feel bad for you, sweetheart. Never had a grandmother come home to cook you food and give you advice you didn't ask for? I mean, it's not like I get all of that either with my current profession, but it was still nice when I was younger."

"Look," Ember said, tossing her a dress. "I don't need your pity. I have my mother, and she's all I need. She's all I've ever needed. That's just the way things are here. A mother and a daughter, a lady and an heir. No sisters or aunts and especially no men."

"What a blessed existence," Lucasta said, beginning to shimmy out of the nightgown. "I think I'd probably starve to death if I didn't have men in my life, even if I absolutely despise them." Ember snorted.

"That's dirty, Lucasta," she said, purposefully staring at the armoire as Lucasta changed, humming a soft tune Ember had heard in temple once.

"It comes with the profession," she responded, and something hit Ember on the back of the head. She turned around to find the crumpled nightgown at her feet, Lucasta dressed in a short red dress instead.

"Looks good on you," Ember said truthfully. "Better than it does on me, honestly."

"Aw, thank you. I appreciate that. I appreciate the dress, too. It's far nicer than the clothes I own. Can we eat now? I'm starving." Ember stared at Lucasta a moment more.

"Sure," Ember said. "Any requests?" She needed to change, too, and she picked a dress in the same cut as Lucasta's, but in black rather than red.

"Fruit," Lucasta said with a small smile. "We don't have a ton of fresh fruit in Vyx. And I don't make enough to afford to buy it. One time, someone paid me with an orange instead of ovum. I ate half and sold the other half for fifteen ovum. Fifteen. For a half-eaten orange. So you can imagine that it's not exactly something I get all that often."

"Phoenix above. I didn't realize it was like that," Ember said. "My mother and I work on finances together, and I do a lot of the food. Fruit is never that much here. Maybe two ovum for an orange? During the winter the price jumps to about six since we have to have them imported from the far continent. Berries are cheap, too, as are apples, since the middle continent ships them to Eiad in droves. We drown in apples for about a week here. Apple pies, apple tarts, apples showing up on our nightstands and in our office drawers. It's a lot of apple. Luckily, they're my mother's favorite," Ember said with a chuckle.

"That sounds amazing," Lucasta said, following Ember as she led her downstairs. "We eat a lot of jam to get our fruit intake. Jam is cheap in comparison to fresh fruit. But I still don't get a lot. I mostly eat bread and stew from the tavern. It's not half-bad if you have a hardy stomach."

"I love jam," Ember confessed, leading Lucasta into the kitchen and calling for one of the servants to come tend to them. "So all you requested was fresh fruit? We can provide far more than that here. How hungry are you?"

Lucasta shrugged. "Starving. I didn't eat dinner last night, which is pretty normal, but I'm ready to eat whatever you put on this table. It could be honey-dipped flies and I'd probably scarf them down like a madwoman. Don't judge me for my eating habits, please."

Ember laughed. This odd girl was a good distraction, keeping her mind off Verity.

"I like to eat too," Ember confessed. "So let's order a lot of food. I don't have any obligations today, do you?" A nagging voice in the back of Ember's mind strongly disagreed, screaming that Verity was the priority, but Ember was in desperate need of at least a short break.

And, quite honestly, she wanted this girl to be her friend.

Lucasta shrugged. "Sort of. I have to pay my employer. She's the reason we can dance on tables in the tavern. Most of the women in my profession in Vyx, and around, work for her. We all live with her, too, but that's all she provides. A leaky roof over our heads. No food or anything. Just that, and we owe her fifteen ovum a week. It's a lot for most of us girls but, hey, it's better than sleeping on the street. At least our bodies are only violated when money changes hands."

"I can pay," Ember offered. "How much would it be to completely get out of paying her?" Lucasta scoffed.

"I have a contract with her for the rest of the year. Nearly nine months."

"Fifteen a month... nine months...one hundred and thirty-five ovum. That's pocket change to the houses, Lucasta. I'll send somebody to pay for your contract, and you won't have to worry about her."

Lucasta grinned. "I think this is the beginning of a very beneficial friendship for the two of us," Lucasta said, and Ember couldn't help but silently agree. "Now, please, let's eat."

Thirty minutes later, Ember and Lucasta both clutched their stomachs and groaned as they shoveled a couple more bites in their mouths.

"Phoenix," Lucasta said, licking her fork. "To eat like this every day. Imagine."

"Amazing, isn't it?" Ember asked, stabbing a piece of pastry and swirling it around in her sugar.

"Truly. I'm going to eat pastries until I explode." Ember giggled.

"We should try that one day," she suggested. "Have a pastry-eating contest." Lucasta gave her a soft smile.

"Can I tell you something?" she asked, touching the daisy tattoo on her arm. It seemed to be an unconscious gesture, but Ember followed her fingers all the same.

"If you'd like," Ember invited, flicking her eyes back up to Lucasta's face.

"You have to pay my employer today," she said, then seemed to consider what she was going to say next. "She... might know something about the rebel group." Ember stood quickly, her chair screeching on the floor behind her.

"Why didn't you tell me last night?" Lucasta looked nervous, not quite meeting Ember's eyes. Ember's hands twitched, and she balled them into fists when Lucasta stared down at them.

"I didn't want to be wrong. I was just thinking about it last night, and— Look, all I'm trying to say is that this woman knows things. And people. If you want to learn something, she's the first person I'd go to."

"Why aren't we there now?" Ember asked, already striding out of the room and leaving Lucasta to scramble after her.

"You can't go in there like a war storm," Lucasta called after Ember, feet slapping on the marble as she tried to catch up. Ember peeked into the kitchen, searching for Roland. "She's not like a regular prostitute. She isn't even a prostitute. She's a really rich woman who owns a lot of women and men. You can't talk down to her. I know that's what you're used to, but brute force won't work against her."

"I can talk down to whomever I please. I outrank everybody except the royal family. And brute force always works," Ember said, locating Roland in the foyer. She rushed to him, even as Lucasta continued protesting in the background.

"I need to go back to Vyx," Ember said, and Roland nodded once before going for the door.

Lucasta beat him to the handle, her hand closing over it a second before his did.

"No," she said. "She doesn't live in Vyx. That place is beneath her."

"Then where is she?" Ember asked, rounding on Lucasta. "Stop withholding information from me, or you can consider your debt to this woman to double." Lucasta paled at that, but to Ember's surprise, it seemed her resolve only hardened. "You honestly think that scares me? I've spent the last three years of my life selling my body to pay back my debt to her. I've been dealing with this for a long time, and if these few hours have been nothing than some sort of fever dream, then I can live with that. But I'm not going to allow you to go barging into her house and demanding answers from her. I know that's how you're used to dealing with things, and I know you outrank her. That's incredibly obvious. But it doesn't matter. That's not the right way to approach her if you want answers. Trust me." The last two words were the harshest of all, as Lucasta stared Ember down. Ember squirmed uncomfortably. It was rare that someone spoke to her like this, and she'd never been spoken to disrespectfully by a houseless person before. And it was clear in Lucasta's eyes that she didn't fear the consequences that Ember could lay out upon her for the way she'd just spoken.

It was almost as though Lucasta knew Ember wouldn't do anything to her.

Almost as if she knew Ember was becoming weak.

"Fine," Ember said, spinning around and looking at her. "What do you suggest, then?"

"This seems like an awful lot of money," Ember said, rummaging through her coin purse once again. Thousands of ovum clinked inside, enough, Lucasta insisted, to buy her employer's knowledge, as well as Lucasta's freedom.

"She's an expensive woman," she said, shrugging. "You of all people should understand that." Ember flipped a coin between her fingers, not saying anything as Lucasta lapsed into silence.

Lucasta had given Ember a piece of the puzzle—a rebel group who was operating out of the south. But she hadn't been able to give a name to them, or even completely confirm that they had been the ones that had taken Verity, Alex, and the lord of House Olor, Nevis Corvu. That somehow made it that much worse. Instead of just a list of possibilities as to where Verity was, there was now a dark, faceless group that had kidnapped her mother.

Hopefully, Lucasta's employer would be able to give Ember the rest of the information.

"We're here," Lucasta said, her voice thick with something that almost sounded like fear, although it was clear she was trying to mask it.

"You don't have to come in," Ember said, clasping the money pouch shut and tucking it into her pocket. Lucasta shook her head, looking up at the house.

"No, you'll want me there."

Ember wanted to assure her that she most definitely would neither want nor need Lucasta there, but the other girl's nerves were rubbing off on her, and she said nothing as they walked up to the front of the house.

It was surprisingly grand for someone who wasn't part of the houses, done up in a fake version of the stone that the Phoenix Palace was made up of. Windows were thrown open on every floor, and from the topmost, Ember could hear a woman singing.

If one could even call it that. It sounded like somebody was attempting to strangle a cat while a piano plunked sadly in the background. Ember cringed as they walked up the drive— she felt as though her ears were going to bleed.

"It's one of those days," Lucasta said, striding straight up to the door and knocking on it. The singing continued, but the door opened, revealing a young girl dressed in gray and green.

"Hello," she said, peeking up at Ember.

"Tell your mistress that the heir of House Draco has come to pay her a visit," Ember said, pushing past the girl and into the house. The girl scrambled after her.

"You can't come in unless you have an appointment." Ember spun around, crossing her arms and staring down at the girl. She had allowed her sleeves to fall back, putting her knife on full display.

"I don't require an appointment, do you understand that? I require your mistress for something, and I will not hesitate to march myself up those stairs and find her without you. We can either make this very easy, or very painful. It's your choice."

The girl gaped for a moment at the knife, and then at Ember's face, before turning and rushing away. Ember turned in a slow circle, taking in the house. Faux-marble floors, wallpaper that was peeling at the top and bottom. A few chairs decorated the foyer space. It had all clearly been nice before, but it had faded with time, and nobody had put in the money or work to get it freshened up as the styles changed. Ember dropped her sleeves, frowning at a scuff on the floor.

"This way," Lucasta said, leading Ember out of the foyer and to the right. The space opened into a large sitting room, complete with a gigantic portrait of a grinning woman over the fireplace.

"Phoenix above," Ember muttered, staring into the woman's eyes. They were empty, and although Ember knew that could've very well been the painter's fault, it didn't seem like that. The artist had been able to perfectly capture the folds of the dress she was wearing, to highlight in sharp detail the daisy the woman held in one hand, and the way dark curls spilled down her back. Beautiful, to be sure, but dull.

Lucasta, by comparison, glowed.

"That's her," Lucasta said, coming to stand beside Ember. She tugged on a lock of her hair, looking up at the portrait with thinly-veiled disgust. "A real treat, once you get to know her."

Ember turned to Lucasta, to ask her what wrong this woman had done against her, besides the obvious, but a loud voice filled the sitting room, and both girls turned as one.

"Ah," the woman from the portrait said, looking rather thinner and with hair that was now peppered with gray. She was still in a fine dress, but it was nothing compared to the clothes Ember was wearing. A small, yapping dog was held like a furry baby in her arms.

"Who are you?" the woman asked, looking at Ember with an unimpressed eye. Ember tried to channel her mother, to think through what Verity would do. She would've flashed the tattoo on the back of her hand, but as Ember didn't have that, she instead pulled her sleeve back again, revealing the knife constantly strapped there.

Unfortunately, this didn't get much of a reaction out of the woman, even as the dog barked obnoxiously at Ember and Lucasta, looking rather like an ugly rat.

"I don't let my girls carry weapons, so you're going to have to leave that at home when you go out."

Ember scrambled for words, completely flabbergasted, as the woman turned her attention on Lucasta, who trembled.

Trembled.

Something inside of Ember sharpened.

"Oh, you," she said. "You were supposed to be my desert flower. My mouthful of water in the sand. And here you are, bringing me more girls I have to take care of."

"How dare you," Ember said, keeping her voice low. "How *dare* you."

The woman looked back over at her, still looking unimpressed. Was she completely stupid?

"My dear girl," she said. "If you've come to me for help, then you're in no position to think of yourself highly."

"I," Ember said, drawing herself up, "Am Ember Ignis, the heir of House Draco, daughter of Verity Ignis. I understand that you have information about where my mother may be, and you're going to tell me all of it."

"Oh, please," the woman said, sitting dramatically in one of the chairs. The dog curled up on her lap, squinting at the girls through watery eyes. Ember and Lucasta sat across from her, Lucasta's hand gently brushing Ember's in reassurance. "Do you know how many people I meet who claim to be the heirs of one of the houses? Try something more original next time."

Ember unsheathed the knife from her arm and threw it, sticking it in the cushion beside the woman's head in one movement. It sliced off a dark curl as it sailed by, pinning it to the seat.

Now, she looked slightly uncomfortable.

The dog hadn't even reacted.

"The next one goes in your head," Ember said. "If I wanted to grovel at your feet, I would. But I won't allow you to disrespect me, in this house of fake wealth and fake luxury.

You understand that I could have you hung for the very way you looked at me, correct? You have no idea who you're dealing with right now."

The woman let out a shaky laugh. "Oh, dear. A few knife tricks and some strong words don't make you an heir."

At this, Ember pulled the money pouch from her pocket and dropped it on the table, the coins inside barely clinking from how packed it was. The woman eyed it greedily, and Ember knew she had her trapped.

Everybody had a weakness, and a temptation they couldn't resist.

"All of this will be yours," Ember said, pulling the pouch back to herself as the woman lunged for it. "For two things. The first of which is this girl's freedom. She is no longer your employee, do you understand that? Her debt is paid." Ember pulled enough of the ovum out of the pouch, sliding it across the table. The woman tucked it in the top of her dress and stared at Ember.

"Before we begin with the other part," Ember said. "I'd like to know your name."

"My true name is of no concern of yours, little one, but you may call me Madame Daisy."

Ember rolled her eyes but moved on from the ridiculous name.

"Fine. Daisy. I recently became aware of a rebel group that may be operating out of the south, and I was also told that you could give me more information on it. The name of the group, perhaps? The leader, or leaders?"

Daisy leaned back in her seat, eyeing Ember's coin pouch as she began speaking.

"There...have been rumors of a rebellion stirring in the south. This far north, I believe that there's nothing actually concrete. That's all I know."

Oh, as if Ember was supposed to believe that. Daisy looked nervous, and Ember leaned over, pulling her knife out before grabbing the little dog with her other hand. Ember placed the tip of the knife against the dog's chest, praying she wouldn't have to harm this innocent animal. He was hideous, but she didn't want to hurt him.

But there was real fear in Daisy's eyes now, and she sat forward, stretching her arms out for the dog. Ember took a step back, handing the dog over to Lucasta, who looked down on it uncomfortably. It settled quickly in her lap, apparently unconcerned with having moved to the other side of the room. Daisy flexed her fingers like a child, whimpering softly.

Ah. Perhaps the money wasn't Daisy's true weakness.

"I'm assuming you're going to be a little more open with me now, yes?"

"Give me my dog back," Daisy said. Ember swung her arm around, the knife slicing a small tuft of hair off the top of the dog's head, and stopping just short of Lucasta's chest, who had barely flinched.

"Answers first," Ember said. "And then the dog."

Daisy buried her hands in the folds of her dress, sighing dramatically. "There is a group—it's not exactly a secret. It's actually rather laughable how the lot of you in the houses have no idea about what's happening in your own country."

Well, that certainly came like a blow to the face, but it wasn't getting Ember any closer to answers.

"My mother," Ember said. "Verity Ignis. Where is she?"

Daisy shook her head, eyes trained on her dog. "I don't know." Ember dipped the knife in the dog's direction, and Daisy threw her hands up, her words coming in the form of a screech that sounded an awful lot like the singing from earlier.

"I'm telling you the truth!" Ember exchanged a glance with Lucasta, and the other girl gave her a small nod. A truth.

Ember hesitated for only a moment. She wouldn't usually trust Lucasta.

But she didn't have another choice.

"Fine." Ember sheathed the knife up her sleeve but didn't give the dog back. Not yet. Daisy still had more answers than she was letting on; she could play dumb all she wanted, and she was good at it, but Ember knew that there was something else.

"You know something," Ember said. It wasn't a question, but it warranted an answer nonetheless. Daisy didn't say anything for a long while, her eyes fixed on her dog, who was currently asleep in Lucasta's lap.

"There is a man. A drunkard. He often mutters about a group who have named themselves after the Bear." The Bear. Of the twelve houses, the first had not always belonged to the Dragon. Originally, it had been the Bear's house, the Phoenix's most dedicated protector. Until the Bear turned on the Phoenix, attacking her. The Dragon had saved her, and the Bear had been banished.

To name a rebellion after it was a clear sign to both the royal family and to the Phoenix Herself.

"Where can I find him?" Ember asked, scooping the dog off Lucasta's lap and holding it under her arm.

"Let me get you an address," Daisy said, snapping her fingers at the young servant who was standing against the wall, pretending not to watch the conversation. "Bring me one of the cards for the Perfumed Palace."

Beside Ember, Lucasta cringed at the name.

"Is that all you know?" Ember asked. "I'm not going to threaten you again—you already know what I could do to you. So just tell me the truth, Daisy."

Daisy shook her head rapidly, her arms held out for her dog like a child begging to be picked up. Her eyes were watering just like her little dog's. "That's it. Just leave me alone. I don't know anything else."

"That's the truth," Lucasta whispered, standing up beside Ember. Ember dropped the dog in Daisy's arms, striding past her and to the servant girl, who handed her a glittering piece of paper. Ember tucked the address into her pocket, fingers brushing the still-full money pouch.

But she had given Daisy both her life, and her dog's life, back. She owned her nothing.

There was no further debt to be paid.

TWENTY-THREE

ASHER ROLLED A DAISY between his fingers, worrying the stem almost into nonexistence. He dropped the flower, turning around to pluck a new one. He desperately wanted one to last until he could give it to Juniper, but she was late, and flowers littered the ground by his feet like a beautiful massacre. He could feel the cold eyes of the palace gardener on him, but he ignored the man. It was early spring—there would be more flowers. And far prettier ones than daisies.

Asher checked his watch, disappointed when he realized Juniper was nearly fifteen minutes late. If he got to twenty minutes without seeing her, then she'd been held up at work, given some useless task by the Phoenix, who seemed determined to keep them away from each other.

Asher let the next daisy fall, grinding it into the dirt as he checked his watch obsessively. He began to itch for a drink but shoved the urge down as he waited for Juniper.

Asher nearly cried when Juniper walked outside, a book in one hand and a glass in the other.

"What's that?" Asher asked, peering at the glass.

"Alcohol," Juniper replied slyly. "I desperately needed a drink, so I got one of the head maids to slip me a bit."

"Can I have a sip?"

"No," Juniper said. "The last thing you need is a drink."

"What do you mean?" Asher said, sticking his bottom lip out in a pout.

"You're busy working on some important palace assignment, aren't you?"

Asher sighed and leaned back on the bench. "No. I'm actually skipping an important palace meeting right now, to be honest. My father wants me to sit in a stuffy room with the stuffy house leaders, and talk about the price of sugar. What do I care about that? There are plenty of people in there who care more. Besides, I've been busy."

Juniper took a sip from her glass, clearly savoring it. Asher envied her for a moment, but then pushed it away.

He didn't need it.

He just had to keep telling himself that.

"Busy with what?"

"Busy with cutting down on my drinking. I'm down to four glasses a day."

Juniper grinned. "That's really good, Asher," she said, taking his hand in hers and squeezing it lightly before releasing it. The touch sent chills through Asher's body.

"It was about time," Asher said. "Was it bad?"

Juniper swirled her drink for a moment before responding. "I can't say for sure. You started cutting down after we met. I'm sure it wasn't good, though. I'd ask your parents if you're really interested in learning how bad it is. Or maybe your liquor supplier. I'm sure they can give you an entire book of what you've had in the last few years."

Asher snorted and shoved Juniper a bit.

"Very funny," he said with a glare. She grinned up at him, draining the rest of her glass and placing it by her feet.

"Whatcha got there?" Asher said, taking the book from her.

Juniper shrugged. "I borrowed it from the palace library." "That's not allowed."

"You're the prince," Juniper countered. "You can just excuse me from my public execution."

Asher handed her the book back. "A copy of Eiad history? Phoenix, you must've picked out the most boring book in that entire library. Besides, doesn't everybody know how Eiad started? The Phoenix cleansed the world in fire, left, and then gave the patron animals humans to look after. I mean, we've fought a few wars here and there, but for the most part it's just king after queen after king. Same thing with the houses."

"I'm reading up on the Phoenix Wars," Juniper said. "I knew we'd fought against the far continent hundreds of years ago, but I hardly knew what the reason was. The motive, for both sides of the battlefield."

"What did you find out?" Asher asked, although he already knew the entire history of Eiad and the far and mid continents.

"Sal worships pagan gods, as does Tali. Humanoid gods. When they sent diplomats here, one of them spat at the Phoenix Flame. One of the devout pushed him in, and it started a war. Until…" She trailed off, finding her place in the book to keep reading.

"Until?" Asher cocked his head at her, hardly hearing what she was saying but completely enthralled by her being so passionate about something. He hadn't realized how important history was to her.

"Until Eiad was able to sway some of the mid continent to their side. Most of the countries have the same religion, and they worship animal gods too. Not the Phoenix, but others. Their main god is a falcon. With the mid continent's power and proximity to the far continent, Eiad was able to turn the tide of the war to their side. Right up until the mid continent decided to switch sides. The far continent was shinier, prettier, and the mid continent decided they wanted that instead. Eiad was still able to crush them, though. Some say the Phoenix Herself came down to end the battle, but most think that Eiad's soldiers simply set the others' campsites on fire. When more than half of them couldn't escape, they surrendered, and they doused the fire."

Asher hummed. "Interesting."

"Very interesting. I never really looked into Eiadian history before, I guess. Especially not as far back as the Phoenix Wars, or even when we fought to free the mid continent from their dictator. Nobody talks about the old wars for some reason."

"They're dreadfully boring," Asher said. "We had to go through all of them—multiple times—during tutoring. For some Phoenix-forsaken reason, they thought that would help me rule the country one day. I can carry a conversation over whether or not we should've backed the current leader of the mid continent, or what we could've done differently during the Phoenix Wars, but I can't sit through a financial meeting without finding the bottom of a whiskey bottle. Besides, most of those stories are simply that. Stories that make up our religion. I'm fairly certain that half of the wars we learned about didn't really happen."

"Religion is important in this country," Juniper said. "It's probably a good thing if you're seen as more devout than you actually are. The people won't trust you if you have smooth palms." She nodded knowingly at his palm, which now had an ugly red scar over it. His other hand, however, was completely bare of scars. He rarely gave blood.

"I'm seen as a lot more than I actually am, so it wouldn't take much," Asher joked.

"I'm seen as a lot less than I actually am," Juniper said.

"Not to me," Asher said, swinging his arm around her shoulders, relieved when Juniper snuggled into his side.

Asher let out a breath and soaked in the moment.

Ember settled into her bath, closing her eyes as warm water lapped her shoulders. She and Lucasta had decided that tonight was *not* the night to go to the Perfumed Palace—which was, as it happened, a harem. One that Lucasta had spent time in, and wasn't interested in going back to. She hadn't provided any further information, and Ember hadn't pushed her on it.

So Ember had immediately decided that, because she wasn't going alone, Viper was going to have to come with her, whether he liked it or not.

Daisy was stupid, yes, but not so stupid that she would purposely lead Ember astray. There was little doubt in Ember's mind that there was a drunk man who frequently hung around the Perfumed Palace, or that the rebel group had named itself after the Bear. She had no reason to doubt any of that.

But she *did* doubt that it would be easy to find the answers that she truly wanted. Verity's location.

Answers weren't going to come in this bathtub, however, and Ember quickly finished, wrapping a towel around herself and pulling her hair into a small plait. She rubbed the space between her eyes before stumbling out of the washroom, feet slapping on the cool tile.

It had been a long day. Tomorrow would be much of the same. Keep following clues until they eventually led Ember to Verity. One way or another, she was going to find her mother.

Ember lit a candle on her bedside table, the small light only illuminating the space directly beside her bed. Her knife lay beside it, her constant protector. Ember's nightgown, in the drawer of the table, went on, and she hung the towel in the bathroom before climbing into bed. She turned, slipping underneath her duvet. For a while, she laid there on her back, forcing herself to breathe slowly, trying to get herself to relax enough to fall asleep. The faster she was asleep, Ember reasoned, the faster she could get back to working.

She considered, for a brief moment, asking Lucasta to come into the room with her, just for comfort, but she grit her teeth, letting out another long breath. She could handle this.

Ember blew out the candle, the smell of smoke gently filling the air.

She rolled over, letting out a long sigh as sleep continued to evade her.

And came face to face with a man.

Ember screamed, pulling away from him so quickly that she rolled off the bed, hitting her head on the corner of the bedside table. The candle swayed dangerously, and Ember caught it before it could fall to the floor. She scrambled for her knife, her hand closing over the handle. She turned it on the man, lifting it high above her head with full intentions to plunge it into his chest.

But it was far too late for that, for the man was already dead.

He clearly hadn't been dead for long—there was no stench surrounding him, or any visible signs of decay. Ember ran her eyes over the part of his body that was visible and not covered by the duvet, but there were no signs of blood. He looked peaceful, too, which made it seem like he hadn't been strangled or bashed over the head with a large object. Ember set her knife down, ripping the duvet back to reveal the rest of his body.

And promptly turned away.

He was stark naked, not a single scrap of clothing covering his body. Ember gagged, rushing to grab a towel from the bathroom and she tossed it over his sensitive parts. There was still no blood, even with more skin being revealed. He looked, as far as Ember could tell, as though he'd died in his sleep.

This man was familiar, too, something about his face and his build that reminded Ember of someone else. And she'd most certainly seen this man before, but it was vastly different seeing somebody clothed from head to toe, awake and speaking, versus seeing a man naked and dead, lying in her bed without warning.

Her eyes drifted to his fingers, the right one clutching something round, and the left splayed out upon the sheets.

A finger missing.

Oh, Phoenix.

Someone was knocking on the door, but Ember ignored it. She had to know.

Ember scrambled for her box of matches, hastily relighting her candle. She held it close to his face, staring into his dead eyes.

Blue's eyes, sharp and silver.

This was the missing lord of House Olor, whose finger had been found still wearing his house ring.

Bile rose in the back of Ember's throat, and she retched, stumbling away from the man's body again. She couldn't stand to be near it anymore as the thoughts rapidly running through her head were telling her things she couldn't bear to think. She stumbled into the bathroom, breathing shakily as she braced her hands on either side of the sink.

"Ember!" Lucasta's voice came, desperate from outside the door. Ember's stomach twisted as she stared at herself.

This was a threat. Pure and simple. A very blatant and very bold threat. And Ember had no doubt that it was from to the people who had taken her mother. Ember felt like she was suffocating, as though the unnamed threat looming over her head had only gotten closer and bigger.

Ember forced herself to relax before going back out into the room, lighting the rest of the candles to optimize the light.

"I'm okay!" Ember called to Lucasta, her voice trembling, and heard the other girl sigh in relief, although Ember highly doubted she believed her. She would explain soon, but not now. She needed more answers, and Nevis Corvu held them.

She forced herself to ignore his left hand, and instead focused on opening his right hand, to reveal what was inside. Two things had been clutched in his hand: a piece of paper which fluttered out, and the other clunked when it hit the floor.

As soon as her hand closed over it, she knew exactly what it was. The smoothness of the skin, the crunch it made as Ember dug her fingernails into it.

An apple.

Verity's favorite fruit, the one that made the perfume that was constantly surrounding Ember and the entirety of the Draco Estate.

She unfolded the paper, fingers shaking as the words shined up at her.

Leave it alone, Dragon.

Or she's next.

Chapter

Twenty-Four

ASHER PACED THE GARDEN, plucking flowers at random for Juniper, as he had done yesterday. They had started meeting almost daily, when Juniper was on her lunch break and Asher was skipping meetings. Right now, he was missing the weekly palace meeting. They didn't need him there.

They ate lunch together in the back of the garden, usually on a stone bench, but sometimes they sat in the dirt together. Neither one of them spoke of their almost-kiss, and for that Asher was grateful. He didn't want to have to think about *that* particular failure.

Juniper was already waiting for him when he arrived, a book in her hand and one on the bench beside her.

"You've replaced me with a book? Again? Did you take this one from the library, too?" Asher joked, coming up to her with two plates of food.

She placed the book in her hand on top of the other one and took the second plate from him.

"I had an idea," Juniper said, moving the books so Asher could sit. He squinted at it for a moment, vaguely recognizing the title, but then dismissing it. He'd read a lot of books. He couldn't be expected to remember every one of them.

"An idea, huh? About what?"

"About those missing people you told me about. The house leaders. I think usurpers might have taken them."

"Usurpers? Really? Does it have something to do with your new book?"

Juniper nodded.

Asher kept his mouth shut about the fact that one of the missing people had been found—the lord of House Olor, who had shown up, dead, in Ember Ignis's bed. Nobody knew how he'd gotten there, but it was fairly clear that Ember hadn't done it. She didn't have a motive. Asher had no doubt that she was laying out the details in the palace meeting right now, explaining how, exactly, a dead man had ended up in her bedroom without her knowing. He'd seen her before the meeting started—paler than usual, her eyes wide and haunted. He couldn't imagine the fear. The paranoia. Somebody had broken into her house and left a body in her bed.

But Asher's attention was fully on Juniper.

"It's a history book. I took it after finishing the other one yesterday. The one about the wars. Stuff like this happens every hundred years or so. That's what the book says, at least.

So this will be the first time it's happened in, like I said, a hundred years. Before your father was born, and before your grandfather became king. Usually these rebels gather themselves under something called the Order of the Bear. In honor of the thirteenth patron. I don't think they kidnapped anybody last time, though. They were stopped pretty quickly."

"I learned a little about it in tutoring. It clearly hasn't worked before, though. So why would they try again?"

"I don't know. It seems idiotic to me. I'm surprised they were even able to take Lady Ignis. The Dragons seem quite… formidable."

Asher chuckled. "They are. Especially Lady Ember Ignis. She's…truly a Dragon wearing a woman's skin. I'm pretty sure Ember wasn't born, honestly. She was forged out of iron and fire and hatred. Born out of the Phoenix Flame, maybe."

"She certainly seems like it. I've seen her in meetings and at dinners. She always seems displeased with everybody around her. Turns her nose up at people who are beneath her. Except for the royals, of course. Even then. You should see the way she looks at you when you drink."

"That's because she *is* displeased with everyone."

Juniper erupted into giggles, prompting Asher to laugh as well. "Like she has a stick up her ass."

Asher snorted and clapped his hand over his mouth, causing Juniper to laugh harder, leaning forward and spilling some of her food in her wheezing.

In a few moments, the two of them were clutching their sides, laughing so hard they could barely breathe. Asher wiped a tear from the corner of his eye before noticing the way Juniper was looking at him.

"Juniper?" he asked.

She leaned in a little closer, all laughter gone from her face. "Were you going to kiss me? The other day?"

Asher pursed his lips before answering. "Yes. I thought you wanted to. But you didn't."

He had dropped his voice to nearly a whisper. A lock of Juniper's hair had fallen out of her bun and now fell across her eyes. Asher reached his hand out, hesitating before brushing it behind her ear. She shivered under his touch.

Her eyes were two orbs of pure emerald when they were this close. There were small flecks of gold in them, he noticed. Asher could hear her breathing and was afraid Juniper could hear his heartbeat. His curls were too far in his face, and his palms were sweating and Juniper was so close to him. If he even moved slightly, their noses would bump, and his mouth would be on hers.

Asher had never kissed a girl before, never been kissed by one. He didn't really know what he was supposed to be doing with his hands, with his mouth, with his hair. He pushed his curls back with one hand and gripped the bench with the other. Asher let out a long, slow breath, moving the hand in his hair to hers, twirling the lock in his fingers.

"You can kiss me," Juniper whispered, and Asher leaned in, hesitating for a moment. Juniper closed the gap, and they met in the middle, mouths touching in a quick peck.

Phoenix above, her mouth was soft. Asher pulled away, grinning. Juniper was smiling, too, and when her hand covered his on the bench, he leaned back in for a more sensual, slower kiss, lingering on her bottom lip. She tasted like honey and lavender.

"That was nice," Juniper murmured.

"It was nice," Asher agreed, taking his hand off the bench and putting it around her waist, pulling Juniper closer. It felt right, to hold her so close. She gently nuzzled into his chest, humming softly.

"I have to get back," Juniper said, with a hint of sorrow in her voice.

"No, you don't." Asher leaned in again, and Juniper rewarded him with another quick kiss, before pulling away. The lack of heat from her body was immediately apparent, and Asher resisted the urge to draw her into him again.

"I really do have to get back to work."

"I'm the prince. I can excuse you."

Juniper shook her head, but she was still smiling. "I'll meet you here for lunch tomorrow," she said, before taking her plate, and her books, and walking off.

Asher watched her as she walked away, unable to stop grinning.

Chapter

TWENTY-FIVE

"Vax," Asher said. "I have something important to tell you." The snow had all melted in the cemetery, and the ground was slightly squishy as he made his way toward Vax's grave. For the first time in a long time, he didn't carry two bottles in his pocket—only one, for Vax.

Asher couldn't deny he wanted a drink, but he forced himself to resist the urge. He didn't want that to sway how the rest of his day was going to go. He ran his hand over the knife at his side as he located Vax's grave.

He settled beside the headstone, leaning against the one that faced it. Hazel laid at his side immediately, and Asher ran his hand over her head unconsciously. He tried to figure out how to phrase what had happened exactly, but the words tumbled out in a mess of words and laughing.

"We kissed. Vax. Juniper and I kissed. Just yesterday." He let out a long, contented sigh. "And it was. Amazing. Electrifying." Asher couldn't even form more words to describe it, as he didn't even know how. His emotions were all messed up, twisting together like a knotted ball of yarn. Things seemed to be happening all over the place, and Asher closed his eyes for a long moment. "She's really great, Vax. I think... I think you would've liked her a lot. I haven't told her about you. Not yet. But I will, and I'll bring her here." Asher stood, brushing dirt off his pants. If he hurried, he could catch Juniper between her shifts.

A soft noise sounded behind him, like a string being plucked on a harp. He turned his head slightly to discover the source of the noise, when something whipped by him, slamming into the bottle he'd just left. A blur of brown and red that had passed only inches from his nose. Liquor soaked his shoe from the shattered bottle.

Asher looked down, furrowing his brow as he dipped to pick up the arrow. It was poorly made, but the tip was still sharp enough to kill, and Asher suddenly realized that it had been meant for his head.

He whipped around, searching for the shooter, but there was nobody in the cemetery. Siliros, on the other side, was still there, unharmed. Hazel was also unhurt, but her hackles were up, ears pricked as she searched for the source of the noise.

Asher took a step forward, dropping the arrow as he slipped between two headstones. There were footprints on the ground, sunk into the mud, but Asher couldn't tell if they were his or somebody else's.

"I'm armed," Asher warned, unsheathing his knife. "I recommend you show yourself. Now."

No response. His only answer was the sound of Hazel as she came to stand beside him, nose to the ground as she sniffed. But it was clear that all the water from the snowmelt was confusing her.

Asher whistled for Siliros, and after a moment the horse trotted over. Asher hauled himself onto his back, using his newfound height to sweep the cemetery once again. Nothing moved, and he coaxed the horse, Hazel at his side, out of the gate, and let it clang shut behind him.

He rode quickly.

Fear had crawled its way up Asher's throat the further away he got, and by the time the palace came back into view, he was breathing quickly, heart pounding in his chest.

Somebody had just tried to kill him. And they'd almost succeeded, too. Asher already knew that he had gotten lucky, but his mind—which had been thinking of Juniper almost non-stop recently—was now consumed by few rotating questions, that overlapped each other until the noise in Asher's head was deafening.

He slowed Siliros to a walk once he could see the palace. He wasn't interested in going in just yet, but he had to get away from that place, from the assassin in shadow. There was no doubt in his mind that the person had absolutely been aiming for him. His father had told him stories of his life being targeted before, and given him warnings about it, but Asher had never thought it would be so soon. He wasn't king.

There were obvious reasons to murder him. Asher was well aware of that fact. He was crown prince, and an only child, and both of those reasons painted a decent target on his back. To kill him meant to end the royal Cinis line. No other children were available to take his spot.

He arrived at the gate, barely sparing a glance at the guard. A small look revealed a bow on the woman's back, and Asher immediately stiffened.

"Are you alright?" the woman asked, squinting up at Asher's face. He forced himself to relax, at least slightly. One look at the woman's quiver showed that her arrows were brown and...red.

Of course they were. The wood would always be brown, and one of the main colors of House Phoenix was red.

"I'm just fine," Asher said. "Could I...see one of your arrows? Do you mind?" The woman looked confused, but did as he asked, handing one of them over. Asher sighed in relief. This arrow, while the same colors, was nothing like the one in the cemetery. The quality between the arrows was night and day, as this one was slicker, slimmer, and better quality. But both arrows would fly straight, and Asher couldn't help the fear that rolled in his stomach as he handed the arrow back to the guard. She dipped her head in respect, slipping it into her quiver. Asher peered closer at the quiver, at the intricately marked designs on it.

Something was familiar about it, something familiar about the animal's head that was stitched into the leather. Asher's hand went to his belt, to the knife that hung there. He glanced down at it and stiffened once more.

They were exactly the same.

He still couldn't tell exactly what it was, but it was most certainly something fearsome. On the guard's quiver, the creature's mouth was open in what seemed to be a roar, two rows of sharp teeth exposed.

Asher shook off the sense of unease that surrounded the creature, looking toward the horizon, where the sun was just beginning to rise. He urged Siliros on through the gate, not giving the guard and her arrows a second glance.

TWENTY-SIX

MBER STUDIED VIPER, SITTING against the wall during the palace meeting. The king was rambling about something to do with the temple asking for funds, but she was more interested in the way he seemed to speak to himself and then scribble notes on a small piece of paper in his lap. He was attentive, careful in his note taking, and surprisingly attractive. The sun had caught on his white-blonde hair, and Ember couldn't help but notice that Viper had started wearing it naturally, not slicking it back in the outdated style he had favored only a few weeks ago.

Ember's heart fluttered, and she immediately turned away from him, cursing softly. She didn't have time to think about the way Viper's hair looked. She was supposed to be acting in Verity's place, and her mother always paid close attention to what the king was saying. She smoothed the front of her shirt and turned her full attention on the king, even as something in her stomach desperately tried to pull her eyes back toward Viper.

Suddenly, a terrible noise filled the room—the sound of glass shattering from brute force. It showered over the house members closest to it—Aranea, Corvus, and Passer—and they all scrambled away from it as something skidded into the middle of the table and lay there, face down. Chaos exploded in the room, guards who had been standing against the wall herding the royal family into the back corner, protecting them first. One made his way towards Ember, but her attention was on the object that had landed on the table.

With trembling hands, Ember reached out, flipping it over, before she, too, fell back from it.

"The Order of the Bear," she whispered, staring down at the brick that had been carved into the symbol of the people who had taken her mother. The guard escorted her toward where the king and queen stood, both praying softly as Asher stared blankly at the wall, one hand resting on his hound dog's head, while the other was clenched around a knife that hung from his waist.

Phoenix, what were they doing here? Viper wound his way through the group, pressing himself against Ember's side.

Stay calm, he mouthed, and Ember nodded, still feeling shaky. One of her hands twitched, and she pressed it against her side. A scream came from the outdoor ballroom, the sound almost matching the one the window had made when it shattered. With a silent word, the king pointed two of the guards out of the room to investigate, although Ember's mind was still spinning as to *why*. Weren't there more guards? Where were they?

A minute passed, and then two. The king sent more guards out, leaving only a small handful to protect the houses. Ember brushed her fingers over her knife, a steady weight on the inside of her arm, but didn't unsheathe it yet. There were sounds of a vicious fight outside—flesh meeting bone, the grunting as someone was hit—and the court seemed to freeze as one. If Ember had to guess, she was one of the only ones in the group who was armed. The king sent out the rest of the guards, and Ember almost screamed. Didn't he understand what he was doing? The danger he was putting them all in?

Words were screaming behind her teeth, lashing across her mind, but Ember could barely breathe. Barely think.

They're here. They're here. They're here.

She quickly looked around the room, counting the weapons. She was armed, of course, and Asher had a knife, as well as the brown-and-white hound dog, who was growling in the direction of the doors. The four members of House Vulpus who were present—Lady Scarlett, the heir, Vervid, and Bat and Hawk, each had a set of throwing knives. But that was it; a total of ten, maybe twelve knives between all of them. No bows or crossbows, and certainly no spears or swords.

One of the female guards let out a horrible cry of pain from the hallway, and the king threw open the doors, revealing the woman on the ground. Her throat had been slashed, blood pouring from it like a macabre fountain. Not even the Phoenix could save her now. The woman was growing paler by the second, even as the king stooped over her, whispering a gentle prayer to the Phoenix. A common prayer for the dying, to help ease their pain and make their transition into whatever lay beyond life easier.

There was another scream and Ember's curiosity, although strong, was not enough to draw her to the courtyard. Her mind was screaming that something was desperately wrong, and if she went to investigate, she would find something she never wanted to see.

More guards poured from the halls, and the king straightened, moving to speak to them as Feather and Asher trailed in his wake.

Ember watched them move as Viper came to her side, following her gaze toward the king and the guards.

Ember jumped at the sound of a sword being drawn from its sheath, and she watched as one of the guards pointed her sword at the king. The hound dog let out a mighty bark, but Asher grabbed her collar, hauling her backwards. He pointed a finger at the door, and the dog trotted toward it, tail between her legs as she whined softly. She laid down in the doorway to the meeting room but made no further movements to protect Asher.

The female guard still had the tip of her sword on the king's chest.

"It's time to go outside," she said and pulled something from her pocket, pinning it to her shirt.

Ember didn't have to get any closer to know that it was a Bear pin. The guard jerked her head once, and the guards behind her moved toward the houses, surrounding them. Ember's hands twitched, and she reached for her knife, but Viper's hand dropped on her arm, a steady weight that stopped her from grabbing it. He slowly slid her sleeve down to further hide it.

"Not yet," he whispered. "Don't give away your advantage." Ember gave him a small nod as the soldiers pushed them forward. A glance to her right, at the guard standing there, revealed her worst fears: the Order of the Bear had completely infiltrated the palace, as all the soldiers standing around them had silver pins on their shirts.

Traitors, Ember thought. She would get back at them for this; they would face the highest punishment for turning their backs on the houses and the Phoenix.

They pushed through the front doors, and the guards marched them toward the middle of the courtyard, where Ember forced herself to the front. She stopped short as she took in the scene in the front of the courtyard, at the object that had everybody's attention.

It was a crude remake of a metal hanging tree, commonly used by the houses to punish criminals in a merciful way. This one was clearly made by amateur hands, as the metal was clumped in some places and too thin in others. Plus, the entire thing was on wheels, which had been drawn by two mules. The house hanging trees didn't have wheels. They were permanent. Two palace-grade prison carriages flanked either side of it.

And, perhaps, the most horrifying part of it were the bodies splayed out in front of the hanging tree. A man and a woman, both in palace guard uniforms. They had been the voices behind the horrible screams that had drawn the court out, and they had died for no apparent reason. Arrows stuck out of their backs, blood soaking the space where they lay.

The court cried out in shock but were silenced when a woman's voice rose over the crowd.

"Silence!" Half the court fell quiet. The other half continued to screech. "Be quiet, all of you!" That shut everybody up enough, but Ember was already forcing her way closer to the hanging tree, pulling her knife from her arm. Now she'd use it to kill whoever these traitors thought they were.

"Drop the knife," someone said, and Ember looked around wildly, finding an archer perched up on one of the beams, pointing a flaming arrow directly at her head. She and the man glared at each other defiantly. She didn't want to drop the knife. But she also didn't want to die by fire. She clutched it harder, considering her options. Ember didn't want to drop her only defense. Her only chance. Viper came up behind her and gently pried the knife from her fingers, allowing it to fall to the tile, where it clunked awkwardly. Behind her, Ember could hear House Vulpus unstrapping their knife belts, as they, too, fell with a loud crash on the floor.

"Just cooperate," he whispered, taking her hand in his. "Maybe they'll go away if somebody surrenders or something."

"Only a coward would surrender," Ember whispered back, shaking her hand from his and crossing her arms over her chest. "And I am no coward."

People began pouring from every corner of the court-yard, completely surrounding the court. All of them were armed, from the smallest throwing knives to broadswords to crossbows. One man even had a hatchet strapped to his back. Someone swooped down and picked up Ember and House Vulpus' knives, carrying them away with them. Leaving the court completely unarmed.

But the people hadn't stopped showing up. Now they were coming into the courtyard from the palace, wearing clothing that ranged from guard uniforms to those of the maids and manservants, and even a few who were wearing aprons or had silver envelopes sewn on their shirts. All of them had silver Bears pinned to the front of their shirts, and they moved to stand with the other members of the Order, even as Ember's panic really set in.

Phoenix above. There were so many of them. How long had they been in the palace? How long had they been watching and waiting for this to happen? Ember swayed slightly, and Viper steadied her with a hand on her shoulder. He dropped it as soon as she was steady again, his eyes fixed on the woman who stood on the hanging tree. "We are the Order of the Bear!" the woman yelled.

Ember squinted at her. A scar covered one side of her face, making her skin look grotesque in the full sunlight. Ember immediately disliked her.

"And we are here to show you what happens when you hang our brothers, our sisters, mothers and fathers. Our wives, husbands, and children have been lost to your barbaric ways! Well, we say, it's time for change! It's time for the power to shift from the hands of the few, to the hands of the many! It's time for you, the 'Phoenix Court' to be afraid!" Her words were met with hollers of approval from the rest of her group, and the court cringed, growing closer together.

"Who?" someone in the court said, and everybody turned to them, finding Lady Victoria Soo squinting at the woman.

"We represent the thirteenth animal," the scarred woman said. "We represent those who are forced to grovel at the court's feet! At the Phoenix's feet! The Bear never forgot the injustice done to it! And neither will we!"

Ember didn't move. She simply stared at the hanging tree, contemplating what they might do with it. Hang someone, obviously, but who?

The answer hit her like a slap in the face, and she stumbled backwards, knocking into Viper.

"What's wrong?" he whispered. She couldn't speak, only shake her head. Viper followed her eyes to the hanging tree, and his face fell when he, too, realized it.

"They won't do that, Ember. They can't." But his tone was far from reassuring, and he placed a protective hand around her waist.

"Whatever you do," he said, "You can't run for the hanging tree. They'll kill you too, and your house will have no leader." His voice trembled. Ember shoved him off her.

"She's my mother. If I get the chance, I plan on rushing the stage. I will not let her die without a fight. I won't die without a fight." The doors behind them opened, and the woman standing on the hanging tree cackled.

"Oh, good. The royal family finally decided to join us. Make sure you give them a front row seat." Asher was shoved into place beside Ember, and she flinched away from him.

"What's going on?" he asked, eyes wide, looking to her for answers. Ember avoided his gaze, but the only other place to look was the hanging tree, or her own trembling hands. He had a knife strapped to his hip, and one of the traitor servants came forward, extending his hand for it. Asher unbuckled it without protesting, and Ember caught a glimpse of the handle, which was carved in the shape of the Bear. She felt another flash of fear—was Asher one of them?

But there was no pin on his shirt, and he looked truly frantic as he gazed at the hanging tree and the woman standing upon it. And if he had been one of them, she realized, he would've already been facing her, standing among his fellow traitors.

"Someone give me answers!" Asher demanded, turning to Viper. "Please."

"They're staging a public execution," Viper whispered.

"Lady Verity," Asher whispered, and hearing her mother's name undid Ember. Her hands were moving so fast that they hit the boys on either side of her.

"We have guards," Asher said. "Where are they?"

"Either betraying us or they've been held up by some other members of this rebellion," Viper answered, looking at Ember with concern, and then the two guards at the base of the tree. His eyes jumped to the traitor guards, who kept their weapons pointed at the court. "They'll be here soon. They have to be." His voice was still shaking, though.

"What if they went to the estates?" Viper whispered, going pale. "My little sisters. Adder and Mamba. Asp."

Asher shook his head.

"They don't have a reason to go for you, or your siblings. What they want are the lords and ladies, and the heirs. We're the ones who should be afraid. We're the ones who should be afraid. Ember and I, and my parents. We're probably the main targets."

Ember crossed her arms, squeezing them tightly with her hands to attempt to quell their shaking.

"Shut up!" the woman roared, and the crowd went silent again.

"I could easily execute the king now," the woman crooned, and her group cheered. "But wouldn't it be so much more fun to make him watch his perfect paradise crumble around him? To force him to watch as his heaven turns to hell? Wouldn't that be better?" This elicited a far stronger response from the group, who stamped their feet and made odd animal calls. Certainly not the calls of any of the patron animals, Ember realized, but of something different. Something awful and primal and feral that made the hair on her arms stand up.

"So instead of the king," the woman said. "I have someone he will surely miss. Two of his favored advisors. First, the lady of House Pardus. The Leopard herself."

"NO!" The scream came from behind Ember, and she knew that if she had looked, she would've seen Lilith screaming for their mother.

"Yes, my dear. You must be the heir. Bring them to the front!" Sounds of struggling came from behind Ember, and then Lilith was between her and Asher. They looked at Ember with desperation.

"I can't watch," they whispered. "I can't." They dropped to their knees, bowing before the woman.

"Oh, my darling. You and I both know that there's a way out of your mother dying. The choice is yours. You are the heir, after all."

"If I swear House Pardus's loyalty to you, will you release her?" The woman and one of her companions exchanged a glance, and a triumphant smile, before giving Lilith a terse nod.

"Release Alex Taya." The door to one of the prison carriages swung open, and Alex Taya fell out, collapsing into her child's arms.

"If any of you are House Pardus, then join us here, at the front," the woman commanded, and Lilith's stepmother and younger sisters shuffled to the front, heads hung. Nobody said a word, but the anger and fear in the air was palpable.

Ember would do many things to save her mother. But if she surrendered, if she gave in, the two of them would be dead anyway.

Dragons never died without a fight.

Chapter

TWENTY-SEVEN

ONCE HOUSE PARDUS HAD made their way to the front, disgraced and traitorous, the woman turned back to the crowd.

"I'm giving the heir of House Draco a chance. A chance to surrender, to join me and the Order of the Bear. She can spare her mother that way. We already have the Leopard, what's one more?" Silence in the courtyard as Ember stared at the woman.

"You're Ember Ignis, aren't you?" the woman said, looking down at her from the hanging tree.

"My name is Lady Ember Ignis. And I would never bow to you," Ember spat, and although she could barely control her hands, and the way her legs were beginning to wobble a bit too, she stood up a bit straighter and held her head high as she and the woman stared at each other.

"I suppose we will have an execution today!" the woman yelled, and there were more animal calls, more stamping of feet. The second prison carriage was thrown open, and Verity was forced out.

Ember had never seen her mother in such a state before. She had never seen her mother any way other than immaculate.

Her hair was matted to her head with what looked like blood and vomit and tangled to the point that Ember couldn't even tell if it hadn't been cut. Her lovely red dress, which she had been wearing when she had been kidnapped, was now torn and stained with dark liquid in various places. Bruises lined her arms and neck, small, finger-shaped bruises, and there were scars around her wrists, where they must've had manacles on her. A scratch above her lip bled over her mouth. They had taken her shoes and even from where she stood, Ember could see the dried blood on her feet. Her nails were scraggly and yellowed.

The worst part, though, was the empty look in Verity's eyes. The look of a hopeless woman. Everything else could be healed with a bit of bandage and ointment. Some rest and a warm bath. The emptiness, however, was permanent.

"Mother!" At Ember's call, Verity perked up a bit, scanning the crowd for her. "Verity!" They locked eyes, and Ember pushed off Viper, taking a few uncertain steps forward.

She had promised herself she wouldn't surrender. But seeing her mother like this, knowing her mother might die in that filthy dress, without saying her goodbyes, without receiving final prayers, was almost enough to push her over the edge.

Almost. Ember stumbled forward, nearly hitting the edge of the hanging tree, but the woman waved her hand, and two of her foot soldiers grabbed Ember's arms.

"Ember!" Verity cried out, tripping as she was forced up and onto the hanging tree. "Ember, my darling." Ember was crying now, tears flowing down her face with no signs of stopping.

Something snapped inside of Ember, and she wrenched her arm from one of the guards, using it to punch the other in the nose, blood spurting on her hands, warm and sticky. He fell back with a grunt, and Viper immediately tackled him, keeping him pinned and punching him as Ember slammed the other man's head into the hanging tree and rushed it. The woman on the stage whistled, and more rebels appeared, surrounding her. Then Viper was beside her, taking care of one of the larger ones as she shouldered her way up the stairs. Desperate to save her mother from swinging. She had to try.

"Enough!" the woman yelled, and three rebels tackled Ember as one, keeping her down. Her breathing came in short pants, and she could barely lift her head, but when she did, she saw Verity looking at her. With something akin to pride.

"You are a Dragon," Verity commanded as her neck was slipped into the noose. She wasn't fighting anymore, even tipping her head slightly to allow the rebels better access to her neck. Ember couldn't understand why she wasn't fighting any more—why was she so desperate to die.

She looked back into Verity's eyes, and she understood. Verity had already fought; she had already tried to free herself and get back to Ember. And now, she was a broken woman, standing there in her red dress, with those empty eyes. But

Ember would not allow her to die yet; she would not give up on her mother's life.

Ember thrashed underneath the rebels, but they held fast. "You were born of the Phoenix Flame, crafted from steel and vengeance. Dragons do not surrender. Do not surrender, Ember. Fight to the last. I love you."

Ember screamed, a horrible, hoarse sound born of all her anger and sadness, choking out her last words to her mother.

"I love you too." The trapdoor swung out from underneath Verity, and Ember's scream doubled as she watched her mother's neck hang at an unnatural angle, her eyes already glazed over and empty. The snap of her neck was a sound Ember would never be able to forget, the way it crunched unnaturally as the light drained from her mother. Ember couldn't catch her breath, fighting for control as she attempted to wrestle her way out from underneath the three guards, all of whom were cheering. Cheering for the woman hanging from a noose that was made for someone far below her status.

Cheering for the death of a woman who had never deserved it.

Ember's vision began to spot as she looked at her mother, slightly swaying in the breeze. She kept screaming, kept clawing and scratching and biting and something snapped in her eye, clouding it with blood. The smell of death surrounded her, and the only noise was the cheering of the rebellion, and that was beginning to be slightly muffled. The only thing she could hear, over and over again, were her mother's last words.

Crafted from steel and vengeance. Steel and vengeance.

Ember screamed once more before her vision went out completely, plunging her into the darkness.

Vengeance.

Asher was gaping at the hanging tree, where Lady Verity remained. Swinging in the breeze, tattered red dress shifting around her bare feet. Gaping at Ember, who was screaming and thrashing until she lost her breath and passed out under three rebels. A fighter.

And then one of the rebels shouted, warning the others, and the world erupted into chaos for the third time in one day.

The royal guard was there, swinging their swords and cutting down rebels and traitor guards. Steel met steel, and arrows rained from all angles as the two groups launched themselves at each other. Asher turned just in time to see one of the true palace guards sink a spear into a traitor's stomach, but in return, she received a flaming arrow in the back of her head, shot by a man crouching in the rafters. It was mass chaos, and as Asher watched, rooted in place, more guards poured in, mercifully free of silver Bear pins. They outnumbered the rebels—not by much, but it seemed to be enough, as more bodies with silver pins littered the ground than the others, and several rebels had already taken flight. He pulled a knife from the body of a guard and stood there, looking around wildly. Asher could see Captain Moreci, his face bloodied and bruised. There had been a fight for them to even reach the courtyard. Was the Order truly that powerful?

"Capture some!" Asher's father yelled from where he stood, completely safe, behind two guards. "We want them for questioning!" Four guards tackled rebels at his words, keeping them captive underneath their bodies. At this point, Asher couldn't tell which guards were with them and which were not. He couldn't see any more Bear pins, but there was always the chance that they had taken them off to attempt and blend back in with the true guards. It was all a bloody, vicious disaster. The smell of blood choked the air, drowning out Asher's senses as he scanned the courtyard again. His hand clenched around his knife.

Asher, with a stab of fear, suddenly saw his father lying on the ground and ran toward him, only to find that he had curled up on the floor, and he was sobbing, whether from fear or distress over Verity Ignis, Asher couldn't tell. He immediately looked for his mother next, finding her in the corner, two guards standing in front of her. Protecting her. Her eyes were fixed on something over Asher's shoulder, her expression one of horror and immense relief, and he turned, finding the source of her gaze.

The hanging tree, with Verity Ignis still swinging from it.

"Go!" the woman on the hanging tree screeched, and the rebels immediately took off, fleeing back to wherever they had initially come from. Leaving their companions struggling underneath the guards. In their haste, they even left the hanging tree, Verity still swinging from it. Someone grabbed the House Pardus members, forcing them along too. The guards that had been holding down Ember were gone, leaving Ember underneath her mother's body, as though they had died together. The woman remained for a moment longer, a finger pointed directly at Asher's father.

"This is not the end," she said, and although she didn't shout, her voice carried. "You started this war, King Whelyn, but we will finish it." She turned and fled as her counterparts had, leaving behind those parting words.

Viper Trunca was on the stage, then, hoisting Ember up into his arms and looking around frantically.

"Someone help me!" Asher should've gone up to help him but was secretly, selfishly relieved when Blue Corvu of House Olor walked up to the hanging tree, refusing to look at Lady Verity's body. Paying it respect by not staring at it.

"We need to cut her down," someone whispered, and Asher nodded.

"I'll do it," his father offered, finally standing. Tears had tracked down his face, and Asher turned to see Feather's eyes, narrowing at his father. He knew she was thinking about what he had told her. But at the same time, Asher couldn't help but feel as though now was not exactly the best time to work out those issues. "Someone help me with her body." Two bodies, one still breathing, and one that had taken her last breath only moments ago. Two dragons, one made out of pure fire, and one made of ash. Two women with vicious gold eyes and sleek black hair.

Two women forged of molten gold and black stone.

Asher needed to do something. He felt useless, standing there while the court wept around him and his father handled a dead body. While two people of the seventh and ninth houses carried a broken girl inside to restrain her for when she woke up crying and fighting for her mother. There was no doubt in Asher's mind that Ember would wake up swinging, and they would need the entirety of the army to keep her from slaughtering the rebels in revenge.

He needed to find Juniper. He needed to find her, to have someone to hold. Or someone to hold him since what he had just witnessed was…revolting. Grotesque. Something that, no matter how hard he tried, he would never be able to forget.

He slipped through the crowd and back into the palace, which was surprisingly untouched. It seemed entirely normal, except for the servants weeping in the halls. Asher realized that they had been betrayed just as much as he had—those were their friends who had stood amongst the rebels in the courtyard. Potentially their families.

The young House Vulpus twins were holding each other, crying softly. He wondered how much they'd seen, how much they'd heard. Asher extended a hand to them, but then pulled it back. They didn't want his sympathy any more than he wanted someone else's.

Asher walked through the palace in a daze, unable to stop thinking about what had just happened. He passed by the conference hall, and Hazel trotted at his side, a comforting presence in a sea of unknowns.

Juniper had been right about the Order of the Bear. He'd kissed her only days before he'd watched someone die in his own home. The kiss lingered in the back of his mind, a sweet memory soured by the events of the day.

He passed Viper and Blue in the hall, seated outside of one of their guest rooms. One of the few rooms that locked from the outside. Locking Ember in. Someone must have shown it to them, thinking that the only person they were protecting Ember from was herself.

They made eye contact, but Asher moved on, unable to summon words to say to them. What could he say to them? Sorry you just watched someone die? Sorry that it was Ember's mother? Sorry that Ember was no doubt going to be a wreck whenever she woke up, that she would probably lash out at those closest to her?

No. He kept going, making his way down to the servants' quarters. In the kitchen, where Juniper was consoling a group of younger servants.

"Thank the Phoenix," she whispered when she saw him, pulling him into a long hug. "I've never prayed for anything to stop as much as that. Not even my brother's sickness. That was awful."

"Did you watch?" Asher asked.

"No. But some of the other servants saw, and those screams... Word travels fast around here. It's an awful thing that happened."

"It's more awful if you were forced to watch it," Asher said. Juniper simply nodded, and they stood that way for a long time, quietly crying and holding onto each other, as though the floor would fall out from under them if they didn't.

Chapter

TWENTY-EIGHT

EMBER WOKE UP IN a room decorated with blue flowers. The walls had blue flowers, the vase beside her held them. She was sure, had she looked, that the carpet would've been blue too. The comforter that was covering her was a deep, ocean blue, the color most saw as gentle. Even the ceiling was patterned with blue flowers, repeating over and over again. Blue was never a color she liked much. It wasn't a Dragon color. Not harsh enough for Ember's taste, and certainly not for past Dragons. There were no windows in this room, she noticed in some back corner of her mind, but didn't care. She could see perfectly well with the lamps placed around the room.

She stared at the ceiling for a while, completely transfixed on tracing the patterns with her eyes. She didn't know where she was, and quite frankly, she didn't care.

Ember could feel some sort of restraint holding her to the bed, but she shimmied out of it in an instant, looking down to find she was still in the same clothes she had been in when...

Ember collapsed onto the floor, vomiting up the little that was in her stomach. She retched until her head spun and her hands shook, and then stumbled her way to the bathroom, splashing cold water on her face. Ember looked up to discover that she was a disgusting mess. Vomit dripped down her chin, onto her shirt, which was stained with dirt and somebody's blood. Her hand hurt, and when she looked at it, she discovered a piece of metal wedged into the meat of her palm. Metal from the hanging tree.

Immediately she was sick again, into the sink, but nothing came up. Only dry heaving, her body desperately trying to throw up something that wasn't there. The image of her mother, in a torn red dress, with hair matted with vomit and sweat, stumbling out of a prison carriage. Smelling of piss and vomit. And her empty eyes. But she would've taken that image, that horrible, awful image, over the one of her before she passed out.

Her mother, swinging from a rope around her neck. The sickening sound of her bones snapping played in her head over and over and over again. The way her eyes glazed over, the light draining from them. How Ember had not even been given the chance to apologize to her mother for all the wrongs she'd committed against her.

She had not even been able to say goodbye.

Or to tell Verity how much she loved her, and how afraid she was of taking her place.

Ember looked up, meeting her own eyes, but all she could see was Verity, and she screamed, tasting blood in her throat.

She slammed her elbow against the mirror, shattering it. Her elbow began to bleed, but she ignored it, picking up one of the largest shards. She stumbled back to the main bedroom area, sitting on the bed, the glass in her hand. She ran it across the pad of her thumb, testing the sharpness. It glanced off her finger, cutting it wide open. Ember placed the trembling piece of glass to her wrist, and before she could hesitate a moment longer, she scored it across her skin. Blood gushed up, red and sticky and metallic, the pain a welcome relief. She made another cut beneath it, watching her own blood bubble up to greet her.

Ember cut her wrist again, almost smiling now. What a welcome distraction it made, that pain. She made another cut, watching as her arm turned red and the bedsheets beneath her began to stain.

Control. She needed the control, and she had no other way to get it. There were no knives for her to throw, no music for her to dance to.

Physical pain was easy to control.

She deserved to hurt, for not saving Verity.

She glanced up, holding the bloody glass, before standing and going to the door. Ember let the blood from her arm drip to the carpet, leaving a red-brown trail behind her. She tested the knob a couple times before discovering that this blue room was like the Draco Estate's black room. Ember screamed, kicking the door as hard as she could.

"Let me out!" Her voice cracked as she kicked it again, barely feeling the pain that came from bashing her foot into a wooden door. She was becoming numb. "Please!"

To her complete surprise, the door swung open, and Viper came in, closing it behind him. Ember backed away from him.

"Viper," she choked out, falling into him, and he caught her.

"Where the hell did this blood come from?" he asked, catching her and guiding her back to bed. She could see now that the restraints were nothing more than a pile of blankets, with a sharp and bloodied piece of glass resting on top of them. Viper noticed it too, then looked at her arm and ran into the bathroom. A string of profanities flooded out the door before he came back with a towel.

"I can't think," she whispered as he wrapped her arm with the towel. He went back to find another, then pulled a knife from his pocket and began cutting her sheets into strips, wrapping her arm tightly with them.

"I know," he responded. "I'm not asking you to think. I'm asking you to please not hurt yourself. Phoenix, Ember, this is a lot of blood."

"It doesn't hurt."

"I'm not going to argue with you, because you're unstable. I thought we had completely Ember-proofed this room. I never imagined you'd break the mirror." He dropped his head in his hands for a moment but then, immediately raised it again, gently turning her arm over in his hand. There were deep, black circles underneath his eyes, and he shuddered as his thumb passed through the blood on her wrist.

"Viper?"

"Don't worry about me, Ember. Just let us worry about you, okay?"

"I don't want you to worry about me."

"Right now, Ember, nobody is concerned about what you want. We're concerned about what you need."

"You locked me in," she said, voice breaking as she reached for her piece of glass. Viper delicately set her arm down, then moved the glass out of her reach. When he spoke, his voice was clogged with emotion. His eyes shone.

"I had to, Ember. Don't you understand? We didn't know how you'd be when you woke up. Especially when you didn't wake up yesterday."

"Yesterday?"

"It's been two full days since you passed out," Viper said.

"Did they get her body?"

"Yes. They've recovered it. Don't worry. Please try to go back to sleep. I'll come and check on you later, okay?"

"Bring Lucasta," Ember said quietly. "She's all alone at the Draco Estate and—"

House Draco. Her house. Verity's house. Verity, who was the lady of the house, who ran it perfectly, with the right amount of firmness and kindness. Who made sure everybody was happy and paid and fed and still managed to be the king's best advisor and make time for her daughter. Verity, the true Dragon.

Verity. Her mother. Swinging in the breeze, her body as limp as a doll's. Ember's stomach turned, and she pushed Viper away as she began dry heaving again.

"You need some water," Viper said, standing and taking her shard of glass with him. "I'm going to send somebody in to clean up the rest of that glass and bandage you properly. Please stay in bed, Ember. I'll be back soon."

Any other day she would've protested, would've fought against him protecting her.

But she was tired.

So ridiculously tired.

Two days of rest had done little to heal her body or her mind.

And as Viper closed and locked the door behind him, Ember fell back into an uneasy sleep, her dreams full of images of blond boys with kind eyes, a woman with a scar, and a hanging tree.

Chapter

TWENTY-NINE

SHER COULDN'T SLEEP, NO matter how many times he
asked the Phoenix to help him. The events of two
days prior kept running circles in his mind, keeping
him awake and anxious. He'd even gone in to check on Ember
the first night she'd been passed out, after the execution. But
she hadn't woken from her slumber, murmuring softly as she
slept. He hadn't gone back, fearing that the next time she
would be awake.

Awake and furious, like a beast uncaged.

He and Juniper had hardly seen each other either as the
entire palace seemed to be moving slowly since Verity's execution.
Most of the house families had chosen to go home, to lock
themselves in and wait for his father's summons. Three remained,
two heirs and one lesser son—Ember, Viper, and Blue—the

boys taking turns caring for Ember for reasons Asher didn't understand. Viper clearly had an unrequited crush. He didn't know what relationship Blue and Ember had, but he figured it had to be pretty strong for Blue to continue to stay behind and guard her. He realized, too, that Blue's father had been the first victim of the Order's wrath, and that there must've been some type of kinship between Blue and Ember, their parents' deaths linking them together.

These were the things he used to distract himself with as he paced the palace halls at night, a glass bottle in his hand. Asher had taken to drinking a bit again. Not as much as before but… still. And right now he was alone with his thoughts, and he didn't have anything better to do. Hazel trotted faithfully at his side, tail wagging. He hadn't allowed her out of his sight in days, terrified for her safety, and he was now letting her wander a bit more, allowing her to take in the sights and smells of the palace.

There was commotion in the hall Ember was in, and Asher quickened his pace to catch Viper coming out of it, a bloody shard of glass clutched in his hand.

"Hey," Viper said. Asher noticed the significant lack of respect in his tone but brushed past it. These past few days had been bad for everybody, and he didn't expect Viper to be worried about formalities.

"Hey," Asher said. They stared at each other for a moment before Asher nodded at the piece of glass, drawn to the blood dripping off it.

"What happened?" Viper hesitated, and Asher watched emotions play out over his face—unwillingness to tell him, and the duty to do so because Asher was his crown prince. The duty won out.

"Ember woke up and shattered her mirror. She used it to cut her wrist. It's...bad. I'm going to call someone to bandage her properly and clean up the rest of the glass, before she can do something else stupid."

"She already *did* do something stupid. Is she still awake?"

Viper shook his head. "I made her go back to sleep. She seriously needs to eat and drink some water, though. She kept trying to vomit, but nothing would come up."

"Do you think she'll ever recover?"

Viper leaned against the wall, rubbing the space between his eyes before answering. "From the death of her mother? The only family she has? She will, eventually, although it'll leave a scar. But not today, and not tomorrow, and not next year, or the year after that. Especially not the way it happened. It was gruesome. Barbaric. She's falling apart right now. She has to piece herself together, and nobody can do that for her. So don't try to do that. Ember is strong enough to put herself back together if she truly wants to. If she's ready to. With whatever means she needs to employ. Whether that be a pilgrimage up Mount Saffi, or throwing knives until her arms ache, so be it. But right now, what she needs is space and time, so please don't go barging in there to bother her."

"I wasn't going to."

Viper crossed his arms. "Look, Prince Asher. I don't know if you know this, but Ember—she wanted to be your friend. Both for political reasons, and for personal. She doesn't have many friends, you know, and I think she expected that you, of all people, would understand that."

"She told you that?"

"She didn't have to. It's obvious. So just keep that in mind if you go barging into her room, asking questions that she doesn't have answers for. I'm going to go find a maid now. And some bandages. Goodnight, Prince Asher." Viper brushed past him, heading into the dark hallway, and Asher stood, completely dumbfounded by his last comment.

He began heading to the temple, hoping he'd find Juniper there. To get to the temple, though, he had to pass the garden. He decided to step out for a moment, breathing in the fragrant air as Hazel began sniffing around near the door, not straying far from his side, as though she understood his anxieties. The hotter it got, the more flowers bloomed in the garden, and by the end of spring it would be a mix of different colored sprays. For now, though, only a few flowers were open. It was still early spring. Asher strode through the garden, heading to his and Juniper's bench. Perhaps he could sit a bit and relax. Think.

Voices floated toward him, and Asher stopped in his tracks. He hadn't expected anybody to be out here. Hadn't his father mentioned something about an enforced curfew for all staff?

"It went better than expected," someone said. "Especially with her daughter passing out like that. It was quite a spectacle. They certainly won't be forgetting us anytime soon."

"It was unnecessary to kill her. They were already scared when you took the Leopard. You could've just taken her back with you. You were a little dramatic," the other person answered, her voice soft and familiar, and Asher clapped his hand over his mouth to stifle his gasp.

Juniper.

"Maybe. They'll definitely be looking for us now," the first girl said.

"Pick up camp and move then."

"Not until you break Tyvish, Riley, Morgan, and Rabbit out. I want you to be able to find us."

"I don't think you understand how difficult that's going to be. This prison is like nothing we've ever encountered. Even with the rebels that are still stationed around the palace we're still going to have a hell of a time getting in and out of it. You'll need to ensure our ride is ready for us, so we can bolt as soon as we've got them." Asher took another step forward, breaking a branch under his foot, and Hazel trotted towards his side, her hackles raised.

"Shut up. Shut up right now. Someone is here."

"Run," Juniper hissed. The other girl took off, disappearing into the night. She was nothing more than a black blur, leaping over shrubs as she dashed for the wall.

Juniper stood, turned around, and froze when she caught sight of Asher. Her eyes went wide, pupils blowing out with fear.

"Asher, I can explain," she said.

Asher backed up a step. "What the hell, Juniper."

His eyes went to her shirt, where a silver Bear-head pin glimmered over her heart.

"It's not what it looks like."

"What it looks like is that you had a hand in Verity Ignis's death. Is that true or not?"

Juniper hesitated for a long moment, and Hazel barked at her.

She jumped away from the dog, not meeting Asher's eyes. "I... It's... It's true. But you don't understand. You have to let me explain."

"How much of it was a lie?"

Juniper stepped forward and reached her hand out. She dropped it at his look, along with her eyes.

"What?"

"How much of us was a lie? Did you actually want to kiss me, or were you just trying to get close enough to sink a knife in my chest? Is that why you always felt the need to remark on the guards? Because you couldn't tell if they were just as traitorous as you?"

"Asher," Juniper said, voice breaking. "All of that was real."

"I don't even know what to say to you right now. I can barely even look at you."

"Let me explain," Juniper said. "Please."

"Fine. But you better consider your words carefully before I allow Ember Ignis to have her way with you. I'd bet on the fact that she wouldn't make it merciful for you. Come with me. I don't want this to turn into a spectacle." Asher turned around and left, knowing Juniper was following.

He was furious, his anger a rioting, live thing in his stomach.

Juniper, part of the Order of the Bear? That would've explained why she was so confident the rebels were the Order of the Bear and not something completely unrelated.

And then, all of a sudden, something clicked.

Ember had accused Juniper of attempting to poison him. She could've been right. And he'd called her crazy. He whipped around, not caring how his voice carried in the hallway. If there was going to be a spectacle, so be it. It would keep him from having to order her death himself.

"Did you try to poison me?" he asked. Juniper, who was already crying, made a small choking sound, which confirmed it before she even said anything.

"Yes. It obviously didn't work but that was before I knew what I felt about you."

"Save your excuses and prayers for the Phoenix," Asher said, turning around again, stalking up a set of stairs as they climbed toward his room. He could hear Juniper sobbing quietly behind him, and although all he wanted to do was turn around and hold her, Asher wasn't quickly getting over the fact that she had tried to *kill* him. Ember was the only reason he was still alive. He threw open the door to his room, pointed to his desk chair, and Juniper immediately sat. The servant who slept in his room looked up, clearly surprised.

"Please go. Your silence is appreciated," Asher said, with a hint of threat in his voice, and the man immediately complied, darting out of the room. Asher locked it behind him. He'd thought about bringing Juniper here, before. He'd wanted her to see his room, to see where he spent his most desperate hours. To fall asleep next to her on the bed. He'd wanted to walk her around it, to guide her hands over the small piano his mother insisted he keep in the room, to kiss her against the bathroom wall.

And now, all he wanted to do was get her out of his room, away from him. His heart and mind warred with each other—his heart, whispering that this was Juniper, that she'd had plenty of chances to kill him and hadn't seized them. But his mind spoke louder, clearer, saying Juniper had been biding her time, that she had been waiting for the right moment to do him in. Waiting to break her friends out of prison and then murder him.

"Explain," Asher said, striding to his nightstand to pour himself a drink. He sat on the edge of his bed, taking a large swig of it. It burned on the way down, and he relished the feeling. Juniper took a moment to compose herself before speaking. Her leg jogged as she sat there, crying.

"I joined the Order of the Bear about six months ago, when I ran into a group of them near my house. My brother was sick, as I've told you before. Very sick. *Deathbed* sick. We'd even had a priest come in, to pray for him. The Phoenix wouldn't save him, and I needed medicine, but nobody in my family was making enough to purchase that sort of medicine. Definitely not my brother in the temple, who still doesn't know how bad it really was. His prayers did nothing, but the Order did. They offered me a trial run, in a sense—help them steal the medicine and they'd let me join officially. I did it because I was desperate, originally. And then I realized how very right they were. How wrong the house system was. How much we suffered when all of you, the houses, lived comfortably. You have never wanted for anything, where I have wanted for everything.

"My brother healed, thankfully, but only because of that expensive medicine. If not, we would've lost him. So I joined the Order of the Bear, and they gave me an assignment: kill the crown prince. And while I was working on that, working on getting close enough to slip you a poison or land a crossbow bolt in your back, something happened that nobody expected. I fell for the very person I was expected to stick a knife through. And I couldn't do it. I couldn't do that to you, Asher. But I am begging you to take a look around and realize how your people suffer while you sit in the very lap of luxury. I'm not asking you to join us. I'm simply asking you to forgive me."

Asher sat back on his bed, rubbing the space between his eyes. He set his drink down and began to pace the room. Juniper watched him, wiping tears from her eyes.

He considered what she was asking of him. Asher looked at his bedroom, at the plush bed stuffed with goose feathers. His liquor, which was the finest in the three continents. Even his sleeping clothes, which were pure silk with golden stitching. If he had bothered to open his closet, he would find even more fine clothes. Miles away, the Phoenix Crown, which would one day be his, was held in a secure facility. That crown could probably keep Juniper's village alive for years. And yet he was expected to only wear it on the day he was coronated and his wedding.

Asher drained the rest of his glass and turned around to face her.

"Get out," he said quietly. "Go back to bed, Juniper. I'll decide what I want to do in the morning. You don't breathe a word about this to anybody else, do you understand that? Not to your little traitor friends, who we *will* weed out, nor to anybody above you. This stays between the two of us, is that clear?" Juniper nodded shakily.

"You're not going to kill me?" she asked, her tears beginning to dry up. Asher let out a roar of frustration, slamming his hand on the desk, and Juniper flinched away from him. Asher stepped away from her. He didn't know what had come over him, but he was angry and upset and so ridiculously confused.

"I don't know! I don't know yet, okay? I need time to think about this. You can't expect me to just get over this. So please just...just leave. Get out of my room. I'll call you when I'm ready to speak to you again, don't worry." When she still didn't move, Asher snapped his fingers at Hazel, who jumped up from the floor immediately, moving toward Juniper, who stumbled back.

"Asher?" Juniper asked, looking up at him as Hazel backed her into the door.

"Go," Asher said, his voice breaking. "Please, just go."

Juniper nodded, dipping into a short curtsy. She turned and left the room, closing the door softly behind her.

Asher sat hard on his bed, unable to stop the tears that sprang to his eyes.

Asher awoke early and lay in bed for a long while, his eyes fixed on the ceiling while Hazel slumbered beside him. He'd made up his mind hours ago, unable to get more than a few hours of sleep, and he was hoping—praying, more like—that it was the right decision to make. Asher knew he only had two options, and he'd gone with the one that, in his own head, made the most sense. He felt, too, that he could only choose one of the choices—his conscience wouldn't allow him to live with the other.

He'd wanted to call Juniper to his room as soon as he'd made his mind up, but instead he waited, allowing warm sunlight to seep through his windows, and the birds to start singing. Once he could hear the palace waking up around him— servants passing outside his doors, curtains being opened in the halls, the sound of somebody dragging something—he allowed himself to wake.

Asher dressed slowly, leaving Hazel on his bed as he slipped out of the room. The halls seemed empty at first, but as Asher walked, he happened upon more servants, who hastily bowed, murmured sympathies about Verity, and got out of his way. Everybody was still on edge, and it was clear nobody trusted any of their fellow servants. Those who were working in pairs were stealing suspicious glances at each other, but most were working alone, washing windows or attempting to draw dirt out of the carpets.

"Good morning, Prince Asher," one woman said, dipping into a curtsy. "Can I help you with something?"

Asher nodded, looking at the carpet. "Could you point me in the direction of Juniper Farley?" he asked, and the woman gave him a small, knowing smile.

"She's in the kitchens, sir. Already awake and working," she said.

"Thank you," Asher said, moving past her. In a blind haze he moved down the stairs towards the kitchens, and pushed in, where he was greeted by a mess of smells. Asher could pick out baking bread and pastries, no doubt just enough to get them through the day. Already, other servants were busy preparing for the rest of the day—knives flashed quickly through the air as they prepped vegetables, and several women called to each other from opposite sides of the kitchen. He heard orders to send up tea to his mother's room, to send a bit of food up to Ember's. Two young boys even rushed past him, holding two baskets, and they promptly informed who looked to be the person in charge that they had just come back from the stables.

They all worked in perfect, organized chaos, but at the same time, everybody seemed on edge, and more than a few servants jumped when Asher knocked on the wall to get their attention.

"Prince Asher," the woman in charge said, sweeping into a low curtsy. "What an unexpected surprise. What can I do for you, sir?"

Asher swept his eyes over the kitchen, and the now-still servants, but Juniper wasn't to be seen, and he couldn't contain the disappointment and anxiety that spilled into his voice.

"I'm looking for Juniper Farley," Asher said, and several of the servants looked at each other, their glances so quick that he couldn't catch the expressions on their faces.

"She's in her room," the woman said finally. "Boys, show the prince where to go." The two boys from earlier eagerly dropped their baskets and ushered Asher toward the hallway. Memories of Juniper were pouring into Asher's mind from places he didn't know he had stored them, and those green eyes, her enchanting laugh, their kiss flashed before his eyes as the boys left him in front of a door.

He hesitated before knocking, two sides of himself at war with each other. His heart and mind threatened to rip each other apart, and he slowly lowered his hand. Asher drew in a long breath, told himself to stop being so stupid, and knocked, two times, on the door.

It flew open instantly, and Juniper looked up at him, her eyes wide with something akin to panic.

"Prince Asher," she said, dipping into a small curtsy. She retreated a few steps into the room, and Asher followed her in, closing the door softly behind him. Nobody else was in the room, mercifully, and Juniper's nerves seemed to be a tangible thing in the air, especially as she moved toward her bed, where a large bag was in the middle of being packed. Asher's eyes lingered on it for a moment too long, and then turned to her.

"Did you really think I was going to send you away?" Asher asked, sitting on one of the other beds. Tears immediately sprang to Juniper's eyes at his words, but he brought his hand up to stop her from saying anything. "Just listen."

Juniper nodded and sat across from him, her leg jogging nervously as she waited for him to speak.

It wasn't often that Asher truly felt the weight of the power he possessed, but he certainly did now, and he despised it.

"I... This wasn't easy, to be completely honest. I just saw Verity Ignis die a few days ago, and I just saw Ember Ignis scar her own body because of the pain in her head. My family, my court, has all been under this threat of the Order of the Bear for months now. And to think, Juniper, about how many of you were in the palace... You could've killed all of us. The country is going to be in chaos as my father tears it up trying to find you. Ember Ignis is going to raise hell, and I wouldn't be surprised if she starts hunting you as soon as she gets the chance. You're killing people that I've known my entire life—Verity, Nevis Corvu. Your group, whether you personally did it or not, left a dead man in somebody's bed. Your group broke into her house and left a corpse in her bed. Again, it doesn't matter if you physically did it or not—it was your group who did it. She's traumatized. I can't deny that Ember needed a reality check, but it didn't need to be that intense. Not in the slightest."

Asher paused to take a break and held up his hand once more when he saw Juniper open her mouth. She closed it again, and he looked down to find that both of her legs were jogging quickly. Asher reached over and placed a hand on her knee, stalling her leg.

"Relax," he said. "I already said I'm not throwing you out. So calm down."

Juniper nodded, and before Asher could stop her, she started speaking.

"Thank you," Juniper said, her words spilling out in a rush. "Thank you so much."

"I'm not done," Asher said, pulling his hand back. "Let me finish." Juniper's legs immediately began jogging again, but Asher ignored them.

"Your group did all of these horrific things in the name of freedom from my family and my court. And regardless of the intent behind them, they were horrific. You've scarred so many of us with memories we will never be able to lose. So many things we'll all see every time we close our eyes. And yet..."

Asher trailed off, his heart pounding. Was he seriously going to do this? Part of him still felt like this was a bad idea, but the majority of himself overruled it, and he cleared his throat, continuing.

"And yet, Juniper, I can't say that you're wrong. I don't agree with the way the Order goes about things—I certainly don't condone murder or kidnapping," he said, meeting Juniper's eyes. "But I can't disagree with what you're trying to accomplish. The house system is, as much as I've benefited from it, fairly corrupt. You've suffered, and so have thousands of other people. And there's nothing that we're going to be able to do about it until my parents are off the throne, which isn't going to be for a long time. Not to mention the fact that the court is just as bad—Ember holds more power than she realizes right now. Even without House Pardus, there's still eleven of them, and my parents. Outright war would accomplish your goals faster than waiting for my parents, and the generations in the courts, to die.

"So I'll help you, Juniper. I'll help you break your companions out of prison, because without me, you'll all end up like Verity Ignis. And once we've got them out, I'll come with you, and I'll aid your cause." Juniper moved faster than Asher could react, throwing her arms around him.

"Thank you," she whispered. "Thank you so much. You're going to save their lives. You're going to help us save so many lives, Asher."

Chapter

THIRTY

THERE WAS A PLATE of food beside Ember's bed when she woke up. A small roll, a glass of water. Soft foods for a sensitive stomach. Beside it was a small, wooden Phoenix charm that she ignored. The Phoenix had turned Her back on her, and Ember would do the same. What she really needed, though, was to use the bathroom. She swung out of bed, noticed the glass of her mirror-shattering incident had been cleaned up, and took a quick leak in the toilet. With no mirror, she couldn't see what she looked like, but Ember assumed it was nothing good. A glance down told her she was in the same clothes she had been the last time she had woken up, too. This time, along with the old blood, was her new blood and her vomit.

She crawled back into bed, delicately sipping the water and testing her stomach before nibbling on the roll.

Immediately, her stomach recoiled, and she set the roll back down, sticking solely to the water. The glass shook violently in her hand, causing it to run over the sides and spill out onto her shirt. Ember touched her bandaged arm. It hurt like hell, and she resisted the urge to pull the bandages away.

Ember figured the door was locked again, but she got out of bed to try it. She was surprised when it opened under her hand, revealing an empty hallway bathed in sunlight. She stepped out, testing it. Surprisingly enough, nobody jumped out to force her back to bed, and she walked a few more steps down the hallway, bare feet sinking into the plush carpet. Everything seemed beautiful and normal and perfect in this hallway full of sunlight, and she stretched her arms as she passed through the rays. She basked in it for a moment, eyes closed.

The stained-glass windows cast rainbow patterns over her, the shape of a Dragon with wings flared, mimicking the way her arms were outstretched. Red and gold rolled over her body, bathing her in firelight. Her weak arms began to quiver but she kept them up, embracing the warmth the Dragon provided.

"You're up," someone said behind her, and Ember didn't turn, but she recognized Blue's voice.

"I'm going to go get Viper. Stay here, please. Enjoy the sunlight." He turned and disappeared into the shadows, leaving Ember alone again. She sat on the carpet, digging her fingers into it, disregarding anything to do with propriety. If someone walked up on her right then, she had a feeling she would do something completely stupid. Like smile at them.

Ember laid completely back, like a cat stretched out on the carpet. Or maybe a small Dragon. Someone laid down beside her. She knew it was Viper without opening her eyes, because he simply laid there, breathing in time with her. He didn't feel the need to say anything to her.

After a moment, his hand covered Ember's, and she allowed it to rest there, a comforting weight. It helped ease the shaking, at the very least. His thumb brushed the back of her hand, reassuring her.

They laid there for a long time like that, holding hands in the sunlight. Ember enjoyed it for a brief moment, before her memories came shooting back in a torrent.

Her mother.

Swinging.

Neck snapping.

Eyes glazing over.

Ember shot up, her breath speeding as she began to think again. She didn't want to think.

"Ember," Viper said quietly, rubbing Ember's back as she attempted to keep down her few sips of water. When she looked at him, she noticed a bandage around his left hand. Today was a holy day, then. She hardly cared.

"I'm okay," she said, but they both knew she was lying.

"I'll walk you back to bed," Viper offered, and Ember nodded, allowing him to help support her on the way back to her bedroom. He tucked her into bed again, frowning at the mostly untouched roll on her plate and the half-full glass of water.

"You should drink some more," Viper said quietly, handing her the glass.

"I can't," Ember said. "I can't. My hands." She held them out so he could see how violently they were shaking, and he took them both into his bandaged hand, still offering her the glass with his right.

"Please," Viper said. "Ember, you need it. Please. I need you to try and take care of yourself. A little bit."

Ember accepted the glass, allowing him to tip it back into her mouth, and drank a bit more, almost immediately pushing it back toward him. She couldn't stomach it."No more."

Viper set the glass down and released her hands, pulling the comforter over her shoulders. He looked at her sadly.

"Okay, Ember. No more. Try and sleep some more, okay? Blue and I are going to set up cots on your floor, in case you need us during the night. Okay?"

"Okay."

Ember woke, a scream tearing from her mouth. Cold sweat covered her neck and matted her hair close to her head, and she desperately tore it away from her skin, trying to cool off. Blue's cot was empty, but Viper had sat straight up, hair mussed from sleep and eyes drowsy with it.

"Ember?" he asked, rolling off his cot and coming over to her, slipping into the bed beside her. He lay on top of the comforter, giving her space, but being there.

"I'm okay," Ember whispered, but that was another lie, and they both knew it.

"Nightmare?"

Ember nodded, looking over at Viper in the dark. His eyes were going in and out of focus, drifting between being asleep and being awake. A nightmare seemed like a rather tame way to phrase it. Ember had always considered nightmares to be when she was falling from a high place and never hit the ground, or when a hundred bugs crawled their way onto her skin.

Nightmares weren't supposed to show her mother dying hundreds of thousands of times in front of her eyes while everybody she had ever known stood by and watched, not even blinking in response to Verity's screams. Ember had been screaming too, but her lips had been sealed shut, and her cries hadn't managed to break through. All had been silent except for Verity's screaming, and Ember shuddered violently as she thought about it, her hands twitching.

"Let's get out of here," Viper whispered, extending his hand to her. Ember hesitated for a long moment. Where could they go where the memories wouldn't haunt her every step? They clung to her body, to this room, even to the air in the space itself like spiderwebs, and they weren't going away anytime soon.

She stared at his hand for a long while, and then back up at him. He withdrew his hand.

"It's okay," he whispered. "Follow me."

He led her out of the room and into the hallway, which was bathed in darkness and moonlight. The moon, in the shape of a curved claw, peeked through the stained-glass windows, casting light shadows onto the carpet.

"Where are we going?" Ember whispered, feeling her heart lighten slightly as they continued down the hallway. Down the main staircase, and then they were near the large meeting room.

"Shh," Viper said, leading her past the doors to the conference room. They were getting further into the reaches of the palace, where Ember had spent childhood years running around with the other children of the houses.

She had spent hours upon hours hiding from the other children in the cabinets, praying they wouldn't find her and make her search for them. She ran wild until Verity finally decided her daughter was too old for childish nonsense, and Ember had truly become the heir of House Draco.

And now... Viper paused in front of a door, holding it so Ember could go in, looking around and squinting in the darkness.

"Hold on," Viper said, and moved past her, the door closing loudly behind him. There was a *skritch* sound as he lit matches around the room, lighting the place up as he lit the lanterns that hung on the walls.

Ah. A training room. A rather nice one, at that. Weapons, glittering and sharp, hung on the walls, ranging from throwing knives to crossbows to axes. Ember had been in this room only twice before, in the weeks before the Silent Duels, and she couldn't help but have her breath taken away by it all. Targets, in the traditional circle shape, as well as in the form of humans and animals, were stacked on the wall opposite the weapons, leaving the far wall bare. That was where the targets were designed to line up, and Viper was already dragging one of the circular targets over to it.

"Pick your choice weapon," he suggested, and Ember couldn't help but be drawn toward the knives, all sparkling along the wall. She ran her hand across the hilts, pulling out one that was small and thin. When she ran the pad of her finger across the blade, however, it left a small line of red across her finger. It was light, too, the perfect type of knife used for throwing with deadly accuracy. Identical knives flanked it, and Ember picked those out as well, holding two in one hand and one in the other. Her hands trembled slightly, and she willed them to be still. The last thing she needed to do was hit Viper with one of the knives.

"Ready?" Viper asked, moving away from the target. Ember lined up her shot, positioning her feet just so. She released a long breath, squinting at the target to ensure she would hit it and not Viper, before pulling her arm back and throwing the knife as hard as she could.

Thunk. It hit the target with a solid, satisfying noise. It stuck slightly to the left of the bullseye, and Ember swore under her breath.

"Close," Viper said, coming up beside her with a bow and a quiver of wood-and-silver arrows. He notched it, pulling the string close to his cheek. Ember watched him—his chest as it slowly rose and fell under his thin nightshirt, his mouth as he pursed his lips in concentration, his hair, feathery and still mussed from sleep. She had the strangest urge to reach up and run her hand through the blond locks, just to see if his hair was really as soft as she imagined.

He released the arrow, and it hit directly beside the knife she'd thrown, the sound jolting her from thoughts of his hair.

"Weak," Ember said, shifting one of the remaining two knives into her other hand. She aimed it slightly more to the right than the last time and threw it without hesitation.

Bullseye.

Viper whistled through his teeth as he nocked another arrow. "Remind me never to cross you," he said.

"I thought you knew that already," Ember replied, watching as he loosed his arrow and it hit only a hair away from the bullseye. She threw her last knife and went back to the rack for more.

And so they went, alternating weapons until the target was full of them, and Ember's hands were red and raw from holding the knives.

She did not allow herself to stop throwing the knives, not even as tears began to roll down her face and splash on the mats underfoot. Viper did not so much as look over at her, giving her the privacy she so desperately needed, simply loosing another arrow and then waiting until she had thrown her knife again before loading his bow again.

On and on they went, loading and reloading, knives and arrows flying in an easy rhythm that Ember found easy to work with.

Ember allowed herself to relax. And she allowed herself to begin healing, even if it was only in this room, and only with this boy.

Chapter

THIRTY-ONE

SHER SLIPPED ON HIS servant's uniform, putting a bottle of liquor into his pocket. He hadn't been able to sit at Vax's grave since someone had shot an arrow at him, and the last few days had been so full of horror and fear that he hadn't been able to slip out.

But he had to get out tonight. He had to tell Vax about what was going on—about Verity Ignis, about Juniper, about the Order of the Bear and all their threats.

Asher knew the only reason he was so desperate to get out was because he and Juniper were leaving. There would be no more late-night visits to Vax's grave.

He wanted to get in as many conversations with Vax as he could before he and Juniper headed south. He wanted to spend time with Siliros and Hazel and Vax, who for years had been his only friends.

Asher swung a long cloak over his servant's uniform, pulling the hood up and over his head for a bit more anonymity, although he had a feeling the guards standing every five feet would have him pull his hood off to prove that he wasn't an Order member in disguise.

Asher allowed Hazel to trot at his side as he slipped out of the room, using her to prove his identity even further. He carried no weapons after almost losing his knife to the Order, making him less of a threat than usual.

There had been dozens of traitors within the palace guards, but four still stood outside of every door—two flanking it, and two across from it. Asher forced himself to take a deep breath as one of the women squinted at his face underneath his hood, and sped up, jogging down the first staircase. Hazel's tail wagged rapidly, and Asher had the same feeling in his chest; he was finally getting out of the palace.

On the lower floors were more guards, all standing stoically every few feet. He pushed his hood back once he reached the first floor, hoping that a glimpse of his face would be enough to ward off any unwelcome questions.

As he turned to go out to the stables, two guards silently stepped away from the wall, walking a few paces behind him. They weren't trying to hide, but they weren't intruding, and Asher ignored them as he stepped into the stables. They were warmer now due to the spring weather, and a few of the stalls had the top part of their back doors open, letting in some cool night air.

Asher moved for Siliros, who nuzzled his palm affectionately as he opened his stall, leading him out with a handful of oats. Hazel slipped between his legs, whining at Asher's side as Siliros slowly tromped out of the stall. Behind him, the two guards were acquiring their own horses, and he could hear them pulling down saddles and bridles.

He threw the doors open, backing up quickly as Siliros reached for the oats in his palm. Asher gave them to him, swinging himself up and onto the horse's back. Hazel let out an excited bark, already a brown-and-white blur rushing down the road toward the graveyard.

Asher spurred Siliros on, chasing after the dog in the distance. The guards shouted his name, but Asher was already gone, quickly moving through the gate and past the shocked man who stood there.

He passed Hazel, who barked at him, and slowed Siliros, allowing the exhausted dog to catch up and trot at his side.

At the cemetery, Asher dismounted, leading Siliros through the gates as Hazel pulled ahead of him, tongue lolling out of her mouth.

Asher closed the gates behind them, locking them tightly to ensure that the guards, if they figured out where he had been going, wouldn't be able to get in.

Wildflowers had started sprouting around the graves, in blues and reds and yellows that made the normally dull cemetery seem like a more welcoming place.

Vax's grave was also surrounded in wildflowers, and Asher accidentally squashed some of them as he settled beside the grave.

"Hey, Vax," Asher said, placing the bottle of liquor next to the others he had left there. "I'm sorry it's been so long. Some...things have happened."

He leaned back, pillowing his head on his arms, listening to Hazel and Siliros walk around the cemetery before proceeding to explain everything to Vax.

Some of his words came out in a rush, but other words took too long to get out. When he got to Verity Ignis's death, his words stuck in his throat, and when he finally forced them out, they sounded strange and high-pitched.

"They hung Verity Ignis," he said quietly. "Do you remember her and Ember? She's our age. And her mom... They kidnapped her, held her prisoner for a long time, and then when they came to the palace, they hung her." Asher paused, the memory of Verity's death playing through his mind again.

"They were going to do the same to Alex Taya, but Lilith Taya decided to surrender their house over to the Order. We've lost them. And then they asked Ember if she would do the same thing, but she didn't. She refused. So they hung her mother. She's... I don't know how she is, but I know she's struggling. Suffering. And I'm going with the people who did that to her."

Asher didn't say anything for a long time, simply sitting there in silence with the night wind blowing softly through the cemetery. He closed his eyes, allowing himself to fully relax as he lay there.

For the first time in days, Asher felt at peace.

THIRTY-TWO

EMBER WOKE UP THE next day to discover Viper sleeping on a small cot on the floor of her room, Blue curled up next to him. She watched the two boys for a moment, sleeping restlessly, before slipping out of bed to go to the bathroom. Almost immediately, they both woke up, looking around wildly. Viper's eyes went to her hands, which were constantly shaking, and completely rubbed raw from the night before. They stung, too, but it was a good type of sting—the type that reminded her that she was, unlike her mother, still alive and breathing. Her heart still beat a steady rhythm, even as her hands twitched at her sides.

"I'm alright," Ember said. "I'm just going to the bathroom. Go back to sleep." Blue clearly needed no extra persuasion, plopping back down and closing his eyes. Viper, however, sat up, leaning his head against the small nightstand. Ember shut the door of the bathroom behind her, cursing herself for breaking the mirror. She didn't exactly want to see herself, but she wanted to feel like herself again. To feel "normal" again. This time, when she thought of Verity, it didn't immediately turn her stomach, and for that she was grateful.

"Viper?" she called quietly, and he was at the other side of the door in a heartbeat. Ember was surprised he could hear her.

"What's wrong?"

"I want new clothes," she said quietly. "And someone to help me wash my hair and face. Please."

"I can make that happen. You want something simple, I assume?"

"Something of my mother's. Perhaps Lucasta can get it for me, if she's here and not at the Draco Estate. I don't know where she stayed last night."

"She's here, but I can send her back over," Viper offered.

"Yes," Ember said. "Thank you."

There was no response as Viper moved away from the door and out into the hallway. Which left Ember and Blue alone in the room. Blue was half-asleep on the cot when she came out of the bathroom, but she had a feeling he would've snapped awake had she needed it.

"Blue?" she asked, sitting back on the bed. He opened his eyes.

"Yes?"

"Why are you here in my room? Viper said you would be, but... why?" she asked.

"When you...collapsed, Viper asked for help moving you to a suitable room. I offered. And when I saw you lying on your bed after that, I couldn't just go. Plus, Viper would've gone with no sleep if I hadn't offered to take some of the shifts for him. I had to promise to wake him if you so much as turned over in your sleep, but I think I did an okay job. And it's the right thing to do. Then the fact that my father was lost to them as well. We weren't close like the two of you were, but I understand it regardless."

"Thank you, Blue," Ember said, eyes watering. "I know I wasn't much help with your father, and then you come and help me after my mother—"

"Don't apologize," Blue said. "It's okay. You do know what today is, right?"

"No."

"There's going to be a palace meeting today. At temple yesterday, everybody gave blood, and the priestess got a vision from the Phoenix, so they decided it was finally time to figure out what to do. You're not expected to attend, so Viper or I can go in your place," Blue offered.

"I'll go," Ember said. "I can do it. How many days has it been?"

"Five."

"I'll go," Ember repeated, and the two of them sat in silence until Viper came back with Lucasta and another girl in tow.

"Are you okay?" Lucasta asked, sitting on the bed beside Ember. She held her arms open, and although Ember hardly knew her, she fell into them gratefully. She knew she must've stunk, but Lucasta held her regardless.

"I'm so sorry," she whispered into Ember's hair. Ember took a shuddering breath and pushed out of her arms, standing up. Her stomach growled.

"I'll find you something to eat," Blue offered, slipping out of the room.

"Let's get you into the bath," Lucasta said, and she and the other girl headed into the bathroom.

"This'll be good for you," Viper said, as Ember brushed past him to take her bath.

"I hope so," Ember answered, shutting the door behind her. It smelled heavenly in the bathroom, as the maid had added rose petals to the bath. Or maybe it just smelled so good because she smelled awful. It was a relief to shed the same clothes she'd been in for four days, to slip into the warm bath. The maid gently unwrapped her arm, and Ember stared at it. It was undoubtably going to scar, but they had stitched it up, and it wasn't quite as red and inflamed as she'd expected. Lucasta sat on the edge of the bathtub and talked about everything under the sun, how the servants had been since she'd been gone. That was quite a relief too, as Ember didn't feel as though she had to say anything.

The maid's hands in Ember's hair were a blessing, as she combed through the knots and the sweat in her hair. She was gentle as she untangled the knots and made her black hair slick and shiny again. The maid gently helped her rub her skin down, cleaning the blood and dirt off it, taking care with her arm. It was nice to smell like soap instead of her own sick, to watch the dirty water wash down the drain. Her hair was soft and clean, her skin radiant again. The maid had brought her a soft black pair of pants, and one of her mother's flowing orange shirts. It still smelled like her, the crisp apple smell that was so common around the Draco Estate. It was a comfort to put it on, and she rubbed the fabric between her hands as the maid combed her hair and braided it back, keeping the locks out of her face. She declined the offer of makeup and jewelry, choosing to go simple to the meeting.

Ember walked down the halls with Blue, Viper, and Lucasta at her back, comforted by their presence.

Ember had hoped they would've been early, slipping in before anybody noticed her. But instead, they were late, an odd group of four that stumbled into the meeting room. Everybody turned as one to look at them, and Ember shuffled to her seat and sat. Lucasta sat beside her on her right, Viper on her other side. Blue sat behind his mother but provided Ember with a nod that spoke volumes. If she needed him, he would be there. Her fingers twitched as a maid poured tea for her, and she ignored it. She would've dropped the cup if she picked it up now.

"Welcome, Lady Ember," the queen said, and the rest of the table echoed it. "You are the lady of House Draco, now. The Dragon."

"I'm aware of that," Ember said. "I know what I am. I accept my position as the Dragon with pride."

"Good. After Verity's funeral, we'll discuss you formally stepping into your position, with all the pomp and circumstance necessary, but for now, we'll bypass all of that. It isn't the most pressing problem at the moment. We were just discussing House Pardus's betrayal, and how we should approach that." Ember nodded and sank back in her chair. She really didn't want to think about it, how she could've had her mother but not the group that surrounded her.

Had it been worth it?

"I think we should permanently banish them," Lord Charles Palin said, with a clenched fist that he repeatedly slammed down on the table. "They committed an act of treason. Let the Leopard join the Bear."

"There is no 'they' in this situation. Lilith Taya made all the decisions," Scarlett Evet countered. "Their mother and stepmother had no say in it. Had Lady Ember done the same, we would have to banish House Draco as well."

"But Lady Ember didn't," spoke up Amber Forrest. "So House Draco stands with us."

"We can't banish one of the Phoenix's patron animals," Lady Violet Soo, of House Aranea, said. "That's not our place."

"She's right," Scarlett said. "It really isn't our place. We need guidance from the Phoenix before making a decision like that. Perhaps to send a delegate up Mount Saffi, to pray at the true Phoenix Flame."

"We don't have time for that," Lord Charles said. "We need to take action now. If we cower, the Order of the Bear will only grow in size and in power. Their demonstration in the courtyard was not the last time we'll see them. What they did with Lady Verity was decisive. It was meant to scare us. We can't hide in our estates and this palace forever. We have to go on as normal, while quietly gathering an army. Get the temple on our side. They claim to be neutral, but they will join us. We'll send delegations, as you said, Scarlett, but not to pray. To sway the temple. By the solstice, we should be ready."

Ember's stomach roiled as she desperately tried to suppress the memories. She reached out for Viper's hand, and he slipped his into hers easily, grounding her. Easing the shaking.

"It worked," Lord Yvlin said. "We *are* scared. We've never seen a show of power like this from the houseless. Especially not from an organized group like this, with a powerful leader. Nothing public, certainly, and news has spread like a fire in the villages. Surely the upper houseless have mentioned something about them? Not even the temple has the same power that they now wield, even if they won't get involved in something like this. You're right about them continuing to grow, but we have no information on them. They disappeared as quickly as they came."

"They're operating out of the south," Ember said, and everybody turned to look at her. "Their group is located in the south."

"How do you know that?" Lord Ivin Minus, of House Tigris, asked.

"The young woman sitting beside me told me," Ember said, nodding to Lucasta. "She has information."

"She's a nobody," Lord Yvlin countered. "Houseless."

"She's a human being who could help us win," Ember said, voice rising. "And you will listen to what she has to say!"

"Lady Ember!" the queen chastised, but instead of being embarrassed, Ember only grew more defiant. She drew her hand out of Viper's, even as her shaking became worse. She let them see it. Let them see what this had done to her.

"All due respect, Queen Feather, but this court is ridiculous if they don't take information from a willing source. We have somebody who can help. Just because she's houseless doesn't mean she's useless. The Order is houseless, and they certainly aren't useless. They should listen."

"You're right, they should. But you cannot raise your voice in this room."

"I can raise my voice wherever I please!" Silence fell over the table as the queen and Ember stared at each other. There was a hatred in the queen's eyes that Ember matched, fury roaring in her head.

"Lady Ember," the king spoke up. "You need to get a handle on yourself if you expect to stay in this meeting. Outbursts are not helpful right now. We need a calm approach to this."

"A calm approach didn't stop them from murdering my mother!"

"Lady Ember," the queen said. "You are dismissed."

Ember stood, shoving her chair backwards so hard it fell over. Nobody spoke in the wake of that silence, and Lucasta stood too. Viper went to go with them, but she placed a hand on his shoulder.

"Stay and represent my house," Ember said. She gave a defiant look to the rest of the table. Viper gave her a terse nod as Ember and Lucasta moved out of the room and into the hall. Ember staggered against the wall, tears rushing to her eyes, and collapsed there, held by Lucasta as she sobbed.

THIRTY-THREE

SHER WATCHED EMBER LEAVE, her odd female friend beside her. Viper moved into her seat, clearly a representative of House Draco. An honorary Dragon. What a position to have.

He met Juniper's eyes across the room, and she gave him a small, reassuring smile that instantly made him feel better. He dropped his hand to Hazel's head, and she nuzzled into him, providing him a bit more comfort.

"She's had a bad couple of days," Viper said, defending Ember. "And you shouldn't have pushed her like that. You provoked her into lashing out."

"We've all had a bad couple of days," Charles Palin spat back.

"Not like she has," Viper said. "You all have no idea what the last five days have been like for her."

"She wasn't even awake the first two," Yvlin Rostro said.

"As if that matters. When she did wake up, she was immediately confronted with the fact that her mother, the only family she had, is dead. Had been hung in front of her eyes by a group of people that had no justification except for: 'because we wanted to'. So, no. I can almost guarantee that your last five days are *nothing* compared to hers. You're lucky she didn't show you the cuts she made on her own arms when she woke up and had to come to terms with what had happened. Three days of vomiting and shaking and facing those memories are far, far more awful than your three days of lamenting your lives. You went home to relative safety and comfort. She stayed here, locked in a room to attempt and keep her out of danger. We didn't have to protect her from outside forces; we had to protect her from herself. Do you have any idea what that's like?"

"Regardless," Feather said. "She can't have outbursts like that. We are trying, calmly and quickly, might I add, to find a solution to this problem. Anger and fear and hysteria will not help us in attempting to plan our next steps."

"She was in the right," Blue Corvu said, nodding at Viper. "She had every right to have an outburst. Nobody was listening to her when she clearly had something to say. You can't ignore her when you don't like what she says. Ember brought somebody that could give you information, and you shot her down. She's offering you a solution when all you're doing is shouting at each other like children."

"She brought a prostitute into a palace meeting," Lady Nocte of House Ibis said. "I saw the daisy tattoo on her—a clear sign that she's part of a prostitute ring. All of them are marked like that. That's completely inappropriate. If we wanted to open this meeting to the public, we would've. But this was strictly a meeting for the houses, not the scum that Lady Ignis found on the side of the road."

"She isn't a prostitute anymore, and she certainly isn't scum. She works for Lady Ember," Viper said. "Plus, she has incredibly useful information. Her name is Lucasta, and she's been nothing but helpful. She helped calm Ember down before the meeting today, and I have a feeling she's calming her down now. So what if she was once a prostitute? She isn't anymore. If you ignore anybody outside of the houses, you'll never get information."

"Viper is right," Allen Forrest said but was silenced by a harsh look from his father, and sank back in his chair. Asher looked back at Viper, whose eyes were firmly fixed on his parents. They were both squirming uncomfortably, refusing to make eye contact with him.

"Regardless," Charles Palin said. "We need a plan of action. I say we send guards to every town within fifty miles and have them interrogate the locals. See what they know. Use torture if necessary."

"If we torture people, we'll be just as bad as the Order," Asher said, finally speaking up. "We need to go about this a different way. Send spies, maybe. House Vulpus, would you be willing?"

Scarlett nodded. "Yes. My son, Vervid, can go, if he'd like. He's rather good at what they do. I don't want to send the twins."

"Then it's decided," the queen said. "We send the House Vulpus heir...where?"

"Down south," Viper said. "Like Ember said. I'm sure that Vervid can figure it out from there. We'll keep constant contact with him in case plans change."

"We still haven't decided what to do about House Pardus," the king said. "Nor the temple."

"We should do something less drastic than banishment for House Pardus. Maybe we could simply shun the current generation, but welcome Lilith Taya's children, whenever they have them," Scarlett offered.

"As for the temple," Lord Lark Canticum said. "We should send a group up to attempt and sway the High Priest to our side. At the very least, we can keep them from joining with the Order, although I highly doubt they'd do that. At best, they'll come completely over to our side." The table erupted into conversation about it, with Asher's father vehemently agreeing with Lark

Asher kept his eyes on Viper, whose face had fallen when he'd realized he hadn't won a victory for Ember.

Twenty minutes after the meeting ended, Asher was in his room, Juniper at his side as they planned their prison break. Hazel lay at his feet, and he realized with a pang that he was going to have to leave her behind. He had no idea where they were going, and he couldn't subject his poor dog to being cramped in a small carriage for potentially a long time. Siliros would also have to be left behind, as the Order was providing horses and a carriage to transport them to their base, and Siliros was too flashy.

"We'll have to do it at night," Juniper said. "That's the only way to avoid some detection."

"But not all of it," Asher countered. "There are still going to be guards."

"True, but you're the prince. You can dismiss them if you want to."

"Fair. So there's four of them, right?"

"Yes. Tyvish, Riley, Morgan, and Rabbit. Two males, two females."

"I doubt they caged them together, so we'll have to get into four individual cells. And then get back out. What's the plan once we exit the prison, again?" Asher was already well aware of what the plan was, but it helped soothe his nerves when he had Juniper going over it again, helping reassure him that everything had been fully thought through.

"I've been in contact with some Order members. There'll be a carriage from midnight until sunrise waiting down the road. We have to go through the courtyard, there's no other way. We'll just pray that we don't get caught. Pray hard to your god, Asher. Hopefully they help."

"If we do get caught?" Asher asked.

"We fight," Juniper said. "I'll be armed to the teeth, and you probably should be too."

"I'm not killing anybody," Asher said firmly. "I refuse to kill anybody."

"We might not have a choice," Juniper said reluctantly. "It's obviously not ideal if we do have to kill somebody, but if we have to, I'll do it. We're going to try to avoid it, of course, but it could be necessary, Asher. You have to be realistic. You're joining a rebellion, and sometimes you have to do really tough stuff."

Asher sighed, putting his arm around Juniper's shoulders. They'd already gotten into multiple disagreements about this part of the plan; he simply didn't know if he was ready to fight the people he'd grown up around. To kill them. Juniper didn't have a personal connection to any of them, and Asher realized, with just a hint of jealousy, that it was probably easy for her to just see the guards and servants as nothing more than roadblocks in the Order's mission.

Asher couldn't think like that. He couldn't get around the fact that he might have to look somebody in the eyes and hurt them. "I know, Juniper. I just—I can't bring myself to kill somebody. Anything else, but I won't take a life."

She nestled into his side.

"Thank you for agreeing to this," Juniper said. "Your support is important to me. It'll be important for the Order, too."

"I don't exactly want my involvement to be known. It won't look good," Asher said.

Juniper shrugged. "They'll figure it out eventually, when you, you know, disappear."

"Fair. I'll meet you downstairs tomorrow, after your final shift is over. Then, we break your friends out of prison."

"Goodnight," Juniper said, kissing him softly before heading to the door. "And thank you again."

Asher paced his room, stealing glances out of the window every so often. He wanted to sneak out, to go and sit at Vax's grave, but the security put in place after the attack was tighter than ever.

He'd already considered asking his parents for permission to go out to the graveyard, after the last time he'd snuck out.

Some sneaking, he thought, remembering the two men who had followed him. Perhaps he could convince his parents if he promised to go with a group of armed guards, but his father drifted through the halls as though he was a ghost, and his mother was even more prone to fits of rage, frequently lashing out at whoever she first laid her eyes upon. It was lucky for the four remaining guests—Ember, Viper, Blue, and the former prostitute—that they rarely crossed paths with her.

Asher glanced out the window again, looking toward the stables. He had to get out of this palace, though, and say goodbye. He and Juniper were leaving soon, and he doubted he'd have another opportunity to see Vax before he left.

He pulled his cloak over his servant's uniform, although he didn't really know why he was wearing it. It would probably be easier for him to get out of the palace as himself, but it was out of force of habit that he put the uniform on.

Asher left Hazel sleeping on his bed, feeling a stab of guilt when he looked at her. He had no doubt that a similar scene would be playing out in only a few nights, and he left the room before he could hesitate any further.

He was all in on this. He'd told Juniper as much, even if he was already feeling some doubts toward the Order and their plans.

"Stop, Asher." Asher turned at the sound of someone's voice, resisting the urge to hurl profanities at his mother, who stood only a few feet away. Asher crossed his arms over his chest, staring at her as she moved closer.

She took a step forward, and he took a step backwards, getting away from her.

"Walk with me," she said quietly, moving past him down the hallway. Asher sighed, falling in step beside her. There was no way he was going to be able to get out of the castle now, with his mother breathing down his neck. She glanced at him, frowning when she caught sight of his clothing.

"What are you wearing?" Asher pulled his cloak tighter, hiding the uniform from view.

"It's really none of your business," Asher snapped, glancing out the window.

His mother's frown deepened.

"Where's your lapdog? Shame he didn't end up being one of the traitors." Feather ignored his comment, although he could see a flash of anger in her eyes. He'd touched a nerve by mentioning Moreci, apparently.

"How have you been holding up?" she asked quietly, looking over at him. He deliberately ignored her gaze, although he could feel the weight of it.

How have you been holding up?" Asher asked, rounding on her. "I saw you at the execution. I saw that you're happy Verity Ignis died."

"Happy? I was horrified, Asher! Do you think I'm a monster? I loved Verity just as much as anybody else. I grew up with her, you know. She was like an older sister to me. I can't believe you would say something as awful as that."

"Liar. You liar. Admit it, Mother. You were glad she died, because she would no longer be with Father. I already told you I wasn't completely sure it was her, just somebody that looked like her. All I saw was black hair. You jumped to your own conclusions, and you were glad she was dead."

"Stop." His mother's voice, calm and commanding. The voice she used when she sat at palace meetings or dinners with the houses. When she was angry but trying to rein it in. It made the hair on the back of Asher's neck stand up. She usually used that voice around him, when he had done something to displease her in front of the court.

The voice she used when a meeting with Moreci was about to happen.

"Am I wrong?" Asher asked, stopping completely to stare at her. When she didn't respond, he raised an eyebrow. "Am I?"

She stayed quiet, and Asher scoffed.

"Unbelievable. I knew it. You can't even deny it, can you?"

"How dare you," his mother said, her voice a soft, deadly purr. "How dare you suggest that I was glad that Verity Ignis died. You awful, selfish son. You haven't changed, have you? I thought that you had, when you stopped drinking. I was so proud of you. I even protected that brat of a servant you're so infatuated with after Ember Ignis brought her to my attention. But you haven't. You're just as useless as you were before."

Anger coiled in Asher's stomach, and he matched his tone to hers, determined not to let her win this one.

"*Enough,*" he said. "I'm done with you calling me useless. I'm not selfish or awful or worthless. Enough is enough, Mother. I've found my voice, have you realized that? You can't kick me around anymore."

His mother smiled, and Asher's heart dropped. He'd never spoken out against her like this, and he braced himself for a slap across the face. He risked a glance at the guards on the wall, but he wouldn't call to them to protect him, although he didn't know how they would react if Feather did strike him. Would they leap to defend him, as their crown prince, or would they stay in their posts? His mother was the queen, after all, and outranked him. And if she called Moreci...

No. She wouldn't do that in front of everybody.

But she didn't do anything. She simply stood there for a long moment, that sickening smile on her face. Asher stayed as long as he could, then turned on his heel, striding away from her and back toward his room. There would be no way for him to go to Vax's grave tonight, and he muttered a curse because of it. He hadn't been able to say goodbye, after all, and he didn't know how to feel about that.

"You know," his mother said, calling after him. Asher refused to freeze, instead slowing his steps to still be able to hear her. "Maybe you aren't wrong. About Verity Ignis. Maybe I am secretly happy that the insufferable Dragon finally fell. Or swung, rather." He could hear her laughing softly as he picked his pace back up again, desperate to get away from Feather.

Asher said nothing; he was afraid he would've been sick on the carpet if he had.

Chapter

THIRTY-FOUR

MBER SAT IN HER bed, wide awake. The boys were
asleep, and Lucasta was curled up on the bed beside
her, almost cat-like in how her body was bent. Her arm
was outstretched, candlelight rippling across the tattoo on her
wrist.

Lucasta made a small, frightened noise in her sleep,
turning over and stretching out slightly. Her face was contorted
in pain and fear, and Ember watched as she began to whimper,
like a dog that had been kicked.

It wasn't hard to realize she was having nightmares, just
like Ember did. Lucasta woke with a start, her eyes wide with
panic. Her eyes, glazed with fear, slid over to Ember, and she
relaxed slightly, although her chest still heaved as she drew in
fast, short breaths.

"Did I wake you?" she whispered, and Ember shook her head.

"No. I was already awake."

Lucasta sighed, pulling herself into a sitting position as she drew her hair over her shoulder, beginning to braid it quickly. "I understand why you stay awake," Lucasta said, her voice still low, as though not to wake the boys. "I thought I was getting better when it came to the nightmares. I guess not."

"I get them too," Ember said. "But I doubt we have the same ones."

Lucasta shook her head, throwing her braid back over her shoulder, and then held her wrist out, displaying her tattoo.

"I hate this tattoo," she murmured, and Ember instantly realized what Lucasta's nightmares were about.

How could she have possibly been so blind?

"Because of the men?" Ember asked, and Lucasta looked up at her before nodding once.

"There have been hundreds," she whispered. "Hundreds of them. First, when I came here from my home country, Geloj Swesh, I tried to find different work, you know? I worked odd jobs. But I was starving to death and... Daisy found me. She gave me this tattoo, and a room at the Perfumed Palace. Steady work. There's always another man."

Ember watched as she gently touched her tattoo, and then shuddered.

How many hands had slid over that tattoo, how many mouths? Had bruises or bite marks been left on that near-flawless skin? "I can't lay with anybody anymore. I can't... I can't love like that. There's no passion in it. No fire. My people are made of fire, and they would be so devastated to see me like this, but I can't help it. I can only love in one way. In the terms of friends. No romance, no sex. It has ruined me, and I feel broken. I am broken."

Lucasta had suffered, and Ember had as well.

Not the same type of suffering in the slightest, but the pain was there, and it flowed between them, binding them.

"You are *not* broken, but let's cover up your tattoo, anyways," Ember whispered. "There's a tattoo artist who works for the houses. He did mine and Viper's. I'm sure we could get him up here in only a little while, especially if I...incentivized him." Lucasta looked up at Ember and smiled, her wildness coming through again.

Oh, this woman was wicked, a glint in her eyes as she spoke. "Let's do it."

They rushed through the halls together, Ember's hand clutched in Lucasta's. They had already sent a message with the first servant they happened upon, giving her strict and clear instructions, and now they were moving toward the conference room.

Ember pushed the door open, relieved when it was unlocked. She didn't know how much security had increased after the attack, but she and Lucasta had passed plenty of soldiers, although none of them stopped them.

Lucasta had brought a box of matches with her, and moved around the room lighting lamps as Ember arranged several chairs in the back of the room, although she figured the tattoo artist was going to move some things around regardless. She and Lucasta moved lamps over to the chairs, casting plenty of light on them.

Lucasta curled up in one of the chairs, closing her eyes.

Ember sat in the other, her shoulder tingling. Her Dragon was the only tattoo she had, and while she hadn't thought of herself when planning this, she was still slightly intrigued by the idea of a new tattoo, although she had no idea what she would get.

Perhaps Lucasta's tattoo would inspire her; Ember would just have to see.

It took the tattooist only half an hour before he was knocking on the conference room door. Ember stood, rushing to the door and throwing it open. The man respectfully dipped his head toward Ember, and she studied him for a moment. He was perhaps five years older than her, and carried several large bags, no doubt full of the needles and inks he would need. His own body was almost entirely covered in tattoos, colors and shapes and faces blending to create a beautiful portrait.

"Lady Ember," he said and looked past her at Lucasta. "I received your summons. Are you ready?"

Ember shook her head, pointing at Lucasta.

"It's for her," Ember said, turning and moving further into the room, the tattooist following her. "She'd like to cover up one she already has."

The man raised an eyebrow, but said nothing, setting his bags on the table and looking at Lucasta, who evenly looked back.

"I want you to sketch what you want," he said, pulling a chair up toward her. "I'll help you, and then we'll put it on your skin." Lucasta nodded, and the man opened his bag, pulling out a small notebook and a pen, handing them both to Lucasta. Ember watched, fascinated, as Lucasta began to sketch, delicately holding the pen. Her movements were slow, but precise, and for a brief moment, Ember couldn't help but wonder about Lucasta's life before she'd come to Eiad—had she been an artist?

After a few moments, Lucasta handed the notebook back, and the tattoo artist glanced over it, giving her a cautious look

"It's a lot," he said. "It's probably going to hurt pretty badly. Are you prepared for that?"

Lucasta gave him a solemn nod. "I'm ready," she said, extending her arm.

The tattooist opened his other bag, pulling needles and ink pots from them. He placed them on the table, and after pulling on a pair of gloves that had perhaps once been white, but now stained with ink, he dipped one of the needles into a jar of white ink and placed it against Lucasta's arm, directly beneath her elbow.

Ember watched as the tattooist worked, Lucasta's face occasionally contorting in pain before she reined in her emotions once again, although her body was stiff, and her eyes squeezed shut so tightly that it seemed she was on the verge of tears.

But none fell as the man continued to work, drawing white lines across Lucasta's arm, snaking across it and down to her hand, finally ending when he made a loop of white around her middle finger, connecting it to the rest of the design. He stepped back after wiping a drop of blood away, and Ember craned her neck to get a better look at the design.

She couldn't help but gasp at the work that had been done. Lucasta's arm was now covered in thin, delicate lines, each connecting to the other in a beautiful pattern, like an intricate lace, telling a story Ember didn't understand. The white of the ink stood out against Lucasta's dark skin, and the tattoo seemed to glow underneath the lamplight. Her daisy tattoo had been completely covered, and Ember gaped at it for a few more moments before she turned to Lucasta.

"It's incredible," she said, dipping her head toward the tattooist as well. "Does it mean something?"

Lucasta nodded, wincing as the tattooist wrapped her arm in thick bandages, to keep infection off the new wounds.

"In my home country," she said. "Everyone receives a tattoo when they're wed. The men often get tattoos on their backs, large ones depicting one of our gods. But the women get these—a wedding gift, often paid for by the groom's family. It symbolizes that you have been taken, that you are no longer a child, but a woman. I'm not married, but... I worked for Daisy for years. I think that I've earned this tattoo."

Ember gently took Lucasta's other hand, squeezing.

"You have earned it," Ember said.

For a while, even after the tattooist left, even after the lamps burned low and the sun began to stream through the windows, the two girls sat, holding hands. Binding themselves to the other. And unbeknownst to the other, each girl made a promise that day—to protect the other, no matter the cost.

Ember let it steel her heart.

Ember opened the door softly, ushering Lucasta in with a hushed giggle. The boys were still in their cots—a miracle, and a blessing. Lucasta slipped back into bed, immediately closing her eyes and falling into a tentative sleep, but when Ember stepped over Viper's cot, his voice, a low, sleepy whisper filled the room and made her freeze.

"Where did you go?" he asked, and Ember looked down at him as he pushed himself up on his elbows, blinking slowly.

"It's really none of your business," Ember hissed, and Viper rolled his eyes, running a hand through his sleep-mussed hair. Ember had the startling urge to run her own hands through it, to see if it was really as soft as it looked, but she refrained.

"I take it that you're safe," he said. "Lucasta, too. You didn't leave the palace, correct?"

"Stop being such a mother hen," Ember said. "I'm perfectly capable of taking care of myself." Viper sat up fully, his hand quickly lashing out to catch her wrist. His thumb gazed the back of her hand softly.

Normally, she would've pulled away.

Now, the touch sent shivers down her spine.

Ember wrenched her arm from his grip, hating it. Hating him.

"No, you're not," Viper said. "Not right now, at least. But if you really didn't do anything stupid, then I suppose I'll stop fretting. No more sneaking out, okay?"

"It wasn't sneaking," Ember said. "Lucasta wanted to cover her tattoo, and that's what we did. We didn't go out, and if you had been awake, you would've been welcome to come along. Blue, too."

Viper sighed, rubbing his eyes. "You need to get out of this room," he said. "Give me a second to get dressed, and then we'll find something to do."

Ember watched him as he left the room, and then found her own change of clothes—a loose, golden dress, perfect for spring. She left her hair down; she didn't have the time nor the patience to attempt to put it up. Besides, she highly doubted Viper was going to make her do anything athletic. She dressed and shut the door softly behind her, blocking out the soft sound of Lucasta and Blue's breathing.

In the hallway, Ember found herself once again standing underneath the stained-glass, staring up at the Dragon.

There were stories of past Dragons that Ember knew well—her own grandmother, Ferra, had been fierce. Cold. Violent. Verity had said that Ferra, rather than hanging them, gutted those who wronged her alive, but not after torturing them for days. And, if at all possible, Verity's own grandmother had been worse. Ember shuddered. Verity had been cold, yes, but a different sort of cold. One that offered mercy when it was deserved.

Ember didn't know yet what type of Dragon she would be. She didn't know what type of Dragon she *should* be.

Viper took longer than she had expected to meet her in the hallway, but once he was there, he extended a hand to her, his eyes lit with excitement.

"What's this about?" Ember asked, staring at him, skeptical, and Viper sighed, dropping his hand.

"I know you're having a hard time trusting right now, and I understand. But I am going to ask you to trust me. I won't hurt you."

It was tempting, the offer to lean into his trust and be safe.

But Ember had already trusted. She'd trusted that the guards who roamed the halls were loyal to the royal family. She'd trusted that Verity would always come back to her.

"Maybe not trust," Viper said. "Not yet. But I'd still like to show you something, regardless. There are guards—loyal guards—in these halls. And you're fast. You could get away from me if you needed to." He gave her a tentative smile, and slowly, after a long moment, she returned it.

"Okay," Ember said. "Where are we going?"

Viper's only response was a wicked smile that set Ember's heart on fire.

Oh, she certainly couldn't trust him. Not in the slightest.

Viper led her through the halls of the palace just as it was starting to wake up around them. Servants, rushing through the halls with baskets of laundry or cleaning supplies.

They didn't see any of the other lords, ladies, or heirs, but that was to be expected. Ember had a feeling most of them, if not all of them, were back at their own estates, hiding out until they were again summoned by the king.

Oh, well. Let them hide.

Viper motioned Ember down a set of stairs, and for a moment she thought they were going to the training room again, and suddenly regretted leaving her hair down, but no, Viper led her right past the door to the training room.

"Where are we going?" Ember asked, and Viper shot her a dirty look.

"Let it be a surprise," he said. "Don't ruin it for yourself."

Ember made a noise of protest, but Viper ignored her, finally stopping in front of a pair of heavy, wooden doors. The

Phoenix was carved into them, rising from a raging fire near the bottom. Her beak was open in a scream, and Ember shuddered as she turned to Viper.

"Can we go in?" Ember asked, her voice suddenly a hushed, breathless whisper. Viper nodded, pushing the doors open and holding them for her as she stepped inside.

A ballroom.

She'd been here before, but very few times. She'd been fifteen the last time she'd stepped into this room, two, almost three years ago. The king had been throwing a ball for a visiting dignitary from the far continent, and Ember had been allowed to go, although many of her companions hadn't been.

Then, the room had been done up in the colors of both House Phoenix and the kingdom from where the man came—the name of which she couldn't remember. The ballroom had been red and orange and a deep, vibrant green, and it had been glorious.

Now, Ember looked around, taking in the ballroom. It was a long room, rectangular on three sides, and curved on the far wall, which was lined with large, glittering windows, which were letting in plenty of the early-morning light. The floors were a smooth wood, perfect for dancing, and the walls were covered in long, red tapestries, a golden Phoenix in the center of them. Ember stepped into the room, her bare feet sliding over the cool wood, the feeling familiar and comforting.

Phoenix. She missed dancing.

"I've seen you dance," Viper said. "At the ball, for House Corvus's newest baby. You seemed...at ease. Comfortable."

"I love dancing," Ember said quietly. Viper stepped toward her, keeping enough distance that she felt comfortable, extending a hand. Ember hesitated again, and he sighed, although not in frustration or annoyance, and dropped his hand to his side.

"Do you know any dances where we won't touch?" he asked softly, and Ember nodded.

"But we don't have music," she said, and Viper shrugged.

"Envision it," he said. "And I'll follow your lead."

Ember stepped into the middle of the room, her hands flaring at her sides, trembling. She closed her eyes, pushing herself up on her toes and tipping her head back. In the back of her mind, she called a song, strings and woodwinds filling every crevice of her mind.

And Ember danced.

She spun as the strings began, slow and mournful. She was vaguely aware of Viper, standing, watching, but she put him out of her mind as the song picked up, her spin becoming more and more frantic, although she was in complete control. Her feet moved through the steps with ease, her arms stretched toward the heavens.

She heard footsteps as Viper came up, his hands phantoms on her waist. Not touching her, but there. Ensuring she wouldn't fall.

But Ember knew she wouldn't fall.

She never fell.

She and Viper moved like a storm, and when she finally opened her eyes, she found his trained on her face. She leaned forward slightly, and Viper was there, his hands barely brushing her waist. She pulled back and spun away from him, her dress flaring out beside her. Her heart pounded in time to the music in her head, and it skipped ever so slightly when she and Viper made eye contact again.

Ember took a deep breath, gently stepping back toward him. This time, she stood closer than before, and his hands closed fully over her waist. Before her body could register the fire of his touch, Ember pulled away, her fingers running down his arm and lingering on the edge of his longest finger.

They stared at each other for a long moment, gold and blue locked on each other, and then Ember dipped into a short curtsy, watching as Viper bent in a low bow.

Ember turned away from him, drawing in a long breath.

The dance had been a distraction. A perfect, wonderful distraction.

A way to forget.

A way, perhaps, to heal.

And Viper continued to stand behind her, never impatient, never rushing her. She knew that, had she asked, he would've stood behind or beside her as long as she needed. And the weakness, that old, persistent weakness was back, of the overwhelming desire to be held.

Ember squared her shoulders and let out a long breath. Not yet.

But maybe soon.

Chapter

THIRTY-FIVE

SHER ROLLED UP ANOTHER shirt with a heavy sigh. He packed it into the bottom of his bag, on top of a smaller bag that held various toiletries. He folded a pair of pants and put a pair of socks on top of them. Asher looked around his closet, trying to find more clothes he could wear in a rebel camp. His ceremonial clothes he ignored, as well as any clothes with gold stitching. Simple clothing, mostly black and red. He was already in his servant's uniform, cloak swung over his shoulders. Asher placed a small Phoenix charm on the top of his bag, one that his mother had given him for his sixth birthday. He almost left it, thinking about what his mother had said about Verity, but kept it anyways. It wasn't the Phoenix's fault that Feather was slowly going crazy. Maybe the Phoenix would be kind and help them get through this prison break without getting caught. Or killed. He slipped the backpack over his shoulder, taking one last glance around the room.

Hazel was asleep, having barely cracked an eye to see what he was doing. He bent down, scratching her gently between the ears

"I'm sorry," he said quietly, genuinely meaning it. He almost changed his mind as she opened her eyes, ears perking up. "I wish I could take you, but...I couldn't do that to you. I've left a note on how to take care of you, but there are about five servants who already know when and what you need to eat. And they all love you. You'll be okay." Hazel licked his hand, settling back into her bed. Asher blinked back a few tears, forcing them away.

He was about to do what was either the stupidest, or the bravest, thing he'd ever done. He didn't have time to stand there crying.

His palm burned as he jogged down the first flight of stairs. He'd given blood to the Phoenix Flame earlier today, hoping to win the Phoenix's favor for this dangerous night. He'd done it, too, as an apology. To the Phoenix, for turning his back on his position. For being treasonous toward Her. Asher had bled until his head had spun and then the priestess on duty had stitched and bandaged his hand. Maybe it was idiotic to go into this with an injured hand, but he was willing to take his chances.

He waited for Juniper downstairs in the now-empty kitchen, his heart beating a million miles a minute. There'd certainly be questions if he was caught down here, in all black, with a fully packed bag on his back. He hadn't even thought of an alibi should someone find him. Asher was just praying that Juniper, and her rebel friends, would be the only people he saw tonight.

It took her another ten minutes to join him, with a bag of her own. She was wearing a silver bear pinned to her shirt and held out her hand to reveal a matching one, glittering menacingly in the moonlight.

Asher took it, pinning it to his shirt as he glanced over at the guards still stationed on the walls. Mercifully, there were less in this hallway, as servants weren't as high of a priority as the royal family, especially not after the attack.

The cut on his palm seared with pain as the pin rested against his heart, and he suspected he would get no more help from the Phoenix. He'd completely turned against Her now.

"It's time," Juniper whispered. "Lead the way."

The prison was on a lower level than the kitchen, so it took them a few minutes to jog down the set of stairs and reach the imposing metal door. Asher rapped on it a few times, tapping his foot as he waited for someone to open it. A young female guard did, giving him a strange look.

"Your Majesty," she said. "What brings you down here so late? Alone?"

"I need to visit some prisoners," he said. "Clear the prison level. I want all guards to go as far back as they possibly can. In thirty minutes, return to your posts. Can you do that?"

The woman hesitated. "I'm uncomfortable with letting you visit them alone. I'd prefer if you allowed me to go with you."

"Can you follow simple instructions? Or must I get my father? I'll ask you one more time, and if you don't do exactly as I ask, then I'll have to assume you're part of the rebellion. Can you do that for me?"

The woman stiffened.

"Yes. Give me just a moment." She disappeared into the darkness of the prison hallway, and there was a shuffling of feet, and she returned.

"Everything has been done as you asked. Please, come in." Asher followed her, Juniper a step behind him. The door shut with an ominous clanking noise. "The prison log is here," the woman said, pointing to it. "Every prisoner is labeled in it. You should be able to find who you're looking for. I hope everything goes well, Prince Asher. Have a nice night."

She then turned and rushed off into the depths of the prison hall. Juniper was looking around, visibly disturbed.

"This place feels weird," she admitted. "I can't believe they've been stuck here for almost a week." Asher couldn't help but agree. The walls were made of solid metal, as was the circular desk in the lobby part of the room. The doors started about fifteen feet from the desk, each of them solid metal with a small window slit in the top. This wasn't even the highest level. There were stairs at the end of the hallway, descending deeper and deeper down into the ground. At the bottom, there were rumored torture rooms, but Asher had never seen them before, and prayed that they were only rumors. The prison felt *wrong* in the palace, as though it was supposed to exist somewhere else entirely. Luckily, the prisoners they needed were on the first floor.

"Cells 56 and 89," Asher said. "I'll take the boys, since they're farther down. Thank Phoenix they jailed them together. Here's the key for cell 56. Be quick, Juniper." They took off the hallway side by side, until Juniper stopped at her door. Asher kept running, counting doors.

"78, 79... 89." He skidded to a stop in front of it, fitting the key into the lock and throwing the door open. Two rebels looked up at him, both wearing the silver Bear pins. Asher was surprised they'd been allowed to keep them, but the two of them were so filthy, clothes covered in dirt and blood, and Asher realized they hadn't been cared for in the slightest. One gave him a dirty look that he didn't read too much into. He probably wasn't these rebels' favorite person, although he was seriously hoping they would begin to trust him now that he was helping break them out.

"Come on," Asher said. "We're leaving." The rebels needed no other encouragement, jumping up and rushing past him, to where Juniper waited, standing beside the two female rebels. Before they reached the outer door, though, Asher came to a stop. The one man who had glared at him gathered Juniper in his arms for a hug, but she pushed him away, visibly uncomfortable. Asher squinted at them, unable to read their interaction, and the man glared at him again. Asher ignored him, turning to Juniper.

"We need to be really careful in the halls," he said. "I think we should take off the pins."

"We can't," Juniper said. "If we get caught, we want to get caught for who we are. Besides, I have this." She lifted her shirt slightly, revealing two familiar knives.

"That's Ember's knife," Asher said, and Juniper shrugged. "Juniper, you shouldn't have that." It felt wrong to see the Dragon-handle knife in Juniper's hand and not Ember's. She pulled the other knife from her waistband, holding it out to him. Asher smiled grimly as he recognized the knife—it was his own, which he had lost during the attack. He ran his hand over the handle, finally realizing that the animal engraved there was a Bear.

Fitting.

"She's not using it, is she? But we really need to go. I'm not getting trapped here. We won't have another chance, and our odds of getting out of here double if we're armed."

"Fine. Let's go," Asher said, opening the outer prison door and slipping into the hallway, flipping his knife so it fit comfortably in his palm. The rebels were remarkably quiet, barely making a sound as they glided over the thick carpets. By comparison, Asher felt clunky and awkward. They made it about twenty feet, further than Asher had expected, when a guard patrolling the halls stopped them.

"Prince Asher?" he asked, looking at the Bear pin. His eyes darted between the six of them nervously. "What's going on?"

"It's none of your concern," Asher said, drawing the man's attention back to him. "And if anybody asks, you didn't see us."

"Sir, I am required to report suspicious activity to my supervisor. We're especially required to report any Order-related activity, and I think I recognize him from the attack." He nodded toward the man who had hugged Juniper. "I won't feel comfortable lying to her."

"Get comfortable with it, or get comfortable with a noose around your neck," Juniper spat, coming up beside Asher and brandishing the knife at him. He backed up a step, despite being armed with a short sword and twin throwing knives. He could've easily taken them.

"Very well," the guard said, but his face was still contorted with worry, and Asher signaled for their group to move faster. The guard would most definitely raise high hell when he realized what the Bear pins were for. It probably wouldn't take too long, but even still, he sent a quick prayer to the Phoenix, hoping that She hadn't truly turned Her back on him, that the guard would be too stupid to realize it until they were far away from the palace.

They jogged up a set of stairs, hitting the main floor.

"There are going to be more guards up here," Asher said. "So you guys need to let me do all the talking. No more threats. Put the knife away until we need to use it." Juniper and the others nodded, and she and Asher sheathed their knives, and he headed down the hallway, getting closer to the courtyard with every step. Toward freedom.

Toward a new life.

There was a shout behind them, and the group took off as one.

The rebels were quick, despite their neglected state, and one of the other women grabbed Asher's hand to keep him at the same pace as the other rebels.

They burst through the main doors and sprinted out into the courtyard, and Asher thanked the Phoenix that the carriage was there. Even if She was upset with him, he was still going to appreciate the luck She'd given to him. The angry man threw the door open, launching himself and another rebel into the carriage. The slam of the door closing behind them never came, though, and rather someone shouted.

"Stop!" Asher turned, shocked to see Ember standing there.

"Stop!" she cried again. Asher stopped without meaning too, a flood of emotions rushing through him. He hadn't expected to run into anybody he knew personally, and it was hard to look at her. There was confusion and betrayal on her face, and Asher, unable to keep eye contact with her, dropped his eyes to her arm, and immediately regretted it.

The cuts on her wrists, which Viper had told him about, were still bright red. They'd been sewn up, mercifully, but a drop of blood still leaked from one. They were a painful and direct reminder of the suffering she had gone through.

The suffering caused by the very group he was helping break out of prison. The very group he was leaving to join.

Asher swallowed hard, looking up at Ember. She glanced between him and Juniper, and a strange blankness spread over her face, an uneasy calm that those of the court were so good at putting on. A mask, designed to shield any of her true emotions. It was working.

He didn't know if he could still do this.

THIRTY-SIX

E MBER COULDN'T SLEEP, TOO anxious about what she had done during the meeting, although it had been two days ago. She tossed and turned in bed, careful not to wake Lucasta, who was asleep beside her. It had been comforting to have her there when they had first gotten into bed, just as it had been every night this week, but tonight Ember had to worry about her thrashing waking the other girl. Blue and Viper were asleep on their cots again, so when Ember slipped out of bed, she had to do an odd dance to avoid stepping on one of them. Ember pulled on a pair of socks and left the room as quietly as she could

Something was wrong. She could feel it, like a rock in her stomach. For the most part, everything looked normal, but as she continued down the hallway, closer to the center of the palace, the rock only grew heavier. She made her way down a set of stairs, as softly as she could, supporting herself on the banister. Ember had managed to eat a small meal before going to bed, which was a relief for her body. Viper had been happy about it too, nearly crying in relief.

The ground floor of the palace, the courtyard being the centerpiece, was completely deserted when she stepped off the stairs. Ember continued forward, tracing her hand against the fine wallpaper. She was heading back to the temple, the last place she saw her mother truly alive. The woman they had hung was already dead. The sanctuary was eerie in the late hours of the night, completely empty except for the thirteen statues, and the priestess who was slumbering near the Phoenix Flame, who didn't even stir as Ember approached.

Ember walked all the way forward, rounding the Phoenix Flame to touch her hand to the base of the Phoenix's statue. It was far warmer than she had expected it to be, and she pressed her face to it. She expected tears to start falling, but her eyes were surprisingly dry. Ember should've cried enough to fill an ocean, but her sadness was slowly being replaced with anger. Anger that quickly fueled ideas of revenge. Of torturing the woman who'd hung her mother. Ember wouldn't ever forget that woman's face, the way she'd leered when Ember had gazed defiantly at her, refusing to break. Ember glanced up at the Dragon statue, locking eyes with her patron animal.

To be a Dragon, she thought to herself. To rage and kill and take her revenge and it be credited to her nature and not her trauma. If she were a Dragon, her mother would still be alive. A Dragon would've fought harder. A Dragon would've clawed them apart and burned them until they screamed for mercy. A true Dragon would've murdered them all with a thought. With a breath.

And she was trembling inside a temple, unable to keep her own hands from fluttering at her sides.

There was a loud shout from outside the sanctuary, and Ember rushed to the doors, waking the priestess, and flinging them open just in time to see a group clad in black rush past her. She darted after them, her body screaming in protest against the physical activity. She still wasn't as fast as the group, though, and her dehydrated state wasn't helping either. She kept running, though, since she knew there was something wrong with a group that was awake and running this late at night.

She flexed her wrists as she ran, almost unconsciously, crying out when one of her stitches tore. She barely remembered getting them but was smart enough to know she didn't want to go through it again.

The group slammed out the doors to the courtyard, and she followed, finally catching a glimpse of one of them as the moonlight lit them up, illuminating silver bear pins on all of their shirts.

Juniper Farley.

Of course.

"Stop!" Ember cried, skidding to a stop. The group turned, and when she saw Asher's face, the bear pinned over his heart, her own heart sank.

"Stop!" she yelled again, striding toward them, keeping her eyes on Asher. She couldn't help the betrayal that flitted across her face as she looked at him, holding his gaze until he dropped his to her wrist. A mixture of horror and disgust and pity passed over his face as he studied her wrist, but she ignored him.

The four rebels she didn't recognize were boarding the carriage that was clearly waiting for them, but Asher and Juniper stared Ember down.

"Asher?" she asked, hands shaking.

He shook his head. "I'm sorry, Ember. I really am," he said.

Juniper scoffed, tossing her head. "I'm not. Go away."

"No." Ember watched as Juniper began reaching for something at the front of her shirt, and her heartbeat quickened. She wasn't armed, and Juniper was far stronger than her, but she wasn't going to lie down and die.

Not like her mother.

She glanced back toward the doors. She had passed what felt like a hundred guards on her way here—where were they now? Surely they had heard the same cry she had?

She looked back at Asher and Juniper, determined to stall them until the guards showed up.

"Go away, Ember Ignis. I don't want to hurt you. Not yet. But I will." She pulled a knife from her waistline, holding it in a strong grip. Ember took a few steps forward, burying her hands in the fabric of her nightgown.

"I'm not going anywhere until the royal guard shows up. They'll throw you all in prison," Ember said, approaching Juniper. "Except maybe you, Juniper Farley. Maybe they'll give you to me. To let me carve you up, for what you did to my mother."

Juniper snarled, clearly threatened. The knife began to shake in her hand. Asher stood behind her, looking nervously between the two girls. Ember flicked her eyes up to him, unable to stop herself from silently pleading with him.

Help me. Stop her.

Asher dropped his gaze, and Ember looked back at Juniper, swiftly reminded of the first time she'd seen her— gold and green meeting in a clash.

"You're making a bad choice," Juniper said, but there was a slight, almost imperceptible waver in her voice, and Ember smirked, hoping that she didn't notice the shaking of her hands, which she had buried in the fabric of her nightgown.

"Has your god abandoned you? Are you scared now, Juniper Farley?" Juniper's eyes narrowed, and she shifted her grip on the knife. Ember's eyes dropped towards it, momentarily blinded by the candlelight, streaming from inside the palace, reflecting off it.

Ember looked back up at Juniper, whose eyes were still narrowed, and she could easily see the animalistic part of Juniper—the part that had, no doubt, starved and scraped and *survived*.

It was easy, truly, to see the Bear that so clearly resided inside of Juniper Farley, and when she spoke, her voice came out in a low snarl.

"Never."

"Juniper—" Asher said, rushing forward to try and place himself between the two girls, to stop whatever Juniper was about to do, but he wasn't fast enough.

He seemed to realize it a moment too late, eyes going wide as Juniper moved.

Ember didn't even have time to cry out as Juniper leapt forward, burying the knife hilt-deep in her stomach. When she released it, Ember could only stare at the Dragon grinning up at her as her gold nightgown began to turn red. The pain was blinding, all-consuming. Ember choked, grasping the handle of the knife. She couldn't bring herself to pull it out, even as her hands became slick with her own blood, sticky and bubbling. The smell of it, thick and metallic, made her gag.

Ember gaped at the wound as the carriage sped off. She stared at the warm blood beginning to drip to the floor, pooling around her feet and making her socks soggy.

"Oh, Mother," Ember whispered, closing her eyes. "I am so sorry."

Ember Ignis swayed once, twice, and then collapsed, her fingers gripping the Dragon.

Chapter

THIRTY-SEVEN

THE NEWS WAS FIRST spoken by a woman in silver priestess robes, whispering to a boy who had a Snake tattooed on his upper arm. He collapsed with relief against the wall, staring at the girl who had just begun to stir in a bed that she had laid in, motionless, for almost a week.

From him, the words were passed to a boy with shock-blue hair, who whispered prayers under his breath when the Snake boy told him. Passing them in that hallway was a man who wore a guard's uniform, although he wasn't truly one of them.

The guard rushed to tell his superiors, to keep up his appearance, and then rushed downstairs, sending a letter with a spy who wore a small envelope on the front of their shirt. He wasted no time, stealing a mare and urging it down the road.

He rode for two days, and when he reached a small city, he whispered words to a woman with a Wolf tattoo on her forearm, handing the letter to her as her eyes grew wide with shock. She took a horse of her own, riding as quickly as possible.

When she arrived in a rebel-held town in the south, word spread like wildfire. It hopped from spy to foot soldier, to scholar and stable hand, until it finally reached the ears of a girl with green eyes and a silver Bear pinned to her shirt.

When the news reached her, she leapt into action immediately, rushing away from a curly-haired boy and toward the building in the center of the town. Her hair flew behind her as she pushed herself past her limits.

It was not good news in the slightest, and her superiors had to know. It wouldn't do to keep them in the dark about this.

She burst through the door, standing there as a group of people sat at a round table with a map in the middle. A woman with a scar across her face, who had been in the middle of a sentence, looked up, brow furrowing. A question formed on her lips, but the green-eyed girl spoke before she could ask, her words coming out in breathless bursts.

"Luria," she said, leaning against the doorframe. "The spy is back." The scarred girl's eyes widened, and she took a step forward. Expecting the worst but hoping for the best.

"And?" The rest of the table was leaning forward, hanging on to her every word. She took a moment to catch her breath and then forced the words out, although they desperately wished to stay behind her teeth.

"She's alive." The people at the table looked at each other, and murmurs burst out between them, half-formed plans springing into existence as they discussed this new development. Only the girl with the scar, Luria, continued to stare at Juniper, her eyes wide.

"This isn't a sick joke, right?" Luria asked, stepping forward. Her words came out in a breathless rush, as though she hoped more than anything that Juniper was lying to her. "She's alive?"

Juniper Farley nodded, finally regaining control over her breathing.

"Ember Ignis is alive."

ACKNOWLEDGMENTS

Oh boy. Where to start?

Well, I'd first like to thank God, because through Him all things are possible, including the daunting task of writing a novel.

Riley and Morgan, who read chapters of my book during the first draft and liked them. There's actually no way I would've finished the first draft without you two behind me every step of the way.

To Aliza and Lucia, for enduring my endless rants about writing and random bursts of excitement at the dinner table. (30,000 words!!)

To Mom and Dad, for always encouraging my writing, and investing in my future. That genuinely means more than I could ever explain in words.

To Grammy, Grandpa, Abu, and Aba. You've always supported my writing, and your enthusiasm when I finished my first draft inspired me to continue writing my second draft.

To Tita, Uncle Johnny, Luke, Ben, Joey, Little, Riff, and Big Time

To Uncle Ed, Aunt Katia, Lexi, Eddie, Hannah, and Livi and Sophia.

To Hailey, for being my constant.

To Ellen, for getting excited with me.

To Ben, for being my favorite.

To Reedsy Editor, where I wrote my book, and the patient people who work the help desk. Thank you so much for enduring my idiotic questions about your fabulous program.

To Judi Weiss, my amazing editor who elevated this book in ways I couldn't have done alone. You are so sweet, and truly a blessing.

To Theá Magerand, my absolutely incredible cover designer. Your patience with me was a godsend, and your work speaks for itself. I gasped the first time I saw my cover.

To my other friends, whoever I forgot, that supported me through this novel, and through life. Honestly, there's so many of you that it's hard to list them all, but your support genuinely got me through this process.

To Mr. Fisher, for providing me the type of encouragement only a teacher could give. I will never forget eighth grade creative writing.

To Hazel. I love you, and you're a good girl.

To whoever is reading these acknowledgments right now. I don't know why you picked up my book, but I will be forever grateful for it. You have no idea what you mean to me. You are the reason I write, and I will continue to do it if you will have me.

Love always,
Amelia Wood

www.ingramcontent.com/pod-product-compliance
Lightning Source LLC
Chambersburg PA
CBHW070511310726
48976CB00002BA/407